FRIENDS AND PREVIEWERS' COMMENTS

An imaginative tale that takes place in two theaters…Heaven and earth… taking us back to the beginning. *The Angel Chronicles* poses the question, "What-If?" Although in line with scripture, it dares to envision what might have occurred, filling in the blanks with engaging angelic beings while fleshing out our (literal) first family.

Heaven meets earth in this compelling drama. Take a glimpse behind the scenes in the garden. Witness angelic beings battling dark forces that are intent on destroying man. Set in the past, this book will help open your eyes to the spiritual battles and realities surrounding us today. I highly recommend it.

I will never read Genesis the same way again!

Karen Gnitecki,
Women's Bible Study Teacher, River In The Hills Church

Winds Of Eternity does an incredible job at pulling the curtain back and letting us see the unseen. Witnessing the excitement and anticipation of the angels before God spoke creation into existence gives the account in Genesis more depth and a fresh new perspective. Reading the book has left me with a renewed daily awareness of the angels and the heavenly host that watch over us. *The Angel Chronicles* is an amazing revelation and a joy to read!

Kevin A. Miller

This book is totally amazing!!! I love how you hooked me in. I loved it because it captured the essence of Heaven's glory, and allowed a glimpse into the possible thoughts and actions of my favorite creatures, angels. The creative genius described the majesty of Heaven in ways I had never even dreamed of. The imaginative writing is superb and completely allowed me to have an insiders' view of what may await us there.

A total delight!!!

DeShae Ashley, RDH, MS

We have had the privilege of previewing *The Angel Chronicles* and found it to be a fun and interesting read. The characters were compelling and at times whimsical. We found the story to be imaginative, true to the scriptural text, quite deep, but one that can be enjoyed on several levels.

Nancy L. and Chuck M. Green

This unfolding mystery catches the eye and heart. I was moved by sharing its privileged, bird's eye, view of Heaven, and the angels' endeavors as they labor to reconcile creation, and their new assignment to man, which is soon followed by man's lost innocence. I'm sure we'd be amazed at how many times we've been protected, encouraged, and lifted up once again by the angels we have entertained, unaware. I'm looking forward to the next in the series of Winds of Eternity.

Vera Zidermanis, Past President,
Aglow International, Waco Lighthouse,
Aglow International, Heart of Texas Area Board

The story-line of your excellently written book, *The Angel Chronicles*, is awesome! Winds Of Eternity absolutely transports my soul, soaring above the Heavens. It provides such an outlook on that beautiful Golden City that I will never be the same, if I tried. How astounding it is to realize that Heaven and Earth's matters are being taken care of by multitudes of angels, empowered by the prayers and cries from across the ages. Understanding this is the quintessence of a supernatural intervention.

Readers will be challenged to lift their sights a little higher, and be encouraged to discover how hope is, in itself, an ever-increasing power through the help of unseen forces.

I stand as a witness that all this happened to me.

M. W. Kendall, Founder/Int. President Flame
Fellowship International

WINDS OF ETERNITY

The Angel Chronicles

TRACK JOHNSON

Xulon
ELITE

www.xulonpress.com

DEDICATION

We dedicate this to Owen. His sweetness of smile brushed our hearts for only a whisper before eternity embraced him.

TABLE OF CONTENTS

Acknowledgements

We wish to thank the many who have been instrumental in the writing of this book.

Five hugs go out to Auseklis and Vera Zidermanis for their faithfulness in mentoring each of us, along the way. So much of the core teaching we've woven into this work was passed on to us by them. We joyfully give honor and credit, where it is due.

Five amens go out to "Dad" Glen Ewing and his son Robert for listening, so precisely, to the invisible One and obediently paving the way for some of Earth's novices to follow. We relied heavily upon *"The Texas Grace Counselor,"* written and printed by them, from 1947 thru 1973. The amens we award are nothing compared to the reward they received when they joined the "cloud of witnesses."

Five hugs go out to Kris and Susan Hochderffer and Don and Judy Wickham for accepting these two authors becoming 'one' when others were looking with a questioning eye. We also thank them for our close friendship.

Five hugs also go out to DeShae Ashley, Karen Gnitecki, Chuck and Nancy Green, Mike and Tawnya Hogan, Suzanne Hubbart, Linda Leroux, Mitzi Levitt, Kevin Miller, and Dan and Diane Peach, each of whose input added so much to these writings.

A wink and a nod go out to Tree's daughter Kim Hill for sowing the seeds of faith while enjoying her own new birth. Without her major contribution, this work would have been impossible. And to Bari

Peterson, Tree's other witty daughter, it was she who coined our pen name Track Johnson.

Asher Intrater's book "*Who Ate Lunch with Abraham*," Intermedia Publishing, 2011 was not quoted in our writings, but his overall influence was felt as we began the final acceleration leading to completion. We highly recommend it to any serious student of the kingdom.

AUTHORS' NOTE TO READERS

We've had a wonderful time writing this book for you and hope that you reap pleasure in meeting Zukher and the angels in his troupe, while enjoying the view of *the beginning* from a different perspective. To help enhance the reading that lies ahead, we've included some extras.

At the end of the book you will find an extensive 'Glossary of Names' separated into *'Names of the Sovereign'* and *'Names of the Characters.'* Checking these out from time to time may help you to become familiar with our actors. There is also an extensive list of end notes that will enhance your understanding of the basis of our reasoning and clarify some of the nuances of the overall story. However, we won't be offended if you are not into the minutiae, and just read the book to enjoy.

For those of you who would like to delve ever deeper, we invite you to check out our web site www.windsofeternity.com for information regarding maps and images presenting the various locations mentioned in these pages. There is also information about how to blog with the authors. If you are interested in discussing the theological source and development of our speculations, we'd enjoy meeting you online.

We thank you for taking the time to be entertained by an age old story, as told by a new set of characters.

Track Johnson

FOREWORD

This chronicle is a work of fiction, sown throughout with reliable facts and truth. Every effort has been made to see that the personalities within agree with Holy Writ and with selected first person accounts submitted by the few who claim to have seen the invisible world around us. We draw heavily from the first five chapters of the first book of the *Pentateuch*. These chapters offer a reliable foundation, however, peppered with purposeful silence. That silence permits our respectful speculation.

"Winds of Eternity *The Angel Chronicles*" gives a voice to that silence, albeit, one that we hope you will find imaginative, encouraging, and entertaining. More important, that which is articulated fully agrees with the completed Writ. Other than this, we make no claim that our speculative offering is any sounder than others that have been proposed.

Our offering is the view the angels had, while casting a watchful eye upon an important span of Eternity. We took great liberty eavesdropping upon Adam's and Eve's private thoughts and intimate discussions, though angels are unable to read man's thoughts. Here is the angel's chronicle of a hotly debated breadth of Eternity. One in which the angels and a newly created world, along with its inhabitants, effected the greatest impact upon our world today.

Knowledgeable readers will quickly recognize Elohim, Michael, Gabriel, and some of the other characters, whom we lifted from the sacred scrolls of the *Pentateuch*. Though the reality of their existence may be debated or ignored, one thing is true: Each of you now has a chance to place your own footprint upon the "Winds of Eternity." That footprint may be the only evidence that you were real, when others might later debate your existence and beliefs. We, the authors, believe the lifted characters are real and are now witnessing our own touché upon the present fabric of Eternity.

Track Johnson

> *No man knows another save the spirit of man within him. Likewise, man knows not with whom he shares a journey, whether they are friend or foe. 'Be not forgetful to entertain strangers: for thereby some have entertained angels, unawares.*[1]*'*

PRELUDE

At a pin point of Eternity past, obeying Their own counsel, Elohim rejoiced in Their conception and creation of us, the angels. We are the citizens of Heaven; the ministering spirits of Elohim. They share Their kingdom, the Highest Heaven, with us. Highest Heaven is an immense, inhabitable expanse and Elohim reigns here, as the Sovereign Lord. He is the Holy Trinity[2] known as Elohim, Adonai, or El Shaddai. Here, as in everywhere, He is the one true King of Kings and Lord of Lords.

Highest Heaven is a wondrous place of eternal beauty, and its endless energy is the twin sister of unspeakable joy. The Highest Heaven is bordered, in all dimensions, by Eternity. The scope of its grandeur defies verbal or written description in any language, except the language of Elohim. He uses this language to share intimacy with the other Ones that define the Holy Trinity. We, the created angels, know of Their language. We recognize it, but we cannot speak or understand it. The language of Elohim and the concept of the Holy Trinity are two mysteries for which we seek understanding. These mysteries, like all mysteries of Heaven, are recorded in the Hall of Mysteries, about which we have much to say later. Except for Elohim, no eye has seen, no ear has heard, and no imagination can capture, the fullness of the Highest Heaven. It must be experienced to be understood.

Heaven and its citizens lack nothing. Every query, every desire, every stroke, finds its mark. As Tantzer, one of my troupe's notable angels, says, "Every hammer's blow misses the hand."

All citizens of Highest Heaven reach great pinnacles of achievement. Our election is to be fully committed to every endeavor, regardless of what it may be. It matters not whether it is for Elohim, for other angels, or involves other efforts in which we engage. Lairn'r, our troupe's Inquisitor, calls this commitment, "zeal." When Elohim presented the opportunity for us to share a covenant with Him, our election was to choose this, the Kingdom of Light, over all other elections.

During a span of Eternity past, long before man was even a nebulous idea, a snippet of imagination tugged at the depth of Elohim's heart. Heaven's citizens had, yet, no concept of another type of living creature placing footprints upon Eternity. That imprint on Eternity was a reality considered to be reserved only for Elohim and Heaven's angels. This chronicle is a record of our surprising discovery of how utterly incomplete was our knowledge.

Our chronicle begins millennia after what Elohim calls, "The Beginning[3]" and we refer to as, "The Great Awakening." It was then that Elohim created the heavens and the Earth. It was revolutionary! One instant there was eternal nothingness. In the next instant, a great expanse was created. Before The Awakening, we dwelt with, and served, Elohim, living in a matchless tranquil paradise. After The Awakening, while the tranquil paradise continued, Eternity now embraced a fresh perspective…the beauty of an unexplored universe and a world offering endless possibilities.

We settled in to the excitement of the universe before us. Then, after immeasurable light years of this calming, fulfilling serenity, our Sovereign's kingdom was beset by treachery and intrigue. From dry wells within our ranks came unimaginable expressions of antagonism, betrayal, hatred, and unholiness. Anti-Elohim forces sought desperately to poison Heaven. Leading these forces was one who had been one of our very own.[4] An angel of renown and beauty, a cherub, who had risen to such standing that he was granted a measured dominion over Earth and was permitted to visibly rule a kingdom there. However, in the fullness of time, Elohim revealed that this angel was harboring an unprecedented secret iniquity. This revelation is unforgettable, and remains fresh in the memories of those who have remained loyal to Elohim. We have devoted much of the aforementioned millennia, watchfully aware, while looking into all matters associated with The Awakening and "The Rebellion.[5]" Although little is presently known, we patiently wait on Elohim. Our earnest expectation is that more of the mystery of this matter will soon be divulged.

It is well known among Heaven's citizens that Michael had his hands full, wrestling with the numerous squads of rebellious angels. Following their expulsion, he was confronted with the need to diligently address the consequences. When the shaking ceased, the everlasting kingdom remained securely in the hands of Elohim's light and glory. The darkness of Lucifer has been eternally banished.

Or has it?

Details are of the future, still unrevealed. The consequences of that rebellion are sealed, but manifested in the Hall of Mysteries. Until, in the fullness of Eternity, the unknown becomes known, the personified darkness is out there.

Bound to Earth, but lurking and watching for any opportunity that might lead to a reversal of the current state, not to mention "The Final End," Lucifer hovers. He is, now, ever further from his self-righteous aspiration. He roams Earth brooding, while tugging on any seemingly loose thread of Eternity that he can find, trying to tug a snag in its tapestry. His quest is to unravel, and thus destroy, the majestic work created by Elohim.

NOBLE INTROMISSION

The panorama, before Lairn`r and me, defies the considerable abilities of our combined senses to comprehend.

"This doesn't match the glory of Highest Heaven, but it comes close. The darkness shrouding Earth, and its neighboring expanse, is in strict contrast with the beauty of the rest of the universe Earth inhabits," I'm speaking aloud to myself, as much as to Lairn`r. He's resting alongside, as we observe the universe through the Observatory's Viewing Window. Lairn`r nods his head in agreement, his eyes never leaving the window. Stretching out and parading before us, as far as our eyes can see, is the blemished, but still expanding, universe. Our vantage point is just beyond the outer rim of this created entity. Here we are able to witness its present state and its one imperfection, the shrouded Earth, the consequence of Lucifer and the fallen angels being cast out of Heaven.[6]

We often come to this Window at the Observatory, just to observe and speculate about the universe and Earth, created a great span of Eternity ago.

My companion and I, enjoying our own limited hiatus, have come to the Observatory, to this Window. We intend to check, again, the existing state of the creation. So much depends upon the role this panorama will play. Its vibrant colors and ever-changing patterns are a masterpiece worthy of the King of Kings. The beauty doesn't stop with just visual elegance. This creation is, also, always singing melodious notes.

After several moments, Lairn`r allows my presence to distract him enough to speak. "Zukher," he says, "what more have you learned about the current state of Earth?" Among our troupe, Lairn`r is the one who is usually the first to ask insightful questions. Whether he uses this as a learning aid, or he is just being the most ardent student among us, no one knows for sure. He came to the troupe as an angel of some renown. He was the first angel, at least that I know about, to make inquiries regarding comments Lucifer had made, and had taken issue with his conduct. There are so many troupes like ours that I can't be certain there weren't other, equally gifted, angels asking questions, too.

Although we can't see much of it, we know Earth has no form and we can see it is shrouded in darkness. I shudder as I, in passing, recall the evil which was cast to Earth, and which enforces a measured dominion and force of governance,[7] there. We sense there is a change coming, for we see the Seven Spirits of God moving, like forceful waves, across the horizons of that formless globe. Though unwelcomed by Lucifer, they go where they please. Lucifer now dwells there by permission only.

"We must leave if we are to find a good seat. Elohim's announcement made it clear the Banquet will be held in the Banquet Chamber. It will be a full house and we have quite a walk ahead, if we are to be there when it begins. We need to meet Komodo`r at the Mall of Wisdom. Also, Tantzer should be waiting at the entrance to the Banquet Chamber. We are sitting together, right?" I prod Lairn`r along, knowing that all Heaven's citizens will hang on every word from Elohim.

"Yes, and don't forget Gabriel is supposed to join us, too!" he replies, though hesitating long enough to take a final long gaze at the expanse.

We will be joining other angels along the way, so we won't wing our way to the Banquet. A swift footed departure from the Observatory takes us down three flights of the Steps of Ascension and into the Plaza, as we make our trek to the Banquet Chamber. We exit on the west side of the Citadel, formally named the Citadel of Infinite Understanding, into a plaza that joins the Mall of Wisdom and the Court of Measures. Our journey is a familiar passage, one which we make quite frequently.

The width of the Steps grows ever narrower as they ascend, and wind through, the inner corridors of the Citadel. The treads, hand rails, and landings are ornately marbled with multi-patterned swirls. Looking down from the landing on the fifth floor, the floor of the Observatory, those spiraled steps hint at leading nowhere. As we make our descent, we continue our discourse. The pending Banquet means there will be very few citizens ascending the Steps. Most of the increasing width is filled by the many groups of angels joining us, on the way to the Banquet Chamber. They filter onto the staircase, heading down from the numerous floors below. This fully enclosed interior passage radiates with a glorious natural illumination. Dvar HaElohim makes it so, for He is that light. Darkness is not allowed here.

"Elohim has exited Their conclave. They haven't hinted anything to the attending cherubs about what They've discussed. Thinking that They will speak about the past rebellion is simple speculation," Lairn`r continues.

Wanting to address the expectations of Lairn`r, and the rest of my troupe, seems important. Everything in Heaven is abundantly full and that includes our moderate speculation. We are quick and gifted in assimilating small scraps of seemingly unrelated information into a cogent hypothesis or theory. Our conclusions may be wrong, but these times are forgivable because they are rooted, not in impatience, rather in hope.

"Whatever They secretly met about will be soon be revealed. I feel it could be something related to the rebellion. Lucifer probably feels some of the same stirrings we are experiencing about this Banquet. After all, his origin is the same as ours. We angels come from the same source, although the corruption that has been assimilated into his being distorts any light he once had," I muse aloud, as we descend.

Lairn`r waits until we reach the landing on the third floor before responding.

"It should tell us something, though. We recognize you are trying to balance our thinking, cutting short our contemplation of the rebellion, thus losing sight of other issues. Yet, you yourself revisit the situation, once again," Lairn`r smiles broadly, as he delivers his pointed jab at me.

All I can do is smile back. I enjoy our jousts. Trading one gambit for another is stimulating and always pleasant when Lairn`r is the sender and receiver.

We finally reach the bottom of the Steps and exit into the Plaza, the busiest place in all of Heaven. Here, great hosts of angels are always gliding this way and that, toward their various destinations. Now the normally huge numbers are swelled because of the pending Banquet.

"Well, which way do you want to go?" I ask.

Our view of the Banquet Chamber is blocked by the beautiful Temple[8] of Elohim, resting elegantly upon the Temple Mount, rising with grandeur from the Plaza level of the city, directly in front of us. There is only one way up to the Mount and onto the pinnacle where the Temple rests, so going that way wouldn't get us to the Banquet Chamber. It is necessary to go either to the right or to the left. Of course, flying is an option, but it is seldom a viable choice, here in the heart of the city. Those who attempt this have to do a lot of hovering. They must move forward in frequent starts and stops. If all the angels decided to fly to move around this inner sanctum of the City of Elohim, the skies over the City would be filled with wings, making it difficult to navigate. The height of the average angel is from six to eight cubits tall, with the wing span measuring between one and a third to one and a half times one's height.

As we pause, deciding our route, there is action all around us. Some of the angels are headed toward the Mall of Wisdom, some are moving intently toward the stairs leading up to the Temple Mount, directly in front of us. The rest of the angels are dodging others, seeking the Court of Measures, on our immediate left.

"Remember! We are supposed to meet Komodo`r over there, in the Mall of Wisdom. Let's go that way," Lairn'r directs.

"Looking for me?" a commanding voice interjects from behind.

Komodo`r, it turns out, has been waiting for us here and, overhearing our indecision, was simplifying our hunt for him.

"Sorry, it was not my original intent, but I ended up coming on ahead. I started waiting near there, between the Garden and the Mall, just beside the first of the Seven Pillars of Wisdom.[9] After standing there a while, I decided to meditate on the first pillar, the Pillar of Prudence, to see if any new understanding was present. From there I moved on to the Fall of the Seven Waters.[10] The first Water Fall is the Fall of Dispensation. The veil over it had not yet been removed, but I thought I would see if my seeking might be answered. Not receiving anything new, I thought, 'Why not check the Fall of Rest?' Though it, too, is veiled, something significant just might be available. Again, nothing. So I went to the next, and then the next, and then kept going, until I looked up and realized that I was standing not far from where you were coming down the steps. So, well, here I am," Komodo`r says, his words drifting, as he shrugs. He is usually more calculating in his actions than the description he's just offered us, thus his slight confusion.

He needn't explain. The tops of the imposing stone Pillars of Wisdom extend up, out of sight, and can only be seen by angels flying high over the City of Elohim. The sight is truly inspirational. We are all similarly captivated by the majestic Fall of the Seven Waters, the Falls which emanate from the River of Life.[11] We are continually seeking the information that flows from them. Here, since our creation, they have been veiled. We probe to find, beyond these veils, the essence of knowledge for which each of us, constantly, yearns. The veils are very thin, and some spots reveal information, but most is hidden from view and, as well, our understanding.

Having regained his composure, once more Komodo`r gets to the point, "Well now, let me ask both of you then, which way? Do you want to go back through the Mall? Or head through the Court?"

With Lairn`r mumbling something like, "Surprises are not my favorite thing," the consensus is the Court of Measures. Komodo`r really doesn't want to retrace his steps, and since he had found nothing new while there to share with us, it seems wise to go through the Court. So we head to our left and follow along with those angels meandering in that direction.

"What have you been up to?" I ask Komodo`r, as we walk three abreast.

"I have been talking with some angels from my previous troupe, trying to learn something about what Elohim will be revealing at the Banquet. I learned nothing, except that they are as curious as we are about Elohim's cloister, and now the expected announcement. Have either of you learned anything about it?"

"No, nothing," we say, while heading toward the Court.

"It won't be long now, though," I add.

The Court of Measures is a wide, long paved court with sporadically placed fountains and large planters filled with fragrant, multi-colored foliage. Streaming in and out is a branch of the River of Life, a major fixture of the city. Its head waters is somewhere beneath the Temple, but it flows purposefully, touching the city in all directions.

The River of Life sings as it meanders here and there throughout Heaven and on out to the City of Dvar HaElohim now under construction. It is this river that taught the earliest angels how to sing and worship Elohim.

Placed along the various paths, through the Court, are tall columns in the shape of scrolls. Writings upon these scroll columns are the laws, precepts, and principals of Elohim, Eternity, and Highest Heaven. The writings on the scroll columns reinforce our Sovereign's judgments expressing the individual righteousness of each. There are many hundreds of the scrolled columns, each with individual, unique writings. The columns extend well beyond the reach of standing angels, even those as large as Komodo`r.

Vines growing up through the pavement cling to these columns and actually sing an ever-changing, and altogether beautiful, melody. We recognize the various words of song, sung with inviting and alternating tones while, as yet, we do not understand the meaning.

"There, there are those words again," says Komodo`r, as we listen to some of the more familiar verses, while striding by. "'Grace, amazing grace, and soon there will be. It is well with my soul, it is well with my soul,' what can they possibly be saying?"

We walk on in silence, each pondering private patterns of thought. As we navigate along the pathway, we round the southwest edge of the Temple Mount. We are just far enough along so that the Banquet Chamber begins to come into view, rising above the Garden of Remembrance. We can see its roof line and the single spire.

Angels never rush through the Garden of Remembrance. It is a large, continuously expanding, place of powerful impressions, some defying reason. It offers a multitude of pavilions, most of which contain countless books full of records and mementos of past events. Some of them are very personal. Others are volumes of chronicles, similar to this one, covering spans of Eternity. Enticing coverings of scented foliage sing and echo playfully, seducing ears and filling eyes with wondrous long ago views of thoughts, impressions and happenings, accompanied by myriad sensations. These are all parts of the Eternity we share. All senses are touched by these uplifting and quickening treasures. Even delightful, delicate flavors tickle the tongue.

Each angel's senses of smell, sound, taste, touch, and hearing, along with reason and imagination, are affected differently, as we pass nearby. These reactions become even stronger if we pause a while to enjoy the sensory attack. Although the feelings, flooding our senses, are individually unique, they are all taken from Elohim's own senses and point of view. This is true whether the records are personal or cover the scope of a grand event. Through these we are able to fully revisit the past. Certainly this is one of our most pleasant, individually gratifying, experiences.

During our passage, Lairn`r, Komodo`r, and I, want to allow ourselves an opportunity to pause beside one or another of the pavilions, but our compelling desire to reach the Chamber trumps the pavilions' invitations to stay.

"Komodo`r, which entices you most? Mine is the one singing echoes of knowledge that I aquired just after I was created and became aware of my surroundings," Lairn`r asks and answers.

"I would have to say the pavilion next to that one. It induces reminiscence of the disorder and perplexity surrounding the rebellion. Zukher, what about yours?"

"Hmmm, I can't really say. It seems to change each time I come to the Garden. When I am alone, it usually is the Pavilion of Hope. There, the pleasant sensations that I've contemplated, or anticipated, seem to fill my sight. The impression of seeing these sensations is so much more pronounced than any other feelings. When I am with a group, like this trip, it is the Pavilion of Prolonged Proving. It is where the emotion of satisfaction, from overcoming past obstacles that impeded my absolute service to Elohim, is so strong and warm."

In twos, threes, and fours we parade down the Garden pathways toward the entrance to the Chamber. The Chamber is a large, inner edifice lifting high domed ceilings supported at forty-nine cubit intervals by grand arched columns. The outer walls are similarly columned, thus opening the inner rooms to Heaven's constantly balmy weather. The openings on the south and east side of the Chamber look down upon the pavilions of the Garden of Remembrance where we are walking. The openings on the north and east side of the Chamber look down upon the Mall of Wisdom where Komodo`r was investigating before joining us.

Just then, I see those who are awaiting our arrival standing at the foot of the stairs leading up to the Banquet Chamber. "There, over there," I say, while gesturing a little too much. "Gabriel, Klalish, Shtitsen, Sryyab`r, Lez`n and Tantzer. They are all here, so we can go right in."

Greeting everyone warmly, I finally reach Tantzer. I guide him through the rest of the new arrivals, leading him to Lairn`r. "Lairn`r, I would like Tantzer, here, to sit beside you during the Banquet. It will give him a chance to see things from an inquisitor's perspective, if that works for you."

"Sure, fine. I had planned to sit next to Gabriel, but what we'd planned to discuss can wait. Is that acceptable to you, Tantzer?" Lairn`r questions our novice messenger and walks on without awaiting an answer.

Without hesitation, we all begin climbing up the short flight of stairs while chatting with one another, once again. This is a great angelic group. Each is a considerable asset to our troupe. We work well together, contributing to the enrichment of each other, to the greater service of Elohim. We are all the stronger for the special role each one plays. During this Banquet not all of our troupe will sit with us. The tables at the Banquet are not large enough to handle the 100 members in each entourage, so the various troupes are spread out and all are inter-mingled.

I take one last look up at the pillared buttress spanning the opening into the atrium of the Chamber. The primary purpose of the Chamber is for presentations to meaningful gatherings of angels. Inhaling the breathtaking architecture is well worth a frequent visit, even if a banquet is not on the agenda. At the crest of the buttress is a six pointed star, held in a mighty hand that is also filled with small grains of sand. It has been that way for as long as angels have been, but no one, as yet, understands their meaning. There are many such mysteries embedded in the bulwarks and structures of Heaven.

Each of these mysteries enjoys a prominently displayed image found in the Citadel's Hall of Mysteries, located on the third floor, just below the Observatory, where Lairn`r and I had been visiting. All around us are pillars lifting the transparent ceiling high into the upper reaches of the Highest Heaven.

"It won't be long now," whispers Lairn`r.

THE ANNOUNCEMENT

Waves of wonder, once lifted, carry the final evidence of Eternity's winds. They continue their pulsating passage, striking and reverberating from all quarters and celestial domains, some known and some unknown or even imagined, except by Elohim. One of these waves towers above all others. Just as a pebble hitting a tranquil pond, the resultant circles whirl, preceding and trailing it, as far as the eye can see. Its origin was a Heaven-quake which disturbed the stable tranquility reigning over Heaven. The epicenter of that shaking was the short lived rebellion, when a third of Heaven's citizens chose ill-advised loyalty to a cherub, named Lucifer. Together they conspired to overthrow Heaven's rightful Sovereign, Elohim. Whatever Lucifer fanaticized about accomplishing by those actions, we cannot imagine. We have pondered that wretched expedition as high-level reasoning creatures of Heaven, yet we come up with no answers. While very little, if anything, escapes our attention, the rationale for this prideful action is beyond our comprehension.

In the deciding moments of the conflict, with great wisdom and Godly restraint, Elohim preserved the Kingdom, and cast the perpetrators out of Heaven, thus forever sealing their eventual end. Such is the consequence of their disobedience. Their lodgings were quarantined and eventually destroyed. Compatriots and associates of the rebels were proved before being allowed to continue enjoying the liberties offered to all Heaven's citizens. Those found culpable were cast away as reprobates, as well.

From this purging, a vacuum developed where infinite avenues of scholarship were left unattended. While we wait for the Banquet to commence, I voice my wonderings about this, and the considerable chaos following the tsunami, to Komodo`r.

"Komodo`r, do you classify the chaos following the rebellion purposeful or purposeless?" I begin.

Except for some novice angels, all of us know and understand the distinction and nuances of these extremes of chaos. Purposeful chaos is that which serves Elohim's perfect purpose, while fulfilling His will. Purposeless chaos is that which erupts out of dark and suspicious motives. However secret the origin may be, it will be contrary to Elohim's perfect purpose. In our vast powers of imagination, we find purposeless chaos to be distasteful to behold, always insulting one's senses.

"Conducting such an inquiry is an arduous undertaking, since all avenues of thought and reasoning crisscross and change direction. Perhaps we are intentionally prevented from forming a reliable analysis," Komodo`r replies.

"We know that Lucifer's actions and intents were rooted in disobedience and sin.[12] He and his nefarious cohorts plotted to steal the Throne and destroy the Kingdom. Until that conspiracy was revealed, we had never witnessed anything that fit the profile of 'purposeless chaos.' I am theorizing now, but if that which came from Lucifer isn't a prime example of 'purposeless chaos,' then I can't imagine whatever could be." My reply to his comments is well beyond my previous insight, and I realize this, even as I am saying it.

This manifested understanding, just coming forth without forethought, is not uncommon with citizens, and is welcomed whenever it does. For we know that when this happens, HaRuach has just caressed our lips and minds, while swooping by unseen.

"There is a series of complex events that must first occur," I continue, "and they determine which of the two disparate possibilities describe an event. I think, the correct answer is that something can be conceived as purposeless chaos. As the path of the intended chaos winds through Eternity, Elohim passes judgment upon it. If He determines the matter can be transformed, from 'purposeless' to 'purposeful,' then He acts to make it so. If He, in His eternal wisdom, determines that the matter cannot be transformed into 'purposeful' without Him sinning, the matter must still be resolved. The only resolution available, then, is to see that it can no longer exist." As I am speaking this, I am also proving it. It sounds good to me, and my reasoning also agrees, for it seems to resonate. So I continue...

"Lingering purposeless chaos would be infectious and therefore would spread. Stopping it before it spreads is critical. From our point of view, the actions perpetrated by Lucifer and his immoral followers were without any recognizable virtue and, therefore, resulted in purposeless chaos. The chaos created by conspiring to steal the Throne is dangerous enough to require annihilation. Had Lucifer succeeded, this wonderfully rich kingdom, created by Elohim, would have been destroyed. What conceivable good could possibly have come from that?"

Of course our musings are just a prelude to the pending Banquet. Recently, Elohim, our great Sovereign, cloistered in Their secret place...the Temple's Holy of Holies. They proffered no explanation when They went there, but Heaven came to a hushed standstill. Until they emerged, we did what we do. We speculated.

"Was this conclave to address the effects of the rebellion?" Or, my favorite, "Are They going to end Lucifer's future?" They emerged without any explanation, except to give notice that we are summoned to a great Banquet, whose guest speaker will be Elohim.

It is this Banquet, and His imminent address, that Lairn`r and I were discussing while inhaling the majesty of the created expanse.

The Chamber is totally white in décor. The inner columns store powerful curtains, kept hidden from view, which are used to cordon off fractions of the Chamber to facilitate smaller banquets of a private nature.

Our sumptuous Banquet will be one of Heaven's finest. The breaking of bread and the enjoyment of every bite of the nutritious fruits, nuts and berries is most pleasurable, yet merely a sideline to the main course of mutual fellowship and stimulating conversation. It is a delight whose novelty never wears off. Our intoxication comes from the promise of the presence of Elohim and the joy He brings to every table.

The meals are served by troupes rewarded with this privileged commission. Their leaders attend to the serving duties, side by side, seeking only to add to the pleasure of those eating. They freely join in the various conversations, agreeing or disagreeing as new bits and pieces of information are introduced. They then carry the hanging dialog to another table where they infect the present thoughts with those of the previous tables. If the banquet agenda is to include Elohim addressing the notable body of citizens, then much of the conversation is devoted to speculation regarding what Elohim might be about to reveal. That is the nature of the conversation at our table and those around us, based upon the information being carried from there to here.

Seated at the table on my right, and leaning on his elbows, is Lairn`r. He is one of two inquisitors gracing our troupe. Seated next to him on his right are Tantzer and Gabriel, our two novice messengers. Komodo`r, one of our tacticians and Klalish, a warrior angel, are seated next. Shtitsen, an exhorter, Sryyab`r and Lez`n, our scribes, sit to my left.

Bartke, Omán, Mehgen', Dāwīd, Gershom, Alexis, Emunah, and Ha-brit, who is sitting next to Klalish, fill the remaining places at our table. These eight are a special cast of angels whose commissions haven't yet been determined. They spend most of their Eternity mastering various trades and procedures.

Upon his arrival, Michael moves about the Chamber, greeting and embracing those at tables gathered closest to his. He, too, is awaiting Elohim's address. His presence now indicates Elohim's imminent arrival. We are all here. The Chamber is full and at the ready. There is an air of highly charged expectation. A gathering of this sort portends great magnitude. Our assembly continues murmuring amongst ourselves in hushed eagerness, awaiting the appearance of Elohim.

And then the Chamber stills. Our eyes widen as appears, before us, a great light. The glow is huge around the light, so great our eyes cannot discern more than a vague figure in massive folds of satin and gossamer cloth that shimmers and moves with the light…a shifting of pale blues, violet, indigo, yellow. Yes, the colors of the most magnificent rainbow. So bright is the force before us that we are caught in breathless wonder. Elohim!

Then there is a rumble, like that of a distant wave, as it builds upon itself, before breaking toward shore. The resonance is that of a rich bass tone, accompanied by a tender breeze, rustling gently through the light green of new shoots of spring leaf, adorning swaying boughs of a verdant tree. The sound is yet soft and sweet, as is the velvet touch on the petals of newly blossomed floral buds. The tones are blended in a magnificent symphony of vibrations that each angel feels within. This masterpiece reverberates in tune with the angel's own individual frequency. Each angel senses, rather than hears, the words. Yet each one has complete cognizance of what is imparted to him and comprehends, each at his own level of understanding: The still small voice!

"It is true and certain, it is for you…the citizens of Heaven, joint partakers, worthy of these glories…to search out and seek insight into great matters. It is for you, therefore, to seek full comprehension of those things which came to light, when those who were not of us were cast from us, that they might receive their eternal recompense for their labors after the darkness filled them. Understand, their deeds were not wrought in secret. For when, in the fullness of Eternity, those things came to be and they determined to steal that which was not theirs, by subterfuge and deceit, their own darkness betrayed their distorted objective. There is nothing that I cannot know. I knew of their evil intent, even before the universe was created or ever the seed of their mischief was planted. I knew they would choose darkness over light, bondage over liberty, anguish over peace, and sorrow over joy. Those empty cisterns, by their actions, have judged themselves to be unworthy of the state and offices to which they had been appointed. Therefore, it is now right and fitting that others among you fill their former lot."

Elohim pauses. We wait. Michael lifts a scroll from within his cloak and begins to read the names of these worthy within our midst.

One by one, those chosen by Elohim to occupy the voided state and offices, are called forward. There, Dvar HaElohim lays His holy hands upon each of them. He speaks and breathes upon them his breath of knowledge, and thereby imparts giftings and power unto those now invited to that for which they were foreordained.

Elohim again speaks to His citizens who remain attentive to Their ministration, "We have taken counsel together to answer events past. Perpetrators of that past, known by all, are not present in the future. We call all of you to secure that future and see that it finds its appointed end. The struggle of the present will be arduous. The failures and transgressions, of those to whom We refer, only serve to underscore their future absence from Eternity. Any failure on our part, however minuscule, in wisdom, in faith, in word or in deed, purchases an impossible end. The result will be that darkness will hold keys to a dominion over light. We have determined that the unfolding campaign will interlock with the future of which We speak. Now wait, for the appointed crusade begins."

With that, the Amen cups His mighty hands and breathes upon Them. We are enraptured by the wonder of this, as suddenly there appear in His hands small lights, growing in brilliance and size whereupon He, The Almighty, turns His eyes toward the vast opening overhead. Our eyes follow the movement of His own, and there above us, appears the created universe in all its glory, just as we last had seen it. Into the universe Dvar HaElohim tosses the lights which He has held securely in His Hands. These sparkles move, as each proceeds to nestle in an assigned station to which it has been secretly commanded by Elohim. "These stars," says He, "are my Word,[13] written in the created Heavens, as a dictum and a testimony of all that I say and promise here, and that is to come. Let they that hear My voice understand what HaRuach says unto them and the meaning of these words."

With that motion and His declaration echoing in our ears, the Light disappears from view. Some of us sit quietly in awe, reflecting on His words. Others, to afford relief from the gravity of what we'd just heard and seen, chat with anyone who would seem to be listening. Michael stands up and addresses his fellow citizens.

"We are engaged in a conflict of eternal consequence. It is true that this matter requires a great amount of wisdom and careful consideration. The outcome of the circumstances, to which Elohim referred, will serve to prove whether this new dominion, conceived by Them, and so grandly executed, can withstand the test of utter darkness perpetrated upon it. Eternity will judge if our works, while holy and righteous, are sufficient to withstand the evil onslaught. Let us, therefore, resolve and commit ourselves to renew our devotion to the truth, to holiness. Let us stand by Him in steadfast devotion, bringing Elohim's kingdom to Earth. For it is on that untried stage that the coming conflict ensues."

MYSTERY - ELOHIM

"So there is a coming conflict and it begins on Earth!" Komodo`r reiterates Michael's closing narrative.

"Right! And using Elohim's overview as our source of understanding, there are risks to the Kingdom and a prophetic promise of a future, empty of Lucifer, along with those who join that emptiness because they join his past. What does that mean? How is it possible for there to be a future without those already created? They cannot, that is, we cannot cease to exist. Not in all the annals of Heaven is it taught that angels can cease to exist. Will Elohim change the laws of life? The laws by which we exist? I can't see that as a possibility," Lairn`r, ever the inquisitor, is now questioning himself, and he is not yet finished.

"Elohim also mentioned the risk. The campaign involves the danger that should a single instance of faithlessness occur, the Kingdom of Heaven is lost. That is a new concept to be explored," Lairn`r comments, and heads off, down the steps and out into the Garden, shaking his head this way and that. As he makes his way into the dispersing crowd of exiting angels, he disappears.

"Well, he has one thing certifiably correct! These things are certainly new," Komodo`r begins, taking up the challenge of the silence left by Lairn'r's departure. He frowns, as he ruminates on a concept that he wants to put into words. With an "Aha!" look on his face, he continues, "Eternity is measured by the events that transpire, marking the passage of Eternity from one episode to another. Therefore, is it not so, that we angel citizens will remember this passage as the time before, or after, the Rebellion? Whereas Lucifer will remember this time as the era of attack, foolishly and, in his egocentric estimation, his near success of unseating our Sovereign. While Elohim will, no doubt, measure before and after this epoch, by relating to it as 'The Banquet.'

"I think I am going back to my quarters now, but by the way of the Mall of Wisdom. This new teaching might have partially lifted some of the veils covering the Fall of the Seven Waters."

With that, he too, departs down the steps and, turning, heads into the Garden.

"Tantzer," I fill the void, since we have a moment to visit. "I suppose you will return to the city that Dvar HaElohim is building north of us. How is that coming? Has the palace for Dvar HaElohim been completed, so He can take residence there, instead of in the Citadel?"

"Since I have a training session with Gabriel, I will head back to Dvar HaElohim's city directly following that. I am tasked with addressing some acoustics in an audience room in His palace. It is a most beautiful place. Have any of you dropped by to get a look?" Tantzer answers with no indication that he is really about to leave.

Having a new thought, I add, "Tantzer, would you be so kind, before you do that, to take a message to Komodo`r and Lairn`r for me, with my apologies for not thinking of this earlier. Request we gather at the Citadel, in the Mezzanine, just after the worship service later. I would like to have a scribe present. I prefer Lez`n, but our other scribe in our troupe will be fine. Looking into the mystery presented by Elohim, I feel the need to dissect it. I'm moved to outline our thoughts and place them into written form. It might help us later. Tantzer, you would benefit from joining us and adding your comments, as well."

The worship service was glorious, and uplifting. It always is. There is no greater or grander thing to do in Heaven, than partake in the worship of Elohim. It is amazing that Elohim would humble Themselves so much as to allow us a presence before Them just to worship, praise, and offer our thanksgiving to the One that makes being alive, complete. The self-sustaining One, Elohim, has no need to be worshipped as angels think of "need." They have all things, or so it seems, yet They are moved to permit those, so much less than They, to come into Their presence just to worship Them.

This service spurred Lairn'r, Komodo`r, Tantzer and me to endeavor to outline the mystery of Elohim all the more. We are pleased that the scribe, Lez`n, is available to record our musings. Together, we head to find some private space somewhere in the Mezzanine to look into the essence of Elohim.

Lairn'r, Komodo`r, and I have often deliberated our various observations about our mystery, who is our Sovereign. This would be the first such examination that also includes Tantzer. It will prove to be interesting, thus sequestering ourselves for a little while, bathed in the afterglow of the worship service.

I begin, "Our great and worthy Sovereign is too exalted to be encapsulated by a single name. Any such name that may be offered would immediately limit Him as the syllables roll off the lips of the orator. Our everlasting Father, then, must humble Himself to allow us to know Him by a name. Each name by which He chooses to reveal Himself portrays a different facet of His greatness and person. We, the angels, often contemplate the merits and the measure of the multitude of mysteries inhabiting the Hall of Mysteries. All those mysteries pale in comparison to the mystery that is Elohim, the name by which we know Him.

"It would take an orator of incomparable accomplishment to attempt a proper description of the attributes of His greatness. Alas, I am not such an angel. With whom can Elohim be compared? All life is rooted in His eternal breath. When He speaks, Eternity hesitates, so as not to advance beyond any boundaries He wills to set. His word is sacred. Every syllable, every accent, every utterance of Elohim is accountable for understanding His intent. Nothing in His word is ever wasted and always finds its mark. If His focus is joy, then the result is joy, unspeakable and full of glory. If His focus is peace, then His words gently caress the flower of His eye. Never overlooked is His hand of mercy and His rod of correction, each of which equally survives all scrutiny.

"He is light. He is mercy. He is holy. Every breath, every thought, every desire, every will is righteous. No region is neglected by His inspection. Even darkness is light before Him. In our analysis of this prime mystery we are pondering the darkness of Lucifer and his fallen angels, and the question of that darkness, while we recognize that angels do not die. Elohim never makes a mistake. If He did, then Lucifer would have dominion over Elohim. We passionately embrace our covenant with Elohim, recognizing the significance of every assigned task He commands.

"Elohim has no beginning and He has no ending. He is vastly different from anything else we know. We have great difficulty comprehending the idea of Elohim's eternalness. The vastness of Elohim also includes Their Oneness and yet more than One. For Elohim is One…Elohim is also three Ones…acting in concert as a single determination, without any competing differences. These Three are perfectly flowing through Eternity as a single river, though mostly separated into three branches that combine when Their wisdom determines a course of action. When the branches are combined, the river has a body, soul, and spirit…and each branch is holy and, therefore, the One is holy."

Komodo`r begins, "I, Komodo`r, too, have devoted much time contemplating the mystery that is our Sovereign. Our mighty Sovereign is limited only by His omnipotence, omnipresence, omniscience and omnibenevolence. These four constraints guide Elohim and each of them mitigates the others.

"By His omnipotence He exercises limitless power. Though His power is limitless, it nevertheless operates in voluntary concert within the constraints of His omnipresence, omniscience, and omnibenevolence. Such is the wisdom of our Sovereign, who wields His unlimited power over all of creation.

"In His omnipresence He is everywhere. Our sovereign simultaneously exists everywhere in Eternity...past, present, and future. He hears and remembers the simplest whispered prayers offered in Eternity past, so that He may keep the promise of that prayer in Eternity present or future. Likewise, His omnipresence answers a future plea, in Eternity present or in Eternity past.

"In His omniscience He enjoys unlimited knowledge. He possesses knowledge of the past, present and future and, therefore, exercises His will based upon past, present, and future realities.

"In His omnibenevolence His goodness knows no bounds. The mystery here rests in the depth of this spring of life, and though we have witnessed some of the dimensions of His omnipotence, omnipresence, and omniscience, we have not plumbed the depth of Elohim's omnibenevolence. All testaments available to us here in Heaven lack demonstrative examples that reveal the magnitude of His benevolence, although we know it is limitless.

"Finally, it is important to note that as great as His omnipotence, omnipresence, omniscience, and omnibenevolence are, these characteristics do not eclipse Elohim. He remains the preeminent One in all things."

Lairn`r begins, "We have been blessed, over a great span of Eternity, with major insight and understanding of the absolute righteousness of Elohim. Though the depths of His righteousness are still being fathomed, we are fully confident that much of what was once a mystery is now to be revealed. Elohim's judgment, pronounced upon Lucifer and the fallen, erased any lingering reservation we might have had. Elohim established the law, whereby an action, or cause, bears a resultant effect. The loyal citizenry of Heaven voluntarily embrace these laws by which we are judged. We cannot conceive of existing any other way. Eternity judges us according to these laws. The independence from these laws, sought after by Lucifer, is not something we seek. Rather, we seek the full manifestation of the treasures and riches which are promised to those who surrender to the majesty by which they are endowed.

"Elohim has instructed that there is a mystery that remains regarding righteousness that no angel citizen has known existed. It was not one discovered by any of the angels. The revelation of its existence was the subject addressed during a major audience we had with Elohim. He asked us, 'Do you see a mystery in My righteousness?' At that time I knew of none. I looked around the chamber, and studying the countenance of each of my compatriots, it was obvious that they didn't know of one either.

"Our reply to Elohim was, 'No Lord, we see no mystery in Your righteousness.'

"With a pleasant smile playing upon His face, Elohim went on to explain, 'The mystery is this. Eternity judges My righteousness differently from the laws governing cause and effect. This righteousness is established by the reward from a much grander law. The Law of Faith.[14]'

"What? You might say, 'What does this mean?'

"Elohim went on to instruct us, 'I judge all things by the evidence of things not yet witnessed. I judge things that are not, as if they already are. I judge Eternity future in Eternity present. That is the power of the Law of Faith. Thus, my righteousness is the product of faith, and is based solely upon the assurances from Me, that everything I say is true and righteous. Even though, temporarily, these things do not yet appear to be.'

"Elohim went on and, as an example, used the presently unfolding strategy in which all of Heaven's citizens are engaged, 'We promised you, the citizens, that Heaven will be purged of Lucifer and his horde, even though all giftings and assignments given unto them are without repentance. This is consistent with My law. Yet evidence of them will cease, even though they are eternal beings.'

"Elohim said that They have a bold plan. If we, His faithful citizens, follow this plan we will not only fully understand the magnitude of His omnibenevolence, but we will also see the final sentence upon Lucifer and his followers," and so Lairn`r concludes his oratory.

Tantzer adds, "I am delighted to endorse the elucidations of my colleagues. I have listened to each of them as they have commented upon the mystery of Elohim. Lez`n has recorded their individual observations. The offerings of Zukher, Komodo`r, and Lairn`r are worthy for their depth of insight, incisive knowledge, and profound consideration of these revealed mysteries. Though I cannot begin to reach their heights, my position as a novice affords me a perspective I may eventually lose, as Eternity fills my own reservoir of knowledge. The others focused upon the serious face of the mysteries of Elohim. I, on the other hand, concentrate upon the lesser notes in this melody that resonate the mysteries of Elohim. I do not limit the elegance, or the inspiration, their perspective offers, but I am filled with the pure enjoyment, the fun of Elohim...His wit and cleverness.

"Through my eyes, I see an obvious readiness upon the face of Elohim, to burst forth with robust enjoyment, as He relishes Eternity's events passing in review. My observations convince me that the magnitude of His omniscience, omnipresence, omnipotence, and omnibenevolence place no burden upon the infrequently alluded to mystery of Elohim, that is His omnisentience.[15] His omnisentience and Their often referenced attributes are abundant fruits of His soul. Their omnisentience amplifies the magnitude of Their pleasure and grief over individual circumstances His other four attributes encounter. I suspect, that hidden in the mystery of Elohim, is a wellspring of sentiments that will take the rest of Eternity to reveal."

This may, indeed, be one of the longest pronouncements from Tantzer that we've ever heard!

He continues, "This leads me to my second novice observation. What is the source of Elohim? We, the angels, draw sustenance from Him and He defines who and what we are, but from what wells of sustenance does He draw waters? Who and what defines Him? These mysteries we offer are but minimal observations of a Sovereign that, by His own nature, unwillingly defies such observations. When we need encouragement, we are encouraged by Him. When we need promises to give us direction, Elohim abounds with words of promise and assurance. When we need faith, Elohim reveals a hope within us that defies our ability to reason. This hope is the forerunner of faith, from which all things exist. Faith, in turn, bears the fruit of virtue, and virtue supports knowledge. Knowledge then sustains self-control and self-control is the ancestor of patience. From patience comes god-likeness and that is the river from which benevolence flows.

"This observation being true then, when Elohim needs a promise where does He turn? When Elohim has a promise, but needs hope to rest His faith upon, where does He look? When Elohim is deprived of Godly essence, necessitating virtue, so as to once again energize all of creation, where does He begin the excavation in search of that treasure? Where does Elohim search for the knowledge that has yet to form within His omniscience? When all of Heaven cries out for the hand of Elohim to act and His own counsel is to wait, where does He find the self-control to endure the pressure to act rashly?

"So I ask an answer to the conundrum that is the mystery of Elohim. He always was, is, and ever shall be, but what is the fountain or spring of life from whence He comes?"

After this Tantzer rendering, Tantzer sags a little, coming to rest in an empty chair that just happens to be close by.

Lez`n closes the record of our trifling observations. Turning to Komodo`r who is standing near Tantzer, he states concisely, "Thus it is entered into the book."

With that the voice of Adonai fills the chamber, "I Am. I came of Myself, from Myself, and return unto Myself. There was none before Me and none shall come after Me. If I came of another then that entity would be the omnipotent, omnipresent, omniscient, and omnibenevolent one filling Heaven. By Me all things exist, and there has never been, nor ever shall be, a moment of Eternity that I was not present... forever proving all that would come after. I swear by no other greater than Myself...I bear witness that My Word is true; Eternity bears witness that My Word is true; all creation bears witness that My Word is true. These three agree. If I were to deny My Word is true, I would be a liar, a thief, and a destroyer of all that was, all that is, and all that is to come..."

The area where we've gathered is heavy with silence, as Adonai, the author and finisher of Eternity ceases speaking. He defines mystery and true revelation of mystery. It is altogether right, and fitting, that He add the Amen to our musings.

LET THERE BE

The Hearing Center is an immense room capable of holding a multitude of angels. The wing span of the angels gives the word "immense" special meaning. Attending angels must climb the Steps of Ascension through the heart of the Citadel to reach The Hearing Center on the sixth floor. The Steps lead past the Mezzanine, then on past the Hall of Mysteries which occupies the second floor. They must continue climbing past the Observatory on the third floor and through the inner Antechamber on the fourth. Occupying the fifth floor, the Throne of Grace which is under construction, is the scene of boundless energy. Projected over the floors below, the vast space on the sixth floor is dedicated to the Hearing Center.

Elohim will be addressing the angels crowding the Hearing Center. The seating is already filled by the time we arrive. We will be part of the overflowing, expectant throng standing next to the walls. Michael, the archangel, won't be directing this session. He will be waiting on the Lord, like the rest of us.

After the invitation came forth, I had little chance to talk with other troupe leaders. I am thinking that some mysteries and unanswered questions will now be addressed. While it isn't rare for Elohim to address us, it is always a memorable occasion when He does. Since the creation of the expanse, and Lucifer's rebellion, troupes have been searching the Hall of Mysteries, and all of Heaven, for anything we can learn about what lies ahead.

Angels work diligently at pursuing knowledge. We spend much of our ministry investigating the mysteries that abound, each sealed by Elohim. When an angel, or troupe, unlocks a mystery or a portion thereof, that revelation becomes unsealed, and recognition of that achievement is recorded. Much like an angel craftsman cutting facets in a precious stone to release the exquisite color and brilliance locked therein, or an angel setting free the form of a magnificent statue buried in a hunk of Heavenly stone, so the angels embrace revealing Heaven's secrets. It is upon these records of achievement that maturity accrues to the individual angels, thus advancement in the ranks results.

We have learned that the expanse Lairn`r and I had been staring at, so long ago, is continuing, unhindered, to enlarge. Also, that the laws of governance over the panorama remain fixed, unaffected by Lucifer's tantrum. Only Lucifer's blemished domain and its heaven are impacted.

The creation of that expanse brought into existence a new dimension, and a new table of laws. One of them is called the Law of Time. The Law of Time differentiates its measurements in the expanse from Elohim's measurement of time in Heaven. It introduced wondrous opportunities for investigation and depths of knowledge to explore.

That new dimension incorporated a law defining boundaries, as most laws do. The scope of this time law, when activated, included the universe and Earth. Knowledge of its existence drew the citizens of Highest Heaven into another interesting conundrum. Learning how to use the law's precepts to account for a small span of eternity, when addressing one another, had become a necessity. Previously, as all know, our time had been measured by event propinquity.

We look forward to learning the reason for this particular measure of time being created.

In unison, without an announcement, we all recognize that Elohim is now present in the Hearing Center. An instant hush overcomes the room. I realize that my entire being is filling with unspeakable joy. The joy begins in the inner middle of me and radiates, soon spilling over upon my lips. I yield then to this irresistible fervor and my voice rises to sing hosannas in a language I have not learned. Every angel present joins the chorus in worship and adoration. The circle of our worship radiates like a wave, until I hear the voices of all of Heaven joining the refrain.

The angels are standing in eager anticipation. It is obvious that something very big is about to happen. The wonder of a coming together of angels for a momentous delivery from Elohim is felt like a magnificent rise of power too heady to describe.

Now, an eternal instant seems to hang, waiting for everyone to reach total attentiveness before moving on. The moment Elohim seemed to be awaiting arrives. The blemish within the expanse that Lairn`r and I had been contemplating before, suddenly appears and Elohim declares...

"Let there be light!"

"Lucifer must be furious because this had to have caught him off guard," Lairn`r whispers at my elbow.

"His hatred makes it so. He is defeated again," I reply, not wanting to prolong the discussion. The absence of God's glory which is, by itself, one with the fallen angels, is not something upon which I want my imagination to linger. Not for an instant.

Behind me I hear a grunt from Komodo`r. He never lacks an opinion, much of which is expressed in sound, rather than in words. "Nothing to say, Komodo`r?" I challenge over my shoulder.

"The presence of God's grandeur says it all, don't you think?" was all he could come up with.

The action before us hadn't ceased during our interlude. The three of us refocus to witness Elohim seeing the light and declaring it good. He then follows this up by separating the light's brilliance, from the absence of it. Elohim then names the brilliance, *day*. He also names the absence of light, *night*.

Listen. Elohim, again, speaks. "Let there be a breadth of sky and let it divide the expanse above from the Earth below."

"Did Elohim give the expanse a name?" I ask Komodo`r.

"Yes," he answers, "heaven. You need to listen and quit letting your imagination run like you do," he chides me, playfully, returning my earlier challenge.

This creative effort happened in an instant here. But we know that upon Earth the creation has taken one Day…the second day.

As the second day is ending, we are joined by Tantzer.

"Well?" he asks.

"Where have you been? Have you been watching these wonders unfold?" I answer his open-ended query with my own.

"I was over there, across the Hearing Center. Have you heard that Elohim wants us ready when the new presence is created? New commissions are being defined over there, even as other new things are being created. These creations will need us immediately. Earth is the place over which Lucifer has a measured dominion. This creation will be in his domain," Tantzer brings us up to date, using an unusually serious tone.

New presence? What is this that Tantzer knows, that sounds foreign to us? This novice angel, in his lighthearted manner, acquires all sorts of information not privy to the rest of us. He is simply included in conversations and the dissemination of information, since the troupes don't take him terribly seriously. Hearing about this new presence raises all sorts of questions.

"Are you ready to reengage Lucifer?" Lairn`r asks Tantzer. Not waiting for an answer, but turning to me, he seems to shudder at the prospect, and asks, assuming that some of us will be assigned to Earth, "Will Michael lead the angels that are chosen to go?"

With that communal observation, we wonder which angels will be readied for their passage from the Observatory to Earth in order to engage the enemy.

We again grow quiet in anticipation, as a new cycle is about to begin.

As before, we hear or rather feel, the words of Elohim, "Let the waters under the heaven be gathered together unto one place, and let the dry land appear." He follows this by naming the dry land, Earth, and the gathered water, Seas.

As Elohim continues to draw from His imagination, He speaks, "Let the Earth bring forth grass, the herb yielding seed, and the fruit tree yielding fruit after his kind, whose seed is in it, upon the Earth."

At Elohim's command, and in full view of us all, the Earth brings forth that which was spoken. In unison, Lairn`r, Tantzer, Komodo`r, and the rest of the angels join Elohim in declaring it good in beauty and splendor.

With this, the third Earth day comes to a close.

We are enthralled by the creation taking shape before us. As He pauses, we pause, as well. There is new knowledge flowing within the River of Life.

Elohim continues, "Let there be lights in the breadth of the sky to divide the day from the night. Let them be for signs, and for seasons, and for days, and years. Let them be for lights in the breadth of the sky to give light upon the Earth."

We watch as two great lights appear: the greater light to rule the day and the lesser light to rule the night. His word creates the stars, also. Elohim sets them in the breadth of the sky to give light upon the Earth.

Again, in unison with Elohim, we see that it is good.

The fourth Earth cycle drifts to a close and there is, again, a pause in the action. We take this intermission to reflect on the symphony conducted by the master director, our Sovereign.

During our contemplation we are occupied, as well, with this prospect of travel to Earth. Which of us, we wonder, will be assigned the task of battling with the fallen angels, who now exercise dominion on Earth? Before, when the fallen angels were cast out of Heaven, they crashed onto the Earth and wreaked havoc on the unprepared and undefended piece of the universe. They proceeded to turn the once pleasant surroundings into a formless mass, clouded in the absence of Elohim's glory. This time, with the emerging creation, angels will be sent to combat those evil spirits, thus preventing a similar result manifesting on this reformed Earth. There will be angels chosen, no doubt, to guard the new presence. Who will they be?

Our thirst for knowledge about what we just witnessed is great. The expanse we behold is continuing to increase. Within the expanse the birthing of new globes and features continues. It seems the creation process of Elohim is never ending.

The greater manifestation of the glory of Elohim: A new day, a new testimony, new assignments, new knowledge, new objects. Such wonders move us to interrupt His process of creation to spontaneously worship Elohim. Heaven echoes the sound of this worship.

"Let the waters bring forth abundantly the moving creatures that hath life, and fowl that may fly above the Earth in the open space of the sky." It is, hitherto, Elohim's greatest declaration. The fifth day sees an abundance of life come into being. Each unique, each made after no other living thing. Yet, with their creation, they come with the ability to propagate life like unto itself.

God created great whales, and every living creature that moves, which the waters brought forth abundantly, after their kind, and every winged fowl after his kind.

We watch in a kind of trance, caught up in feasting with our eyes. Elohim saw and declared it, too, is good. He blesses them, saying, "Be fruitful, and multiply, and fill the waters in the seas, and let fowl multiply in the Earth."

Thus the work of Elohim, in the fifth cycle, is complete.

In anticipation of the next Earth day, a silence now settles over the venues of Heaven. It's always interesting to me that mulling over Elohim's words and wonders is as thrilling as the initial introduction. As I reach the most savory portion of what has transpired, I see Michael beckon to me with a nod of his head. It's a motion I recognize immediately, as a result of working with him on so many projects.

Approaching Michael, after wending my way through the crowd, I see a scroll in his outstretched hand. He smiles, and hands it to me. Reading these orders defined on this scroll, against the backdrop of this momentous creation, I am pleased to learn the purpose of my troupe's formation. Elohim has chosen us to be the primary source of ministry to the yet-to-be created presence.

I return to my place, lost in my own thoughts. I'm speculating if my covenant partners are wondering what Michael wanted of me, however, I will keep my counsel until Elohim's creation is complete.

Lairn`r has no questions, and is sitting with a puzzled look.

Tantzer is mumbling, seemingly to himself, about how fast this is happening.

Ever vigilant, Komodo`r is standing guard over nothing.

The rest of our troupe is busy with one thing or another. Some have assigned duties to complete before the sixth Earth cycle begins. Others have the liberty to enjoy the expectation. Since the judgment of the angels in rebellion, there has been continuous activity, most of it associated with this forthcoming creation. Now I can feel, all over, the quietness and the waiting. It is palpable, this anticipation.

At the entrance of the sixth Earth day the Seven Spirits[16] fearlessly begin moving across the surface of the breadth of sky above Earth, thus indicating that everything is ready. The instant has arrived.

Once again Elohim speaks forth, in concert with the Seven Spirits.

We hear here, but Earth hears there, "Let the Earth bring forth the living creature after his kind, cattle, and creeping thing, and beast of the Earth after his kind."

Suddenly there is movement upon Earth in a variety of forms. The spoken word of Elohim brings forth an abundance of unprecedented life. It is so, for He creates the beast of the Earth after his kind and cattle after their kind, and everything that creepeth upon the Earth after his kind. Elohim again sees that it is good.

"Zukher, this is it?" Lairn`r asks, speaking just above a whisper.

"Keep silent!" directs Komodo`r. "Wait for it!"

"TJOTL[17] is my strength," blurts Tantzer. His personality, coming forth in this particular instant, is interesting.

"Well?" Lairn`r persists. We aren't ignoring him; rather, we have our own thoughts racing through our minds and forget to listen.

And Elohim declares, "Let us make man in our image, after our likeness: and let them have dominion over the fish of the sea and over the fowl of the air, and over the cattle, and over all the Earth, and over every creeping thing that creepeth upon the Earth."

Elohim creates man in His own image, in the image of Elohim creates He him; male and female creates He them. And Elohim blesses them, and says unto them, "Be fruitful, and multiply, and replenish the Earth, and subdue it: And have dominion over the fish of the sea, and over the fowl of the air, and over every living thing that moves upon the Earth."

Then Elohim says to the man, "Behold, I have given you every herb bearing seed, which is upon the face of all the Earth, and every tree, in which is the fruit of a tree yielding seed; to you it shall be for food. And to every beast of the Earth, and to every fowl of the air, and to everything that creepeth upon the Earth, wherein there is life, I have given every green herb for food."

We look upon this scene. "It is so," I breathe in awe. "It is so," echoes Lairn`r. "It is so," Tantzer and Komodo`r sigh together.

Elohim looks upon everything that He has made, and it is good. And the evening and the morning are the sixth day.

So Elohim forms man of the dust of the ground, and breathes into his nostrils the breath of life; and man becomes a living soul. The foretold presence is now before us, standing upon Earth.

THE APOKÁLYPSIS [18]

"What is man? Who is man? The angels need to know!" Lairn`r asserts his interest.

"Why is man? What is his purpose? What does this have to do with the unfolding battle plan?" Komodo`r counters, revealing his area of interest.

"Have you noticed any similarity to man in the Hall of Mysteries?" I say, getting everyone back on track, heading toward our favored estate of learning. "There will soon be vast stores of knowledge about them, don't you think? With man's creation, Elohim's knowledge will begin to flow from the Throne."

"They aren't really much different from us, are they?" Tantzer chimes in.

Thus a season of joyous speculation begins immediately upon Elohim's rest from his most recent glorious works.

"Elohim said that man is a living soul. We don't have a soul. That is a big difference!" Komodo`r states, with emphasis. "Let's begin there, then. Since Elohim has a soul, man is like unto Elohim, and unlike us. When Elohim created him, He said man was made in Their image."

Lairn`r asks the question we all want to dance with, "What does it mean 'in the image' of Elohim? After all, aren't we 'in the image' of Elohim?"

Venturing carefully, ignoring the comparison of man to the angels, I choose to compare man with his Creator and state, "When we see Elohim appear before us, might not we be seeing the image of man, as well? Elohim, while three-in-one, appears as One entity to us. That is because all three Ones act in absolute unity.

"When Elohim speaks, we hear one voice because at that instant the three Ones are so united that we cannot distinguish which of the three is speaking.

"Therefore, man is three-in-one. When we see Elohim we see man. When we see man we see Elohim. There are many other facets of these two images that correspond, as well.

"Elohim is eternal. His being is eternal, so the soul of Elohim is eternal. That means the soul of man is also eternal. The soul of man cannot cease to exist.

"Elohim is a soul. Man has a soul. In fact, man's soul houses his personality, is one with it.[19]

"Elohim is a spirit. Man has a spirit. In fact, man's spirit is the essence of the spirit of Elohim. He breathed that into him.

"When Elohim appears He has a form. Man has a form. In fact, in our imagination, when we place these two forms side by side, they look similar."

"Right," agrees Komodo`r and turns with a smile of satisfaction. He must have discovered some new revelation. "Man is made a little lower than we angels are. That means his nature prevents him from seeing the Heavenly realm, unless he is temporarily granted the ability to do so. His physical senses have limits. His physical travel is limited to the physical realm. He is unable to travel from place to place, as we do, certainly not as swiftly, either. Nor has he wings with which to fly."

"I agree, but why would Elohim create such a creature? On top of that, why would He place man on Earth, right there in Lucifer's domain?" Tantzer asks a good question.

Lairn`r's brow furrows, "Why is it necessary to know all of this? Does anyone see a purpose in answering these questions?"

I know that all such questions indicate that there is an answer forthcoming. That is not, to say, an immediate one. At some point, within Eternity, the discernment and insight needed to answer the questions will come.

I see a need to redirect the discussion, "Let's answer Tantzer's question later.

"Lairn`r, I think the simple answer is this…when an asteroid loses momentum and is headed toward creating chaos, our infinite knowledge of astrophysics enables us to make necessary adjustments. If we are to be of use to Elohim in ministering to man, a like knowledge of who, and what, man is will prove equally important.

"In this regard, I have some exciting news for you. I think now is the time to share it. Earlier you may have seen me receive a scroll from Michael. Our troupe's commission is outlined within.

"Elohim has chosen our troupe to be the primary source of ministry to man!"

Much is happening since the host of angels started looking into man's ingress into the noble intromission. Elohim, through Michael, has instructed me to dispatch several of our angels to minister to this creation. For the short term, it seems best to address those demands by commissioning covenant partners who are most spontaneous in their reactions. After we have a better grasp of what will be involved in ministering to man, I'll then execute a long term plan.

There are many celestial and terrestrial laws, interacting and weaving a tapestry of influence, though man is ignorant of these things. The most significant phenomenon is that Dvar HaElohim plans to visit man and talk at length with His creation. We will be permitted to listen, and by this means learn more, and thus improve our ministry to them. The angels have occasional audiences with Dvar HaElohim, but that is in the course of normal Heavenly occurrences. By traveling to Earth and visiting man there, He will be under the hateful, watchful eye of Lucifer and the fallen horde.

Of course, we are fully aware of Lucifer's hatred for us, but now the dark one has a new target for his wrath...man. Man, being created a little lower than the angels, means a little lower than Lucifer. Our speculation is that Lucifer's envy of man, and his realization that man was created with something he covets and thinks he deserves, will fan his hatred for Elohim.

Peaking his fury is man's residence upon Earth, the place over which Lucifer has measured dominance. Elohim has placed a hedge around man, preventing Lucifer access, in the form of a cordon of angels. From our vantage point, high above the expanse under Lucifer's influence, we watch the circling of the dark powers. They explore, ever searching for the opportunity to strike.

Still unanswered is the question Tantzer asked, "Why was man placed on Earth? Man is right under the vengeful eyes of Lucifer."

"Our armies are more than a match for him, and his dark faction, but still the battle flags are unfurled. Their probing continues, night and day. Our forces will repulse each incursion," I reason.

We watch Tantzer, who is sporting a curious look, as he rounds the corner of the golden street. We had agreed to meet here on our way to our preferred Observation Window.

"I've realized something important. Things changed here, in Heaven, at the instant of man's creation," Tantzer blurts out, sliding to a stop in front of Komodo`r's face.

"What are you talking about?" Komodo`r stonewalls. "What's changed? I haven't heard of anything changing. Are you certain of this, or just conjecturing?"

Tantzer smiles at Komodo`r, but otherwise ignores the questions, and continues, "While walking along the garden path, you know, the path that runs in front of my dwelling, I came to this realization. Upon the creation of man, whom Elohim named Adam, several things happened, simultaneously, here in Heaven. So I checked with the angels standing sentry in front of the Temple."

With that revelation, we all pause for details. We know about the significance of the Temple. Its holiness is protected within the Holy of Holies by two armed cherubim, who stand in opposition to any darkness that may try to denigrate the Mercy Seat. Only Tantzer has the audacity to schmooze with these covenant partners, at the entry to the Holy ground.

Tantzer is relishing the attention he has engendered.

"First, a new pavilion appeared in the Garden of Remembrance! In it is a book. It appeared out of nowhere. It just appeared. It is called, 'The Lambs Book of Life.' What's more, within the Temple, something called the Shew Bread also materialized. And a cup, called the Mercy Cup. That Mercy Cup is filled with blood. Someone tested it and it is the blood of man. Furthermore, there are unusual sounds, sounds of movement, coming from the secret Most Holy Place within the Temple.

"That's not all. Twelve thrones appeared in the Throne Room and, along the northeastern shore of the Crystal Sea construction has begun on a very large number of dwellings. Golden avenues and streets are being added or extended," Tantzer says. As usual, Tantzer knows how to finagle his way into another troupe's confidence! He has garnered quite an interesting array of facts. What Tantzer is telling us has undeniably captured our attention.

"I heard the angels, who surround the Throne, singing something about grace. I am not sure what that means, or how it fits in with the creation of man, but that is also different," Lairn`r adds. This final piece of information confirms that Tantzer has accrued his information correctly.

So now we have more questions and more details to scrutinize.

Lairn`r joins our troupe gathered around the Crystal Sea. We haven't seen him, or spoken to him, for several Earth days. His wings are arched high above his head. This usually means he is joyfully contemplating something or other.

"More information about man," he says, smiling broadly. "I have been talking with the angels in the chorus. They are the ones that have been singing about grace."

This time Tantzer is the one asking the question, "Grace is the expressed favor of Elohim, right?"

"Yes, it is the expressed favor of Elohim," Lairn`r readily agrees, and adds, "It is something we will minister to man, for it is directed to man from Elohim. It is measureable, therefore has substance. It is the goodness of Heaven, therefore the goodness of Elohim. It is the atmosphere we enjoy here in Heaven, but containable and portable by angels, and placed upon man. It is not an inheritance or a reward. Elohim generously grants it."

"So, those who are commissioned to minister to man can carry a measure of the goodness, the atmosphere we have here in Heaven, and immerse man in it. That is remarkable," I say over my shoulder, as I head toward the River.

If what Tantzer and Lairn`r say about grace is true, then grace is about Elohim and man, and our understanding about it will increase, as our understanding of man continues to grow. We, the angels, who reside in Heaven, are immersed in Heaven. Heaven is synonymous with God and His nature of godliness. That godliness is part of the divine nature. We have our being in that divine nature. We live in this expressed godliness of Elohim. Now, it seems, so does man. However, man will be able to live in this expressed godliness, while residing on Earth, in a material existence. Even more amazing, man, is a presence, there, in Lucifer's veranda.

What wisdom from Elohim will we find here?

As for the remaining unanswered questions, they remain unanswered.

Tantzer smiles to himself. The information just conveyed to him is incredible, even in this period of incredible things. He holds his peace, though, while Komodo`r continues his dialog. Komodo`r has just returned from a visit to Earth to examine the life below the seas.

"There are myriad life forms below the surface of the seas. And plant life, too. All shapes and sizes. There is one life form that appears to be a rock or stone, but is actually a living creature. Enormous leviathans and, in addition, there are small single-cell creatures that only angels can see. Then there are the various depths of the seas. In some places the depth is as great as the highest mountains upon land. Most of the life forms at those depths are transparent."

Komodo`r had been given the task of going to Earth, accompanied by an army of warrior angels, to examine the life created on the fifth Earth day. Michael had sent him. By making this trip he is the first of our troupe to witness the battles being fought upon newly reconstituted Earth, up close. He is, also, the first to see the incredible beauty below the seas.

Tantzer sees his opportunity to contribute to the discussion, "I have something to add, if I may. I was talking with an angel from another troupe. He had not been around for a while, so I was trying to catch up. Most of the angels in his troupe have been busy constructing a Learning Center to train us to minister to man's young. You will recall Elohim told man to multiply, so they will create offspring. Something the angels have never seen."

HEAVEN ON EARTH

Our summons is unexpected when it comes and we have been afforded only limited preparation. Those selected from our troupe are called to a gathering with Michael. A summons like this is not unprecedented, but assuredly not common, either. When we are called without a hint of forewarning, it usually means Michael has received command directly from Elohim. Therefore, it is important.

As we walk swiftly along the golden streets toward the Hearing Center, my mind is inundated with the events of these seven Earth days. Everything involving Earth is interwoven. Each is like a thread, elaborately entwined with others, to produce an intricately patterned tapestry. Elohim's ways are beyond comprehension, a source of stimulating adventures for one's senses.

Keeping pace with my covenant partners, images of the infinite and ever expanding universe occupy my thinking. I am stirred by the awareness that warrior angels are there, battling the forces of Lucifer.

There, too, is man, just created. I wonder what thoughts he might be having. I suppose we will have to wait to learn this until he shares them with Dvar HaElohim. Another source may be this chronicle once Lez'n or some other scribe records them here.

As we learn more about Adam, we will be able to anticipate his actions and thoughts. This is a necessity, if we are to minister to him. Those assigned to him have already started doing that. To our chagrin, we are aware of the reality that Lucifer will learn to anticipate his idiosyncrasies and intents, as well.

Our stroll ends just before passing into the Citadel. We ascend to the Hearing Center where we are to meet with Michael. He is already there. I look around and everyone except Tantzer is present, but I hear his joyful voice as he is just about to enter.

He slips in next to me.

Michael looks imposing, as he addresses our troupe, "You have been given a great honor by Elohim. A truly great honor. One of you will be given the task to stand guard at the entrance to the dwelling place of the created man. As you guard the entrance, you will be holding a flaming sword."

I look around trying to guess which of our number it could be. My eyes settle upon Klalish. He is a cherub. He has a warrior's stature, and he is experienced in battle. When the horde was cast down, he was one of the first to engage the fallen angels. He wasn't the only one, of course, but he was the only one from our troupe. Standing the post would be an honor, but against whom would he be guarding and where would this post be? Questions, questions, I am beginning to sound like Lairn`r.

With no further fanfare, Michael announces that the honor will go to Klalish. Our troupe gathers, joyfully, around him. Michael quickly leaves the center after making the announcement, only to return in short order to join us, as we celebrate the honor given to one of our number. He has a scroll in his hand.

After the celebration subsides, Michael approaches Klalish. With a smile, he hands Klalish the scroll. It is fastened with three seals. "One," he says, prophesying, "in the fullness of time, will be opened by Gershom, a guardian, yet to be given his commission. One will be opened by Adam, the man. And one will be opened by Zukher."

At the mention of my name, I wonder what this is about. I know nothing about this matter before me. I turn to ask Michael, but he has, swiftly, left the center, again. I will have to wait, as does Klalish, for further enlightenment.

Such mysteries are common here and are part of the glory we behold. Elohim doesn't seek counsel from angels, so we don't always know the purpose for which we've been chosen. With Michael's departure, the short gathering is over. We leave the center, Klalish taking the lead.

"Do you know what those seals are about, or when they will be unsealed?" Lairn`r asks Klalish.

"Yes. Please, tells us," Tantzer adds, with a rush of curiosity.

"Adam, the man, unsealing a scroll here in Heaven?" questions Komodo`r.

Klalish holds the sealed scroll in his mighty hand and, with a resolute look, turns and heads for the entrance. "Elohim be praised!" is all he says, and disappears.

It will be a while before I see him again. The events, foreknown by Elohim, begin to be enacted upon the scene called Earth. The actors in this melodrama are about to enter center stage.

It came to be that Elohim planted a garden in Eden. Now Eden is a certain place, where a footprint within the physical realm, corresponds with a footprint within the Heavenly realm. There, agents of both realms have liberty to abide together.

After Elohim plants the Garden in Eden, He places the man, Adam, there.

"Adam! Adam!"

"I am here," he answers and wonders, "Where is here?"

He hears a profound voice that sounds to him like deeply running rivers, saying, "I placed you here, in a Garden of My making. When you awake, for now you are dreaming, you will see wondrous things."

"Who are you, lord? I hear you, but I don't see you."

"That is because I haven't made Myself known unto you yet. I am the One who formed you and I named you Adam, which means 'man.' I am Adonai Yehovah. I am of the Self Existent One."

Adam awakes and opens his eyes for the first time.

"Are you *Yehovah*?" asks Adam of the One standing above him.

It is then *Yehovah* bends and extends his hand to lift Adam, the first man, to his feet and says "Stand up and walk!"

Adam stands and looks, for the first time, into the eyes of his Maker. "*Adonai Yehovah!*" he says, and kneels before his creator.

"Adam, I charge you to care for, and enjoy, the Garden. By My word, you are given dominion over the plants and animals of the Garden and Earth.

After giving Adam the gift of understanding of the three Great Lights[20] and the comforting Radiant One, *Yehovah* gives Adam a command, "Of every tree of the Garden you may freely eat: But of the Tree of the Knowledge of Good and Evil, you shall not eat of it: For in the day that you eat thereof you shall surely die."

Not long after Adam was placed there, Elohim caused the animals to pass before him to see what man would name them. So it came to be that the names man gave them were what they were called.

While the angels perform their commission of ministering to Adam, the rest of us observe the action. For us, and man, it is a period and place of constant delight and discovery.

It is with awe, that we watch intently, as Elohim creates Adam's help-mate. He does this from the rib of Adam, after placing over him a deep slumber. In wonder, we are watching as the man, Adam finds his mate as planned by omnibenevolent Elohim.

Adam awakens. Slightly groggy, he feels no more disoriented than from a long, deep sleep. He hears a sound beside him...a gentle stirring, a quiet murmur, and distinguishes a scent he'd never known. It is not like the flowers that are sweet, or the wild grasses that are acrid. No. This one has delicate warmth that stirs him. Strange. A feeling he's never experienced before! He opens his eyes and there is a form before him. It is so like him, yet so different. Almost as tall as he, but slight. Curvy, rather than sinewy and hairy. It has gentleness about it. Rounded and smooth, it moves lithely.

The weirdness he is feeling is indescribable, and hovers somewhere inside his chest. Just a defined awareness, yet almost like a pain. His first instinct is to touch her and hold her, but he can't take a breath, for fear she will run away. And he wants nothing more than for her to stay, even if he can do no more than watch her move, in that slow, gentle manner she has. He looks at her face and she is watching him. A small, tentative parting of her lips witnesses the first smile. Adam discovers woman, and in doing so, discovers an emotion he is in need of understanding.

He stares at her and murmurs breathlessly, "Who are you?"

To which she replies, smiling again, while looking up into his eyes, "*Yehovah* has placed me beside you to be your helpmate. He told me you are Adam. And He said we should care for each other."

Together they take their first meal. Together they take their first step into a river. Together they witness their first sunset and gaze into the starry sky. Together they walk in the Garden and fellowship with *Yehovah*. Together they are fascinated by the starry patterns in the heavens. Adam had considered that he would live on with no interchange of thoughts and ideas, other than the visits and animated conversation with *Yehovah*. He is overwhelmed by the wonder of sharing his days with the helpmate *Yehovah* has given unto him.

We, the angels, watch as Dvar HaElohim, Adam, and the woman walk and talk in the Garden. They regularly do so, and their exchanges are many and varied. They talk about the beauty of the Garden, and the glory of Heaven. Lucifer watches from outside the Garden, looking for that thread to pull, but Elohim keeps him at a distance.

On one such day, the three happen upon a unique tree in the midst of the Garden. "That is the Tree of Life of which I told you," Dvar HaElohim says. "Do you remember that, Adam?" He asks.

"Yes, Lord, I remember" Adam replies.

Dvar HaElohim turns to the woman and asks, "Adam has told you what I said regarding the two trees?"

"Yes, Lord, he has told me and I remember what he said," she confirms.

"Do not forget," Dvar HaElohim says, and they move on to discuss other subjects. After the sun reaches its height at the middle of the day, Dvar HaElohim leaves the couple standing there, along the river that flows through the Garden.

"Is that the first time you saw the Tree of Life?" the woman asks.

"Yes, it is beautiful to look upon, just like the other trees in the Garden, but there is something life affirming about it. Maybe that is why *Yehovah* named it the Tree of Life," Adam muses as they walk, hand in hand.

"I wonder where the other tree is. The one I have not yet seen. You know, the one *Yehovah* called, the Tree of the Knowledge of Good and Evil," she says, always curious about the world in which she finds herself. She enjoys their daily discourse with *Yehovah*.

THE HEDGE OF ELOHIM

"What are they up to, today?" Tantzer distracts our standing quorum, as he announces his arrival upon the Observatory landing.

Our commission demands that we devote ourselves to being fully prepared and equipped in order to faithfully minister to man. Our inquisitiveness, as it happens, compels us to dedicate ever increasing measures of our own personal time to knowing more about man. We have revised already full schedules in order to come to the Observatory. Crowded with angels and their wings, we gaze through the single Viewing Window dedicated to Adam, his woman, and the Garden.

Now, this assembly consists of Komodo`r, Gabriel, Lairn`r, Tantzer and me. Komodo`r, who is usually reluctant to engage in small talk, is the first to reply to Tantzer's interruption. "The woman is exploring the Garden, while Adam busies himself close by, gathering sustenance for a meal." The interruption answered, Komodo`r returns his attention to the Window.

Tantzer, ignoring the hint, is just getting started. "Well, you might be interested in knowing that I have been racing a comet I found shooting through Earth's solar system. Lairn'r helped me with the calculations. This particular comet will complete a circuit of streaking through the family of planets about every seventy-five cycles of the Earth around its sun.[21]"

It is obvious to us that Tantzer is very excited about his recent discovery. Without pausing, he goes on to say, "I overheard other angels
talking about holding impromptu contests with various objects pop-
ulating the universe. Racing that comet was my first attempt. It was
a thrill and I plan on doing it again. The only problem I ran into was
when the comet and I passed behind the sun's crescent. I saw a brood
of dark angels rising from Earth's surface. It appeared that they were
headed in my direction. I had no warrior covering, and was heavily out-
numbered. I used my already achieved speed advantage from racing to
escape, and let the comet go. Then I headed here, to the Observatory."

Lairn`r nods at Tantzer, but ignores his reference to the dark angels.
He, instead, picks up the conversation where he left off, "So, Dvar
HaElohim talks about creation during His walks in the Garden with
Adam and his woman. Is He teaching them how they came to be? Do
they understand what He is saying?"

In an attempt to recognize Tantzer's enjoyment following Lairn`r's
dismissal, Komodo`r says, "Tantzer, I'm sorry that I haven't tried the
latest angel venture, using the universe as a place for amusement. I'll
have to try that! And, by the way, the dark angels are incapable of exercising dominion beyond Earth's atmosphere.[22]"

"They must understand what He's teaching them." Komodo`r says,
retrieving our inquisitor's thread of the conversation. "They are
repeating the lessons to each other, days later. We know they are created with great cognitive capabilities. Also, Dvar HaElohim is very
clear and precise when He teaches. Their comprehension of these
things convinces me that they are created with great spiritual reser-
voirs, as yet untapped, that Dvar HaElohim is touching.

"How they look, act, and live is so much like us. There are a few physical differences like the wings and stature but, overall, watching them
is like watching ourselves. We have certain similar capabilities. They
are able to sense the presence of others. While we are capable of seeing
terrestrial and celestial beings with our eyes, as well as our other senses,
man cannot know of celestial beings, unless we manifest ourselves
to them. Therefore, we can stand next to them, or hover above them,
without their knowledge.

"However, they do have the ability of utilizing their soul and spirit senses, if they exercise them, to become aware of our presence. And, here, there is need for caution. If man does, in fact, develop their soul or spirit senses to the point where they can perceive our existence, we must take care. Our obvious differences from them, and the skills with which we are endowed, might give them the misguided impetus to revere us, instead of Elohim.

"This must not be. It is an example of the very perversion Lucifer desired."

"Are there other cautionary concerns?" Tantzer asks, always handy with a follow up. Maybe he will be an inquisitor later.

Lairn`r interjects a change in the subject. "Just as we do, Adam and the woman interact in perfect harmony within the Garden and with Heaven. The rest of Earth is quite different, though. It is unknown if it is possible to maintain this state of harmony, if they ever go outside the Garden. Don't you find that question compelling?" he asks.

His look is directing the first question to all of us, but the second question seems to be to me, alone. He must have noticed that Tantzer isn't paying any attention and is sitting, head bowed, still pondering the first question. Hesitating a bit, I wait on Tantzer or Komodo`r to respond. Then not hearing from anyone, I jump in.

"The Garden is unique in all creation," I offer, while continuing to contemplate the fine distinctions that are suddenly apparent in this new set of circumstances. Everyone inhabiting the Garden, including the animals, is able to interact with the natural, or Earthly, realm and the spirit, or celestial, realm. It is the most unique place upon Heaven and Earth. They have a physical presence in both places, simultaneously. I do find the possibilities endless, and compelling.

Just before tossing this morsel to the others, I recall that Komodo`r and Lairn`r are now old hands at grasping the nuances of the Garden. In fact, their understanding is quite extensive, probably better than mine. Nevertheless, due to the importance of the matter, and recognizing no seeming desire from either one of them to add something, I decide to go ahead and state my analysis.

"It means there is a separation between the Garden and the rest of Earth, and," pausing for emphasis, "it means there is a similar separation between the Garden and the Highest Heaven. The separation is a hedge. The Garden has a presence in both realms. In the Garden, Adam and his mate are within a protectorate created by Elohim, as are the animals therein. That protectorate is independent of the Garden. We refer to it as, 'The Hedge of Elohim.'

"Adam and the woman are moderately capable of interacting with, and comfortable in, both realms, just like the angels. Elohim has established the Garden so that it combines the laws of the terrestrial estate with the laws of the celestial estate."

Satisfied, I sit down and rest my case. Just as Tantzer is about to speak, I add quickly, "Excuse me. I might add, this is all done in perfect harmony and absent of all destructive chaos.[23]" I then turn again to Tantzer, who is awaiting his opportunity.

"Remember, they are subject to the governance of the law of freedom of choice," he says. Therefore, he is breaching the surface of an inscrutability which we have in common with man, but one which is rarely discussed.

Before we can continue, a signal from Lairn`r reminds us that it is getting close to the moment when Dvar HaElohim will enter the Garden for His daily walk with Adam and his mate. Sure enough, right on time, Dvar HaElohim is there calling out to Adam.

"Adam, are you ready?" *Yehovah* speaks, calling out to them, seeking fellowship with His daily invitation.

"Yes Lord, we are ready. Which way would you like to go today, Lord?" Adam asks.

"I don't have anything particular in mind. Why don't you two pick one?" *Yehova*h gently asks, in reply.

"Well, we have a favorite spot down near the river. Let's go there." He hesitates and extends his arm, gesturing to *Yehovah*, and waiting for Him and the woman, to go before him.

Arriving at the spot Adam had picked out, he begins "Lord, may I ask you a question?"

"Of course, Adam, I want to know what you think and what questions you have. In fact, I am so very interested in everything about you both. How close can we become, after all, if we do only that which is important to Me?" *Yehovah* reminds Adam warmly. "Now, what is it that you want to ask?"

"Well, we were talking about this wonderful place, and going over the things we seem to just know. We have this inner knowledge. How can it be that sometimes we know things before You teach us, yet other times what You teach us is totally new?" Adam begins. "When we've mentioned our understanding to You, You agree that indeed our insight is correct."

"I was wondering when you would get around to that. The answer is simple, really. Do you see the birds that fly over our heads?" *Yehovah* says, looking up.

"Yes," Adam answers simply, but his brow is revealing questioning lines.

"Well," *Yehovah* continues, "they just know what to do. When to eat. When to sleep. Where to fly. HaRuach teaches them these things, and it is the same with you. The origin of this way of learning is a product of your being. Your reverence for Abba is the spring from which this comes."

Encouraged by the patience of *Yehovah* and His willingness to answer, Adam boldly questions, "We enjoy speaking with You when You come to visit. We would like You to come more often to talk with us. Is that possible? Would You do so?"

"I am pleased you enjoy my company. I enjoy yours, as well. It pleases Mc to hear you say these things. I am thankful for your friendship." *Yehovah* says, "The truth is, you two can talk with me anytime you want. I may not be visible to you, but that doesn't mean I am not here, or that I don't hear you. I am able to be in many places, all at the same time. Try it some evening, before you retire. Ask me a couple of questions. I will answer them when you ask. Then, when I come to walk with you the next day, I will tell you the questions you asked and the answer you were told. That way you both can learn to trust My presence, even when you don't see Me.

"Here we are at the river. Why is this a favorite spot of yours? " *Yehovah* asks the couple.

"We like the sound of the water and the coolness of the mist rising from the surface. It relaxes us and refreshes us," the woman replies.

"We have given to you all these things to enjoy. We are glad you enjoy them so much. We thought you would, when We created this," *Yehovah* says, revealing the concept of the three-in-One, as they stand by the waters.

Dvar HaElohim's visit to the Garden each day, to walk with the created beings, remains a celebrated event in the Observatory. This present visit begins with just a few of us looking on through the Viewing Window in anticipation of His arrival. Then, once news of His presence in the Garden spreads in Heaven, the Window becomes crowded. There are now so many of us that we must be motionless, so everyone can hear the conversation. His visit that we are observing is not exceptional, although the topic of the conversation is new. We, too, are beginning to better comprehend the blessings that Elohim has provided these two beings.

Once Dvar HaElohim leaves the Garden, the large number of inquisitive angels reduces considerably. Soon it is only Komodo`r, Lairn`r, Tantzer and me, still watching. Except for a leopard, a lamb, a few birds, and the couple, the Garden is still.

"An interesting assignment, don't you think?" Lairn`r doesn't run out of questions.

Our troupe is directed to map a region of space within the created expanse. In the past, other troupes had performed similar assignments. This new chart is the first, since man has been placed in the Garden.

The region of lights that we are instructed to diagram is located several hundred light years away from Earth. Viewable from Earth, it is best viewed from an outcropping of plateaus and low level mountains, west of the Garden of Eden. This region is the midway point of the single land mass formed during creation. The dark blue sky, viewable above that region, features a mosaic of pulsating colored lights. These clusters of stars are the same that Elohim tossed into the heavens, during the great Banquet.

"How long do you estimate it will take to accomplish this task?" Lairn`r tosses the question into the air, to no one in particular, and I assume he is directing his inquiry to me.

"It will likely take several new Earth moons."

With a smile, I think how I now enjoy using Earth references indicating the passage of time. Each of us has adopted Earth terminology because it affords us an opportunity to measure differently. These small hard-to-identify instances of Eternity have now become compartmentalized. Thus, we mark days, cycles of days of rest, new moons and a cycle of Earth around the sun that we classify as a year.

The speed with which we map the region will be slow, compared to how fast Elohim can perform the tasks with which He has charged us. With His omniscience He already knows the number of objects we are about to individually chart. However, there is great knowledge to be gained by His citizens executing the same task. We will create scrolls, recording each object, its size and mass, makeup, distance to Earth, placement within the constellations and their illumination, as seen from the surface of Earth.

We are divided into groups of six angels, each group given a specific duty. We borrow twenty scribes from other troupes, so each of these survey teams has a scribe to record the various matrixes we are tasked to determine. As we travel, the scribes carry hundreds of scrolls upon which are the names that Elohim has given to each of these thousands of objects. We haven't stopped to actually count how many there are.

I direct each of my closest companions to head a survey team and they depart to map the area of the grid to which they are assigned. I take a team of my own. On the scrolls that our team carries, I read the names of the stars, various spheres, and barely noticeable rocks drifting together like belts. These stars will be classified by temperature and the spectra of light, or elements, they absorb. The name of the first sun on our first scroll is Polaris.[24] Its luminosity makes it the brightest star in the constellation in our grid. By our calculations, it is fifteen times bigger than the sun Earth orbits. It is four hundred thirty-three light years from Earth, and is visible from our Earth point of reference.

As we measure, I ponder, "We are witnessing the creation of new objects, bursting forth, filling voids of the universe, while seeing the disappearance of other points of light. Some disappear just as we finish, or are about to start, cataloging and recording their vitals. Why does this region need to be mapped? Is this somehow part of Elohim's plan to fulfill His promise of removing Lucifer from having a future? And what relationship has this to man, who is four hundred thirty-three light years away?"

Our groups gather to take a break and discuss our findings. Komodo`r approaches with a raised eyebrow. He proceeds to relate the phenomenon that had precipitated my previous contemplation.

"All of this creation and annihilation reminds me that we are eternal creatures, and what happens to these created objects cannot happen to us. How is it that Eternity prevents our demise, yet makes it possible for Lucifer, and the horde following him, to forfeit their future? What about man, the most recent creation? Can it happen to them? And, if not, why not?"

Lairn`r is the first to reply, "First: All of creation is surrounded by a hedge of protection,[25] just like that which surrounds the Garden. The creation or destruction that Komodo`r witnessed did not occur accidently. They came to be, or ceased, at the very instant Elohim intended. Second: Everything has a purpose and Elohim keeps it until that purpose is completed. Third: An object, that is neither angel nor man, is not governed by the law of freedom of choice. Fourth: Different from these, and in contrast to my first three conclusions...once created, we have an Eternal purpose, and so, it seems, has man."

"Further," Komodo`r enhances the narrative and adds to the four conclusions, Lairn`r presented. "Three qualities of Elohim shape the divine order governing the scope of His hedge. First: Elohim's will is the scepter of a Sovereign, which includes His Godly desire, His Godly purpose, and a Godly necessity for the entity to be protected. Second: Elohim's way is rooted in Holiness. It is perfect. It is just. Third: Elohim's time is the least understood quality, the knowledge of which He reserves unto Himself. All things that enjoy his fullest protection operate in accordance with Elohim's time."

Tantzer interjects, "I see the truth in what both Komodo'r and Lairn`r had to say. I would like to hear more about this and how it applies to us, the citizens. Since our stated interest is Adam, how does this apply to him?"

I notice that our current respite from our mapping duties is about to elapse, so I play the tyrant and say, "Lets hold off talking further about this, and just meditate upon it, instead. If we have another break, we can examine these things in more detail. We must continue our directive, if we are to finish on time!"

Our mapping proceeds as planned. There are no unforeseen obstacles. A majority of the objects are properly documented and recorded in the scrolls. Gabriel, Tantzer and several other messenger angels, return to Heaven with the bundle of scrolls we have completed. This will update

Michael as to our progress. Tantzer's absence, dictates that we reserve further discussions about Elohim's hedge until his return.

Gabriel, Tantzer, and the rest of the covenant partners that left with the scrolls have returned to us. Their arrival coincides with our continued sortie, so everyone has to wait to learn about their trip. Before focusing my attention on the next star field, I chance a glance at Tantzer to see if his face might give something away.

Finally, our mapping efforts advance to the point where we are certain that following this last interval we will finish and return forthwith to the glories of Heaven. Everyone finds a seat around or upon an outcropping located on the surface of a large irregular rock formation.

"Well! Gabriel and Tantzer will fill us all in about their journey with the scrolls," Lairn`r announces, his voice carrying for everyone to hear.

"Our passage was quite uneventful, actually. The breadth of sky, directly over our location point, west of the Garden, seemed particularly busy. Several of the enemy circle that region. Of course, we were forewarned that that part of Earth is a rallying center for malevolent activity and needs to be treated seriously.

"On our return journey, some wicked ones started toward us as we made our closest pass to Earth, but their attempt was prevented. We were beyond their dominion. I've been awaiting the continuation of the discussion regarding the hedge and its impact upon Adam and the woman."

"Tantzer, the provisions of the hedge which apply to us, the angels, also apply to Adam. Let's wait until our return to further this discussion, since I doubt there is much more we can determine here," I say, to hasten our return to our task and quicken our return to Highest Heaven.

After homecoming with our data, we do not get back to the promised discussion. Dramatic events begin to unfold in Heaven and on Earth which provide a vivid answer to Tantzer's question.

THE HALL OF MYSTERIES

"Asking, seeking, and knocking, when searching for understanding, we always end up climbing the Steps of Ascension," Tantzer says, with an appreciative smile.

He is right, of course. Highest Heaven is huge, and offers so many places to visit and study, yet our troupe spends a great deal of Eternity here at the Citadel. Except for the plaza level, where the administrative offices are, we end up on one of the next three floors: The Mezzanine, Hall of Mysteries, or the Observatory.

The reasons are obvious and worthy of comment. These three floors meet a critical need that we have. That need is knowledge of truth, the understanding of its application, and the satisfaction of a mission of service well done. The latter expressed by Elohim.

Though not all troupes spend as much of Eternity here as we do, it does not mean they are any less worthy, or less faithful, to Elohim's service. It is just that each troupe has a central, shared mission that moves it to act, without analysis or introspection. We don't question it. We don't seek singular self-expression over others, nor do we think that our service places us proudly above others. We have an example of those who did that, and they are not among us anymore. We choose a different path.

"I agree, Tantzer, I think you are right. Even though we are, oh, so familiar, with these three floors, they don't seem to get old, dated, or repetitive. Every visit seems critically important and necessary," I respond.

We have taken advantage of a pause in our various assigned tasks, and availed ourselves an opportunity to come here. Tantzer has asked, and received, leave from his duties at the construction of the City of Dvar HaElohim, so that he, too, can attend. The leader of the important construction effort shows great humility by letting Tantzer join us. I plan on offering him my extra hands to make up for any time lost by affording us this accommodation. Unity and self-effacing cooperation is always the way in Heaven.

The Hall doesn't have an entrance, in the technical sense. Upon reaching the landing on the third floor, one can view all there is, everywhere and everything, at once. All these images, sounds, scents, tastes, sensations and other impressions, simultaneously stimulate our senses.

Straight ahead upon reaching the landing, in a place of prominence, is a presentation covered in dancing lights of the many colors of the rainbow and all the delicate hues, therein. Beneath this shower of light is a representation of a four square city, whose builder and maker is Elohim. It is the city on which Tantzer has been assigned to work, and from which he is playing hooky right now. This multi-dimensional exhibit emanates a harmony of sensations that impacts the visual, auditory, and emotional senses.

To the immediate right of the landing is an atrium from which many vestibules, with compelling images, emerge. Foremost, in the center of one's view, is an image of several spiral star clusters, as seen from a very great distance. It has undergone some changes since Elohim's Banquet, the one when He tossed the Word, as stars, into the Universe. Those who noticed, recognize that the spiral star clusters replicate the tossed stars, resting at their assigned posts. Therefore, at least part of this mystery is "revealed knowledge."

In the vestibules, arrayed behind and through the atrium, one can see images of great beasts that I do not recognize. Some have long flowing locks of hair; others have massive candlesticks; still others are differently sized lights with moons that orbit spheres, which are circling those lights. The Hall has no lack of such, each representing mysteries of the kingdom. Left of the landing stands the image of a great mountain, a mount of truth upon which rests an image of the Temple of Elohim. Much of that mystery remains sealed, as is true of most of the mysteries nearest the landing.

No one has been able to number the mysteries sheltered within the Hall. There is a massive book yet sealed. It speaks the words, "Life and Honor" to those passing by. Arched high above and over this mysterious book is a rainbow. This image, too, is a mystery. It speaks the wonderful words, "Mercy, Mercy." We still lack understanding of these things.

Then there are the ominous images. One, a gruesome creature of some kind, is unknown in Heaven's quarters, or of the Earthly realm. It appeared after Lucifer was cast out of Heaven. Although we haven't received confirmation from Michael as yet, we are thinking it has something to do with the rebellion. That creature is truly ugly, absent any redeeming attractiveness or any appeal. It is one to be reviled and distained. Carrying a great head, it sports a huge jaw. From its nostrils, fire is expelled upon its repulsive breath. Its mouth opens from ear to ear and the teeth are huge and jagged. The shape of the torso is of sharp, angular lines which run up the backbone defining the back of its head and running down the four appendages. Great ridges and pointed surfaces ride down its back and hind quarters.

Michael calls it a dragon.

Citizens learning the understanding of a mystery of an ominous image or part, thereof, renders it transparent. It fades, almost completely, from sight. We all await a gradual shift of opacity in the image of Lucifer, as we've seen happen to other such images. We assume that transparency of Lucifer's image reflects the lack of an eternal future for him.

The creature, known as a dragon, clutches tightly, in its maws, three great keys. Each has writing upon it. The characters of the writing, and the meaning of the words, are as yet unrecognizable to the citizens.

Attached to the belly of the beast is a chord, dividing, and dividing again into many chords, extending out in all directions. These chords carry sustenance that other smaller, like creatures feast upon. Some of them emit unpleasant odors, fouling the space around them. Others produce sounds as objectionable as the unpleasant odors. The dragon, from time to time, devours one of the lesser creatures. This practice has been previously unheard of in Heaven's quarters.

Once devoured, they are replaced on the end of the chord by another lesser creature, which suddenly appears. Thus begins the process all over again.

It appears that these beasts are ugly as is sin, itself. Along with the awful odors and sounds accompanying their existence, the depth of their darkness is so great that they shun the introduction of light.

Created man is the catalyst of a fourfold increase in the number of mysteries exhibited within the Hall. Beginning with man's creation, followed by the appearance of the Garden, new mysteries have been appearing vying for attention there. These eclipse those that are now considered familiar.

The many mysteries of man are set forth in one corner of a huge chamber, located behind the grand atrium. Images here in the chamber will, no doubt, grow in number, since the area is newly constructed. One image is of a device having two circular wheels upon which it rides. We easily recognize it is a chariot. The image is a duplicate of the chariots we sometimes use here in Heaven, in which two, and sometimes three, angels can ride. These are propelled by Heaven's wind. Though not officially accepted, Tantzer has coined a name for them. He calls them "pick-en-um-up chariots." We wonder what will propel man's chariot if that is what the mystery of the image is and what he'll use it for. Since we haven't yet seen it in use in the Garden, we also wonder when it will be invented.

Then there is the image of a huge, wooden vessel that is totally sealed and has one window. Hovering over the vessel is a magnificent rainbow. Nearby, there is a large stone that is not much thicker than our scrolls and there are words written thereon, however, we cannot decipher what those words are. The mysteries are numerous and seem to multiply with our every visit. Another source of angel curiosity is the image of a sword that is larger than man's capacity to wield. Next to it is a 'Y' shaped branch with some leather attached to it, and lying in the same vicinity are five smooth stones.

The strangest view of all is an image of three flaming entities. One is a bush that burns without destroying itself. The second is dancing flames that appear to be over the form of a man. The third is a sea that is covered in fire.

If every one of the intriguing mysteries of man identified by images arranged here were written about within this chronicle, the scrolls devoted to this endeavor would number more than those we used to map the Word of Elohim, written in the heavens.

We are certain that Eternity will eventually reward our patient endeavors, by revealing to us answers to these mysteries, while a banquet of even more mysteries is being prepared in the wings.

THE SEASON OF TRUMPETS

Making another trek through the quiet edges of the Hall of Wisdom, I am filled with anticipation even though encumbered by a heavy load of notes and books. I head toward a secluded bench, nestled against a Pillar of Wisdom. It is always a pleasure giving a lecture to novice angels within our troupe. Angels in a few other troupes have asked that they be able to attend, as well. The discourse will cover, "A Defense of Faith." I am determined to get it just right and this is prompting me to seek solitude, where I can spread out my material and rehearse aloud.

The bench I select for my seclusion is beside a branch of the River of Life, where beautiful, calming melodies emit, as it flows gently along its banks. Other branches of the river that are nearer the Citadel resound with stirring anthems of praise to our revered Sovereign. Such praise is certainly welcome and desirable, but right now the uplifting tones won't help my preparations.

My purpose in coming here is to rehearse. My presentation will be different from this same theme given by me before. That is because recently understood mysteries have reinforced a new line of reasoning.

"Elohim is Lord of all things and by Him all things consist," I begin.

That declaration is one of a string of truths that form the precious and beautiful crown jewels of Heaven.

"Everything made is of Him, by Him, and for Him, and that includes the angels. We consist, our frame work and being, of all that Elohim spoke into existence when he created each of us. Our individual natures, our very person, are the product of Elohim's foresight and faith. At the instant of creation, we came from Elohim's reason, imagination, affection, memory, and consciousness."

The next part of my narrative was contributed by Lairn`r. He has an abiding interest in the material I plan to present.

"We are the product of Elohim's faith, therefore, we conclude that we are the substance of that faith. We are that, which Elohim was hoping for, when He conceived us. Each of us, each angel, is a visible example of Elohim's faith. We *are* faith."

Understanding based upon that conclusion must scrutinize the nuances underlying its reasoning. Here, I will pick up the dialogue, addressing the rebellion and the judgment of Elohim visited upon Lucifer and the fallen one-third.

"In his original state, Lucifer was an angel, as were those who followed him. Now, their state is eternally changed, frozen within Eternity's powerful grasp. In that original state they, too, were of the essence of Elohim's hope, faith and glory. Although they, at one point in Eternity, enjoyed the full extent of Heaven's limitless bounty, they are now anti Heaven itself! Forever evil incarnate, they are a curse unto themselves. When, of his own free will, Lucifer gave himself over to pride, he made it impossible to backtrack.

"What of the source of that substance of hope and faith from which Lucifer and his horde originated? What has become of that? How can that source of perfection be desecrated? Can, as Lucifer argued, Elohim's hope and faith result in those as vile as Lucifer and one-third of the angelic host?

"How did this change in state happen? Is there a path to redemption?

"Those that are fallen, and who are irrevocably cursed, had consisted of all that Elohim placed within them, when each of them came to be. They, too, were of the substance of faith."

I make a mental note here to pause and let the weight of that thought settle in a little... "Now that substance is negative, what one might call, *negative* faith. They stand defiant, but believing in the beneficial rewards of their negative faith as much as we rest in the hope of what we are, *positive* faith. Positive faith that is filled with power can be neither voided nor annulled.

"Not long ago, during the span of Eternity from Lucifer's creation until his rebellion, he became the most highly favored cherub. Respect for him was no different from that afforded Michael. A seed of pride, and a desire for independence from Elohim, found a home in Lucifer, deep within. Iniquity was found in him. When that seed developed, he considered himself to be equal to Elohim. The consequences of that iniquity made evident his envy of Elohim's independence. They revealed, as well, that he coveted worship. These transgressions perverted that which Elohim had created.

"Lucifer's refusal of positive faith has produced an absence of godliness, a fount of oozing lies, deceit, and separation. He is the father of lies. Where there was once peace, abundance and joy, there is now rebellion, deprivation and unrest.

"Lucifer stood defiant, chained before Yehovah to answer for his wicked disobedience. His defense was, 'Yehovah, you cannot judge me for any evil I have done. You created me this way, and though I may be a flawed creature, I am what you created. Therefore, you cannot condemn that which you created without condemning yourself, thereby proving that it is you that is evil and not me. Your Throne and Kingdom are built on unrighteousness.'

"Here, then, are the proceedings during which Lucifer stood before the White Throne of Yehovah, when the reckoning of the rebellion came."

I pause for a moment, as I retrieve from memory the actual censure, as it occurred. Soon I can recall the very proceedings, which I intend to recount.

"You were not there when Elohim created the heavens? Did He take counsel with you? Yet you said in your heart, 'How marvelous are thy works, oh Elohim.' Is this so?" Yehovah asked.

"It is so, Yehovah. It is so," Lucifer answered.

"Did Elohim take counsel with you when He spoke you into existence and gave you the nature of angels; a heart to know knowledge; reason to understand and perceive; a memory to retain that which is knowable; an imagination to see all that can be witnessed? Did you not say in your heart that you, and all angels, are so wonderfully made?"

"It is so, Yehovah, it is so," once again, Lucifer answered.

"Did you not, then, reason that Elohim bestowed upon you great honor, beauty, wisdom, power and knowledge beyond all other angels? Were you not given the jewel of Elohim's eye to shepherd? Yet in your imagination you wanted more."

"Yes, Yehovah. Yes, it is so," Lucifer answered, once again.

"Then, did you not consider all that Elohim had, and did you not see the intimacy that Elohim[26] has? Did you not determine, in your heart, that such passion was perverted? Then you informed others of your judgment, and in so doing, you polluted their minds. You determined that that which Elohim discreetly treasured was evil and, therefore, unrighteous. You changed that which was blessing in your house, and theirs, into a curse. Wherein you had light, by disobeying the law of faith, you were filled with darkness. Because you were disobedient to the law of faith and because a statute of that law is that the Rhema word of Elohim cannot return void, all that was given unto you became a curse, and you are a curse forever."

"Yes, Yehovah. Yes, so it is," Lucifer answered and continued, "When I beheld the passion of Elohim, I knew it to be weak, because I didn't have that passion. Nor did those you have banished have that passion.

98

I determined, then and there, that it was evil and unrighteous. And, I still do. When I ascend to the Throne you now sit upon, I..."

"Silence!" Yehovah commanded. "You will not ascend, nor possess, the Throne that judges you and those who are equally accursed. Your end you have brought upon yourself, for the word of Yehovah unto you is, You and all who have chosen to follow you, of their own free will, shall be a curse and wander to and fro as long as heaven and Earth exist. The passion of Elohim, which you have judged to be evil, will remain a stumbling block unto you and yours. And since you judge it to be evil, your desires and passions shall forever only be unto thyself and it will fold in upon itself. Wherein Elohim's passion gives, yours will take. Wherein Elohim's passion brings life and blessing, yours will bring death and destruction. Your desire will be to the darkness and the desire of those who follow you will be to feast upon your darkness, reveling in evil and cursing. This you will do until the end, when all strife shall cease. When you, and they, will no longer have a future and your past will be no more. You, and they, are now cast forth from this kingdom. Vagabonds shall you be, for so I command it!" Yehovah turned and directed, "Michael, take them to their destiny."

My lecture preparations are interrupted by waves of music from a quartette of trumpets. Their harmonious tones seem to come from all directions, surrounding and inviting angels to enter into action. The tenor trumpet plays above the melody of the lead trumpet, while the baritone trumpet sings notes ranging high above and deep below the melody, but always in harmony. The fourth trumpet, playing with vibrato, causes a rich depth of feeling to move within me in recognition of this sound.

It is when these trumpets pierce my depth of concentration, that I finally abandon my focus. I appreciate the purpose behind the pleasant tones that come from four trumpeting angels hovering high above the Citadel. They are heralding the Season of Trumpets, as commissioned by Elohim.

The timing of the Season of Trumpets is known only to Elohim. Rich in meaningful pageantry, a period that combines angst and anguish; it is also a time of celebration. This is the season Elohim addresses angels who have erred. Some anticipate pardon and will be afforded accord, similar to Heaven's Jubilee, while others meet our Sovereign's wrath.

The opening element of this season is as much instructional as it is an examination of, and absolution for, imperfect conduct. Elohim is perfect in all His ways, but angels are not! We are capable of an error in choice. These are not acts of disobedience, but do require scrutiny and forgiveness. If ignored, free of judgment, purposeless chaos might ensue.

Prior to Lucifer's rebellion, we had the benefit of freedom of will. The liberties afforded us were considerable. However, after the insurgence, a point of no return was reached. Angels, then, were invited to join in a covenant with Elohim, thereby, sealing them in a state of light and in a position of continual growth with Him. The third of the angelic host, who chose the alternate path of Lucifer, were sealed in a state of darkness and growing separation from Elohim.

The closing element of this season encompasses sentencing for sin, willful disobedience, against Elohim. For sin is transgression of the law, as personified by Lucifer and his followers. During this closing interlude the transgressors are brought before Elohim to answer for their sins. The Throne Room, high within the Citadel, is central to the Creator's accountability which emphasizes the Season of Trumpets. Perpetrators of sin, and recipients of the pardons, stand before Yehovah. Yehovah, The Father of Eternity, exercises and executes righteous judgment over all things, bestowing pardons and conferring sentencing.

During the Season of Trumpets, except for the Throne Room, most activities in and around the Citadel, come to a rest. Outside, the River of Life continues to flow, singing and worshipping. However, Heaven's business within the Citadel is paused, only to continue when the trumpets herald the conclusion of this interval.

Each Season of Trumpets, during the second element, Lucifer and sometimes his ilk are brought to the seat of judgment where their murdering, destroying, and thieving deeds are weighed on Heaven's balances. Warrior Angels of Light flank the angels of darkness. These corrupt entities are forbidden to address anyone, except Yehovah.

There is much interest in their presence this season, for it is their first, since Elohim replenished the Earth by creating Adam and the woman, placing them in the Garden. Thus He invaded Lucifer's perceived dominion and lobbed the first volley.

So it is that I gather my lecture writings under one arm and head toward the Citadel, hoping to find a place to observe the proceedings. I plan to store my writings in one of the chambers, so I won't have a wrestling match with them, while attending the action in the Throne Room. This will enable me to avoid taking the time to drop by my quarters.

Lucifer's presence is not the only reason I want to attend. Some members of my troupe will offer their mistakes for judgment.

Climbing the Steps of Ascension on my way to the sixth floor, I am acutely aware that the Steps are unexpectedly empty. Noticeably absent is the bustling crowd of angels seeking admittance to the Throne room. Instead, I find only a few groups of angels along the way, and some of them are headed in opposite directions. None of them is holding a conversation concerning what is about to take place.

"Strange," I mutter.

The answer to that mini-mystery presents itself when I lift the huge gold latch opening the doors to the Throne Room. The vestibule is packed! The angels wedged there aren't budging nor are they moving forward. There is only room for a few more late arrivals. Why they are maintaining their vigilance, I can't understand. They can't see, nor can they hear, what is going on in the Throne Room.

I reluctantly turn around to leave to avoid the same fate, when I hear someone shout "Zukher" above the din of disappointed, murmuring voices. "Over here, Zukher, I saved a place for you." It is Komodo`r and he is jumping up, so I can see who it is calling my name.

"Thank you. I am on my way to you. Stay there!" I shout back, as I begin uttering apologies to those I brush aside on my way to my earnest colleague, standing politely mute, but displaying a knowing smile, in the distance.

This takes a while and requires a multitude of apologies, lest next Season I am obliged to answer for rash judgment this Season. Eventually, I come to rest before my benefactor, waiting with arms crossed. "Komodo`r, how did you know I was going to need a place, or even that I was going to come?" I ask, or rather shout, seeking to show him how deeply I appreciate his gesture.

"Well, I happened to be a few floors below when the trumpets sounded. I immediately headed up here, but when I arrived the room was already filling up."

The room is large enough to hold mass numbers of angels and has regularly done so, especially when the Judgment of the rebellion was handed down. But this is amazing!

Komodo`r continues, "I knew Tantzer was sequestered to stand before Elohim, along with a couple of other troupe members, and since they are of personal interest to us, I was certain you wanted to attend. With the last waves of the trumpets, I was contemplating these things. Then I saw on the scroll beside the Throne that Lairn`r is speaking for Tantzer. I noticed he was bent over a table nearby, so I asked if he knew whether you were coming. He said he didn't know. As we were talking, an angel overheard our conversation and said he saw you way off in the distance, while he gazed from the balcony of the Mezzanine. He said you seemed to be rushing in this direction. Well! I was right! Here you are!" Komodo'r smiles. He is pleased with himself.

Pardoning is first. Those sequestered are seated or standing around in groups, filling the open court before the Throne.

Yehovah enters. Except for the sound of His robes, rustling as He moves, silence rules. The only Worthy Potentate will now judge His citizens and all those who are privileged to watch are excited witnesses to the wonder.

A host of angel scribes are sitting at tables arranged in a semi-arc surrounding the Throne. Each is ever ready, with quill in hand, to record, in the scrolls, every accent and inflection of each statement. These honored scribes are selected from the various troupes' rolls because of excellence in performance of their duties.

Yehovah begins.

"It is needful that all citizens of our Heavenly home divest themselves of errors in judgment. These matters are not acts of disobedience, therefore, it is for the purpose of their personal protection, that all such actions receive careful scrutiny. In so doing we will cause to occur an elimination of a repeated occurrence. The pardons bestowed on the erring citizens today will be accompanied by a strategy of instruction to inculcate righteousness in their future endeavors."

Yehovah's care for us is not lost on those who will be scrutinized this season.

"All citizens seeking pardoning mercy may present their petitions," He continues.

One by one, angels and their attending solicitors humbly approach the magnificent Throne. Although the offending judgments are read into Eternity's record in hushed tones, all witnesses to Yehovah's righteous judgment hear everything because of the acoustics of the Throne Room.

When it is Tantzer's turn, he and Lairn`r approach the Throne. Yehovah breaks established protocol by not waiting for the reading of the alleged misconduct by the appointed scribe. He directs His opening statement to Tantzer and Lairn`r, saying, "So Tantzer, once again we share these proceedings. Do you enjoy our opportunities to meet with one another?"

At this unexpected statement, I look at Komodo`r. His lower jaw has dropped so far, and deformed his face so much, I am not sure it is him anymore. Mine must have been equally contorted. Yehovah is chatting with Tantzer, more as his amused mentor, than his inquisitor and final judge. I must have composed myself sufficiently to smile at this, because Komodo`r tugs on my arm, whispering, "What are you smiling about?"

"Incredible! Just incredible!" was all I can muster in the way of a reply, because the dialog between Yehovah and Tantzer is just heating up. Lairn`r is no longer a solicitor. He is just an equally stunned spectator.

"When it suits you, be so kind as to inform this esteemed gathering of colleagues your version of the events at issue here. Kindly be certain to include any mitigating circumstances to explain your actions," Yehovah thus yields the floor to Tantzer, who seems not to take into account, at all, how public this discussion is.

Tantzer emits a sigh. "If it pleases you, Yehovah, I am honored for you to consider these matters," he says, a hair above a whisper, suddenly realizing how awesome the power of the judgment hearing is. Standing before the elder angels, the novices and his Sovereign, Himself, he feels the need to kneel. However, he knows this is inappropriate and, as he stands there, his legs commence quivering. He takes a deep breath and continues his narrative.

"I practiced, diligently, all of that which I was supposed to say in delivering the message to Adam. Since I knew that I was filling in for Gabriel, I wanted to do what he would have done. Truly, Lord, my primary goal was to perform that which I'd been assigned, gracefully, as Gabriel would have.

"I arrived, as instructed by Michael, appearing in full sight, rather than as a transparency. I swooped in front of Adam. While I did remember to keep a distance of about 7 cubits between us, he was startled and jumped. I forgot, Yehovah, that I am eight point five cubits in height and that my voice is so deep as to resound through walls! And worse, oh dear me," at this point Tantzer visibly shakes, "I forgot to say, 'Do not be afraid! I am an emissary from the Lord with a message for you from Him.'

"Adam's eyes got so wide. And he stopped breathing! I quickly delivered the message, and again, forgetting to be gentle, I spread my wings, the full width of all 17 cubits, and whooshed away in a gust!

"Oh, merciful Yehovah, I looked back as I departed and I saw him fall to the ground! I thought I had been the cause of the destruction of Your glorious creation!"

At this moment there is a titter that runs through the audience of Tantzer's peers and the Lord purses his lips to keep from giggling, Himself! What a joyful angel, this one!

Tantzer continues, "I hovered there until the woman appeared and tried to revive him. When he didn't respond at once, she washed him with some water from the spring. She thought he'd fallen asleep, which is unlike him in the middle of the daylight hours. Adam did get up in a bit of time and then I transferred myself back to Heaven."

Tantzer lowered his eyes in deep shame as he added, "I thought I'd destroyed Your glorious creation in my one, my very first, message assignment! I, therefore, repent my lack of wisdom and ask Your mercy and pardon, oh Yehovah."

At the conclusion of his confession, he kneels before Yehovah and again asks for mercy and a pardon for making the decisions he made, which seemed to cause such harm to Adam.

"Tantzer, arise," Yehovah says. "Go in peace, secure in knowing not only are you pardoned, but once again you have entertained us with your amusing ways and perspective."

All the while, Lairn'r stands nearby, with blushing face and arms wrapped around his middle. I know he is fighting a losing battle, trying with all his might to keep his composure. It is a contest most of us in this assembly share, because we are all about to burst forth in joyful laughter. And the surprising thing is that Yehovah is sharing in the mirth.

Not long after this, Tantzer and Lairn`r move aside allowing other angels the opportunity to stand before Yehovah to petition His pardon. We know that Adam was in no danger of harm from his shocking encounter with this messenger angel, our very own Tantzer. Tantzer was the first angel Adam had ever seen. and we expect there will likely be many such visits ahead.

The mercy and pardon element of this Season continues moving forward, as angels and their solicitors stand before Yehovah. Although all of their offenses are taken seriously, and the pardoning is not always guaranteed, or treated lightly, Tantzer's episode proves to be the most entertaining.

The much anticipated second element, Yehovah's judgment for willful disobedience follows a short break. Yehovah moves from the place of the Mercy Seat, where He administers mercy and pardons, to the White Throne. From here He calls the proceeding to order and judges defendants before sentencing. Immediately following Yehovah's few comments, an angel reads the Testament. The Testament details Heaven's Laws of Governance for Transgressors.

Already established and recognized by all of Heaven's citizens is that, in an act of rebellion, Lucifer transgressed along with one-third of the angelic host. When he was judged in accordance with these laws, along with those who chose to follow him, sentencing was immediately fulfilled and they were cast out of Heaven. Now, during this Season of Trumpets, as it has been each Season of Trumpets since, their actions and petitions are entered in evidence before Yehovah.

Lucifer's entrance is not celebrated, and his sentencing is not mourned, by any of us. Our interest is motivated by an honorable quest for knowledge and understanding, which compels us to witness these things. By so doing, we honor our Sovereign's greatness and He is glorified.

Lucifer's highly choreographed entrance proceeds as before, whereby he is flanked by fully armed warrior angels who are wearing helmets and carrying shields and swords, feet shod. Hovering over this ensemble, moving as one from the defendant's entrance toward its assigned position before Yehovah, are worshipping angels singing praises to our Sovereign. It is an event that is transparent and openly understood.

When the procession comes to rest before Yehovah, the room fills with a great light that envelops the defendant and his guards. It is so bright

I am unable to see Yehovah's face, only His lower torso and arms. His feet are clothed in light which wraps around the grand White Throne.

There, before Him, Lucifer stands, appearing as he really is and not as the angel of light he pretends to be. The great deceiver is capable of taking many forms, but in the Throne Room he stands, exposed, as what he actually is. In his hands he grasps three keys.

"What have you been doing since you last came before me?" Yehovah questions the unrepentant one.

"I have been going to and fro throughout Earth, ruling, reigning, and exercising my dominion over all things," Lucifer replies, in an even tone that masks the hatred revealed in his eyes.

Without hesitation, Yehovah responds, chastising Lucifer for his misleading statement, "Whereas, it is true you have been going to and fro upon Earth that is given for you to do. But you shall not lie to me, your Sovereign. It is written in the testament that has been read. You are the keeper of the keys to death, Sheol, and the grave. You do not have dominion over all things. You have measured dominion, only, over these. You cannot determine access to these three. You are merely the keeper with the keys to keep the locks steadfast, so that escape from them is impossible.

"Dominion over all living things of Earth has been granted to Adam, the woman, and to their coming generations. In addition, upon Earth I have placed a Garden where their dominion is full, complete and already abundantly fruitful."

"Adam, the woman and the Garden are protected by your hedge. I, and my kingdom, cannot enter. If You do not permit us to test these beings, they will prosper, but it is a hollow untested prosperity. The Law of Freedom of Choice is being honored, but they are free to choose what? They choose what to name the creatures, they choose when and what to eat. They choose to sing or dance, sleep or worship. These are choices without consequence. If they were free to choose between serving you and a god of their own creation they would choose to defy you, as I, and a third of your angels, have done," Lucifer hisses with distain.

"You may test their obedience, son of darkness. You may enter the Garden, however, you may not appear before them in angelic form. Your princes and minions cannot enter the Garden, for they have no dominion there.

"Your deeds are grievous unto me, since I replenished the Earth. These will add to your woes and sorrows, when the end comes. You will know misery upon misery when the time comes for you to have no past and no future. Then your only expectation is more suffering, when that which you fear most comes upon you and your sort.

"Leave, son of darkness, and from this time forward your name shall no longer be Lucifer. Henceforth, your name shall be satan."

With that Yehovah ends His judgments for this Season.

The procession, in the reverse order of its arrival, turns and leaves the Throne Room. An angel chorus, singing praises unto Elohim, Sovereign of an everlasting kingdom, echoes in the ears of satan. The last sound he hears, as the door slams shut behind him, is Michael commanding satan to leave Heaven's radiance, once more, and return to the kingdom of darkness from whence he has come. He is escorted by the warrior angels to the shrouded Observatory Window and disappears through the heavy curtain.

The trumpeters high over the Citadel sound, announcing that the Season of Trumpets is behind us. I have little opportunity to consider, retrospectively, what I have witnessed. My pending lecture is just ahead. Leaving the proceedings, I return to retrieve my writings. There is just enough time to go over them once, before departing the area to deliver the lecture. As I walk alone, once again I begin rehearsing the various reasoning of the lecture, aloud.

"A complex doctrine," Lairn`r says, coming up behind me. "To whom are you presenting it?"

"A group of novices has requested some additional tutoring. I was on my way, when the trumpets called us together." With that I continue on, talking to myself as I go.

THE THIRD TEACHER

The woman's moments during the day are filled with discovery. Everything stimulates the senses of the body, the soul, and the spirit. Her eyes are filled to overflowing. There is an abundance of things to eat. The fruit explodes in the mouth and the multitude of varieties please the palate. There are so many duties to perform. The responsibilities demanded of her reinforce the woman's sense of purpose.

The days run together. "Adam is wonderful to be with. There is a sense of togetherness when we talk about who we are, where we are, and what this all leads to. We also spend some of the day talking about what *Yehovah* has been telling us," she thinks as she smiles quietly, enjoying a tranquility that is as natural to her as breathing.

On one particular day, as she is quietly walking in the Garden, gathering fruit for their midday repast, something appears to the woman. She searches her memory for Adam's description of an animal, matching what she sees. It stands on two short legs and has very short arms. It seems to have a triangular head and is smooth skinned, rather than furry. This thing has a very long tail that makes it move in an unusual way.

It is somewhat distant from the path she is walking. Her attention is drawn to it when she hears a rustling of leaves, emanating from within a bush, near one of the trees. As she turns her head she sees it. With a sudden recognition she remembers Adam's description of this strange animal. Adam had named it a serpent.

For an instant she is uncertain about it. She feels, suddenly and without basis, like running away. She turns to leave and hurry back to the clearing, where she knows Adam is busy gathering fruit, as she was, before this interruption. She hears the serpent make a sound, as if it is talking. Since the unusual is a common occurrence, she leaves without any further thought.

Another time, another day, she is interrupted again by the serpent moving in her direction. Once again, she feels like leaving, but decides to let this creature come a little closer. When it is still quite a distance away, she thinks she hears it call to her. With some hesitation, she stands her ground, but remains poised to leave if this creature comes much closer. *Yehovah* has never mentioned that any animals here would cause harm. She shrugs off a vague feeling of consternation. None of the other animals talk to either of them.

With a quivering voice, it speaks, and she listens. "Are you going to leave again, like you did the other day? I called to you, but you turned and left. Why?"

"You made me feel uncomfortable," is all she says, still not sure if she should be allowing him to engage her like this.

"I understand that you might be uncomfortable with me. You haven't seen, or talked, with me before," the serpent whines. "I am not afraid of you. Some of the other animals are wary of you, but not me. I have been watching you for a while, and I decided to try to meet you. I want to help you learn faster. May we talk again, some other day?"

"Maybe," she says. She turns and leaves, thinking, "What a strange creature."

That evening, as she and Adam prepare to retire, she thinks about the serpent and what he said. "A faster way to learn? Maybe I should talk with the serpent again. I'm sure Adam won't mind and I am supposed to learn. Now I have three teachers, *Yehovah*, Adam, and the serpent.

It has been a good day," she thinks, as she closes her eyes after settling in under Adam's arm.

"Maybe tomorrow I will have something to teach Adam, for a change." She smiles to herself as she drifts off into a peaceful slumber.

It is very quiet. Adam is at the other side of the fruit trees, unloading a basket made from vines and leaves which is filled with fruits for lunch. As usual, a lamb grazes nearby, occasionally moving in kind of a dance with Adam. The woman drifts through the area near the center of the Garden. As she walks, she circles that beautiful gnarled tree. The one *Yehovah* warned Adam and her about. The Tree of the Knowledge of Good and Evil.

It looks so much older than the others. She recognizes that it is near the place where she talked with the serpent. It is captivating her imagination. She can see that the tree is magnificent in its splendor. The trunk is rough and dark. The thick boughs are heavy with waxy leaves and an abundance of fruit, providing the most amazing array of golds and pinks, reds and greens. Each piece of fruit looks more appealing than the last.

When looking at it from a great distance the tree stands proudly alone. From one position, there on the sloping green, she can see the top of the tree. Way up there, at its crest, one of the fruits is ruby red, shining in the early morning sun.

"Oh, my," she murmurs. "No wonder *Yehovah* told Adam that we shouldn't eat any of this fruit. The perfection of this beautiful picture would be disfigured. I wonder what that fruit tastes like? Are they different in flavor although from the same tree? Is the green fruit sour and the pink, sweeter? The ruby one looks like it blows out your mouth with too much flavor to comprehend. I wonder..."

Lairn`r is beside himself. Komodo`r is incredulous. I am stunned by the actions of Adam's helpmate. Tantzer is quietly starring at the Viewing Window.

It is one thing to be curious. We understand that motivation, but she is gradually ignoring her own protective instincts and following an all too familiar course. The law of freedom of choice forbids our direct intervention, or Tantzer would just reveal himself again and scare her so badly she would not again think of venturing anywhere near that tree. To do so would mean our banishment from Heaven.

We cannot force her obedience because of the law. Our weapons of distraction, suggestion, and quickening of memories, are not weak. The Rhema word of Dvar HaElohim is the most powerful. He gave that to them when He warned them. If she chooses to ignore that word, it becomes ineffectual and impotent as a guiding force of her behavior. We are shaken and distressed by her questionable judgment.

ELOHIM'S PROPHECY

"You are up early," she mumbles, rubbing the sleep from her eyes. She reaches out, but doesn't find Adam's warmth next to her. Last evening's bedding made from young vines and lush banana leaves is still warm, so he hasn't been gone long.

From somewhere overhead she hears, "Yes," as Adam replies. "Been awake for a while, thinking. You remember when *Yehovah* said we could ask Him questions even when He isn't visible to us? I've thought of a few and I decided to ask Him tonight, instead of during our walk this morning. He said that we could trust Him, and by doing that we would learn to trust Him even more. Do you have any? We could ask Him together, tonight, in the clearing."

"I would like to know if there are any others like us, or are we the only ones?"

Presently, this is the only question she could think of that *Yehovah* hadn't already answered.

"Hmmm," Adam sighs. "You know, that is really a great question. I hadn't thought of that. Now that I think about it, it is one of the more important ones to ask."

He smiles as he watches her stand and stretch. He appreciates her keen insight. Her intellect has proven to be equal to his own. Since she appeared, she has shown herself to possess a quick, sharp wit to go along with her pleasant temperament. "Okay. Tonight, before we retire, let's pray and ask the Lord our questions."

"Okay," she says, while turning around and heading out into the Garden. Then changing her mind she turns back, gives Adam a kiss on the cheek and says, "I have a thought. I want to make a gift for *Yehovah*. Do you think He will mind?"

This surprises Adam. "What an interesting idea. I don't think He will mind at all. If it is okay with you, I would like to give Him a gift, too."

"Sure," she says, "It will be fun." She kisses Adam again, and then walks blithely off, into the heart of the Garden. She knows exactly what gift she will give Him.

Adam shouts to her, "Don't forget *Yehovah* will be here soon for our walk."

She slows her pace. "I'll remember."

She thinks, "I can make it after today's walk. I'll tidy things up here now and later I'll collect the things I'll need."

With this, she returns to the area where their pallet is. She empties a vessel of milk into two bowls, one for the leopard and the other for the lamb and starts straightening the pallet in the meadow where they slept. Soon she hears *Yehovah's* voice calling out with His daily invitation.

"After all this time, we still don't recognize anything in the star field!" Lairn`r sums up our failed attempts.

"We will, sooner or later, in Elohim's time." I remind him, and me, of how things happen.

Lairn`r and I are taking a furlough from our most frequented observation post. We're sitting before a different Viewing Window that looks upon Elohim's star patterns. It allows us a view, as if we are standing at the center of Earth's single land mass,[27] looking up at what we'd earlier mapped.

"The sixty we mapped still remain a mystery. Neither the forty-eight that are viewable from the northern hemisphere nor the twelve, from the southern, seem to mean anything."

Presently, we do understand they are the Word of Elohim, and are prophetic. Beyond that we speculate, more than know, that they are a blueprint of what Eternity will be like when it brings about the final judgment of satan. If confirmed as true, we believe Elohim has set them as sign posts, marking future events.

We turn to leave, but I decide to take one last, quick look at the patterns and then return to my quarters. Suddenly, there they are! A veil has just been lifted from before my eyes! I now recognize certain images formed by parts of the star patterns. My field of view has been too narrow. When I allow my view to include a greater range of stars, with the brighter stars to convey emphasis, I recognize there is an image that appears to be like Elohim and Adam.

"Lairn`r, I see something! It was there all the time! I see a shape and that shape is like Elohim and man, since they are alike. See, over there!" I can't restrain my excitement and point at the stars, while gripping his elbow to turn him back around, so he can see the view behind him.

"Do you see what I am talking about?" I ask, hoping he will confirm what I see.

"No, nothing, just stars, some brighter than others. What are the limits of the field?" Lairn`r answers and then, asks.

I have a thought. I reach into my carry-all bag and pull out the cover to a basket I had in my quarters. It didn't take me long! I remove the center section of the cover, making a hole in the shape of a rectangle. Then I hold it over my head, framing the star field where I recognize the image. Adjusting it in and out, I play with it, until I have it just right. Carefully, I move aside and Lairn`r slides into my vacated space, beneath the securely held cover.

"Now, do you see it? The head of the image is that bright star just beyond where your right thumb is pointing. The legs are spread out and its hands are stretched out, gripping something. I can't quite make it out."

I wait and all I hear is, "Hmmm," from Lairn`r.

"Do I need to draw you a picture?" I ask.

"No, if it is there, I'll see it. I'll see it," Lairn`r says, brushing aside my generous offer.

We wait, and wait, and wait some more, and still Lairn`r is unable to distinguish the image of the erect man.

Finally, I reach out and touch the Viewing Window, in front of the smaller viewing rectangle now in Lairn`r's hand, and trace the outline of the image in the air before his eyes. That seems to work! He reaches out, brushes aside my hand and begins his own tracing of the outline of the image.

"That is it. The word of Elohim is coming alive," I say, while exhaling a sigh of relief. I wasn't imagining it!

"What do you think it means?" he asks, beginning a new series of questions.

The final rays of sunlight disappear behind the far reaching limbs of the fruited trees. Adam is able to see the brightest of the lights overhead. As the sky darkens, the stars poke through the blanket of blue evening. Adam is always amazed at the wonder arrayed before him.

"*Yehovah* is out there and yet He visits us, walks with us, and the warmth of His presence fills us with delight. Night after night, I look upon these lights. I feel, more than I know, that they are important and I long to understand their meaning. During our walks, *Yehovah* tells us to search the stars, for they speak of Him," he remembers, as he contemplates the sky.

"*Yehovah*," Adam prays, "I devote myself to hear their voice. If You would, let me hear them speak, as You say they will."

It is near time to pray and ask the question that had popped into his conscious mind over this day. Looking around for his life mate, he sees her entering the clearing. Together, hand in hand, they kneel beneath the majestic heaven, closing their eyes and bowing their heads before their Maker.

"Oh, great *Yehovah*," Adam leads.

"You enrich our lives by Your presence and we thank You for all the beauty You have caused us to inhabit. Now hear these offerings of thanksgiving, as we prove that which You have instructed us."

Adam turns to give way to his helpmate, waiting for her to go ahead and ask.

"*Yehovah*, what things fill my heart this night. We want for nothing, except that we live, pleasing You. Tomorrow, when You come into the Garden, I would like You to answer the question I have to give You. *Yehovah*, are there any more like us, or are we all there is?" With that she lifts her arms and hands toward the sky in surrender to the heady feeling of the presence of *Yehovah*. She feels Him so strongly she almost opens her eyes to look around to see if He is standing nearby, but remains hushed and respectful on her knees.

Adam, with his head bowed, prays, "*Yehovah*, You know all things and Your wisdom is unsearchable. I acknowledge our ignorance of the truths that are one with You. We are nothing before You, and yet You have taken note of us over all things on Earth. You instructed us to ask these things of You to prove You. We do not doubt Your faithfulness to us, for it is renewed every morning. In submissive obedience, I ask You, 'what is the meaning of the star patterns You have shown us?'"

That evening when, as they fold into each other on their palette, they ask each other what answers, if any, were received from *Yehovah*.

She says, "I think I heard a 'yes' and a 'no!' I'm not sure what that means."

Adam says, "I think I heard that the star patterns are for signs and wonders, and also, tell a story of seasons to come."

Early the next morning, the woman wakes before Adam. She is excited at the prospect of preparing the gift for *Yehovah*. Yesterday she collected a basket of aromatic flowers and leaves. She proceeds to crush them in a large, round stone that has a central depression. She has a smile on her lips, as she works. This display of her joy has become a common expression on her face.

Adam awakens and finding her already busy preparing her gift for *Yehovah*, starts working on his plan. He twists some leaves and forms a wreath. There are a few small florets entwined, as well. He, too, is grinning with the anticipation of surprising their Sovereign. Just as he completes his work, he hears *Yehovah* calling to them, inviting them to walk with Him.

As they join Him, Adam greets Him with his wreath and places it atop *Yehovah's* head, saying, "A crown for our King."

His mate asks *Yehovah* to sit, and with the oils from the fragrant flowers, she anoints his feet. "I crushed these flowers to bring lovely scents to You. We hope You enjoy our gifts of thankfulness to You."

The Vast Unknown

"Today is the day," Adam whispers his reminder to the warm body who has been lying on his arm. "We are still going to walk down by the bluff?"

"Yes," she smiles, as she replies. "I packed some fruits and nuts and they should be enough to get us there and back."

Stretching her arms above her head and running her fingers through her black, unruly hair, she heads for the stream to wash up. Adam watches her go, thinking how wonderful it is sharing life with her. *Yehovah* has been very good to them.

"*Yehovah*, I thank You for this woman for whom I feel such tenderness, and whom I long to understand. May my thoughts and actions be pleasing in Your sight, and hers, this day. And, dear *Yehovah,* I thank You for the answers You gave us, proving You are with us, even when You're not seen by us."

With that, he heads toward a different part of the stream to bathe in its cool waters. They have a long trip planned. Kneeling down to splash water on his face, he enjoys the feeling of the water, as it fully awakens him.

Later, tossing the food basket with their day's provisions over one shoulder, he grabs her hand in his and they head off toward the distant bluff. They have not explored that part of this wondrous paradise yet. *Yehovah* has assured them there is nothing to be avoided or feared within the Garden, except that one tree.

As they explore a new path through the dense growth, they comment that the plants and animals they see on their way look like others they have seen before. Two familiar companions join in this journey, a leopard, that his mate favors, and the gentle lamb. Soon the man and woman lift their voices in song, their hands swinging back and forth. The four of them are noticed, but not feared, by the animals they pass.

One animal, however, plays a game of hide and seek with the exploring party of four. It does the hiding and seeking, never letting the four out of its sight, as it follows them. A serpent.

"Hurry, go and get Zukher. Tell him to come quickly. We may need to act, and his leadership must be involved in the decision," Tantzer directs another novice.

Tantzer has been watching the journey of Adam's small troupe, through the Window. He grows concerned by the uninvited closeness of the serpent, pressing for an advantage.

"What's happening, Tantzer?" I question, before even taking a look through the Window.

"Look!" Tantzer exclaims, excitedly pointing at the scene before him.

"Oh! Okay, I see. Where are their guardian angels?"

Then I see them, moving from a position above the travelers, to intercept the serpent. The couple, enjoying their exploration, is oblivious to any danger. The engagement doesn't last long. Adam's guardian simply stands in the serpent's way, obscuring his view, and preventing his pursuit of Adam and his entourage.

With a commanding presence, he says to the serpent, "It isn't your time. Adonai rebukes you. He commands you to return to your own place of abode, until your appointed time. You are not invited to their journey and there is nothing of which to accuse them, nor is there error." The angel points back toward the center of the Garden and the serpent sulks off, back the way it came.

"Done," I mutter. "Keep an eye out, but that should settle things for the present. The angel used Adonai's authority. The serpent had no choice, but to acquiesce. Tantzer, you were right to send for me. That serpent was just testing his limits. He won't try anything like that again, that far away from his familiar territory."

While my goal is to reassure Tantzer, it was reassuring to me, too, to see the speedy reaction of the angels assigned the task of protecting Adam and his group. The command of Adonai has reinforced the hedge.

By mid-morning Adam's party reaches a low ridge at the foot of the lofting bluff. The journey hasn't taken as long as they had anticipated. Adam selects a couple of nuts and berries offered by the tender hand of his pleasant mate.

"This is fun, don't you think?" he says to the woman. Her nod, as she smiles, is a sweet answer to the question.

They spend the rest of the morning climbing the ridge. Each step offering their exploring eyes a greater view of this new territory.

Adam sings a new song, rising from within his spirit and filling his soul as each word, just pops into his imagination, without any forethought or reasoning. He isn't sure of the full meaning of the words, but his spirit does and that is enough. Someday, or some evening, he will think on these things and see if *HaRuach* will provide understanding. Adam needn't be concerned about forgetting the captivating melody or the words. He and the woman have total recall, forgetting nothing.

Tantzer, once again alone at the Window, hears the song sung by Adam and Eve, joining in their joyous refrain.

"I love thee, *Adonai,* my strength.

You sent from above, and drew me from many waters.

You placed me in a large place because You delighted in me.

You gird me with strength, and make my way perfect.

You make my feet like hinds' feet, and enlarged my steps, so I do not slip.[28]"

"It is good to get off our feet for a while," Adam declares, and reaches out his hand to help the woman settle on the ground next to him. The lamb and leopard move off in search of moist blades of grass or leaves, but not so far as to lose sight of the relaxing couple.

"That climb seemed to grow steeper with each step."

They have reached the top of the bluff just after mid-day, along the way losing site of the view, while climbing under the canopy of trees. Turning in perfect unison, they can see the front edge of their clearing, way off in the distance. Though the area is several hundred paces in each direction, it looks so small from this vantage point. They can see the Tree of Life, recognizable because of the lush, ever-changing hues of green and aqua. There they can also see the forbidden Tree of the Knowledge that is so easy to distinguish from the surrounding greenery.

At the sight of the Tree of the Knowledge of Good and Evil, the woman cast her eyes down for a brief moment, recalling the pesky serpent that seems to be drawn to her anytime she approaches the proximity of the tree.

They then turn to look in the opposite direction, hoping for a glimpse of unknown wonders. They are not disappointed! Bursting forth, in a great panorama of colors, is layer upon layer of tiered splendor. For the first time, man sees what lies beyond the bluff. There are rivers which must be branches of the rivers flowing near, what they now understand to be, the central part of the Garden. Based upon the distant horizons, the Garden is vast. In fact, it is many times larger than they had previously appreciated.

Nestled among the rivers, they can see flocks of colorful winged animals. Adam recognizes the different species, having named them just before they had flown away to their preferred nesting sites. Vapors rise from unseen geysers, and from founts of refreshing water, that feed the Garden and the abundant life flourishing here.

"What is that?" she asks, gesturing with her pointed index finger.

"What? Where?" Adam retorts, not immediately seeing anything, but the beauty they had been relishing.

"Over there, look along my line of sight," she says, now with more urgency.

Adam pauses and changes his focus, realizing that what is distracting her demands his immediate attention. There, off the end of her hand, he sees a thin, tall, white object with what might be a small dancing light flickering over it. He can see what looks like an opening behind the object but nothing beyond the opening or over it.

Adam, momentarily catching his breath, exclaims, "Wow! Wonder what that is!"

Tantzer squints and moves closer to the Window, straining to see what all the excitement is about. He sees the object with the light, too.

"Do you know what that is?" Tantzer suddenly becomes aware of Lairn'r's presence.

Turning, he asks his covenant partner, "How long have you been here?"

"A while. I slipped in as they began climbing the bluff from the ridge. I didn't want to disturb you, so I remained motionless behind you," Lairn`r answers.

"No, I don't know. What is that?" Tantzer answers Lairn`r's question, and asks.

"That is the gateway into, and out of, the Garden," Lairn`r explains. "An angel stands post there as an ivory candlestick with a flickering flame."

"What can it be? There aren't any things like it in the Garden." Adam now takes the lead in questioning the presence of this strange image.

"Let's go check it out!" he urges them on.

"It looks so far away that it will take the rest of the daylight to reach whatever it is, and we won't be able to get back to the clearing today. We will have to spend the night in an unknown part of the Garden. Do you think *Yehovah* will mind?" The woman, now, is taking the lead in caution. Usually she is the first to propose a bold action.

"I feel it is good and will be good for us to learn what this is," Adam voices his certainty with great conviction.

"Okay," she agrees, his faith settling her own consternation.

Quickly gathering their remaining provisions, with the lamb and the leopard prancing ahead, they climb down the bluff on the opposite side from which they had recently ascended. This discovery is an unexpected bonus.

"Who knows, but I might have missed naming something and must be faithful to do as *Yehovah* has commanded me," Adam thinks.

After the sun begins settling below the overhanging trees, they realize that opening a path in this direction is a lot more difficult to accomplish than opening the way to the bluff this morning. They soon recognize that the mystery will not be solved today, so they choose, instead, to use the remaining twilight to find a suitable place to sleep. Soon after giving thanks to *Yehovah* for the day, exhausted, the four companions lie down upon the few large leaves they've found and fall fast asleep.

Tantzer and Lairn`r continue watching. They understand that the unexpected difficulty Adam's party is encountering is a result of their guardian angels, placing some token resistance in their path. This is to teach them that growth in soul strength is as much a part of life as is having everything handed to them as a sign of Elohim's favor.

The canopy of trees and greenery shield the sun's rays from reaching the floor in this part of the Garden until late in the morning. It is quite different from the more open spaces they think of as home. This contributes to their late awakening. It has caused a later departure than they'd planned. With several fruits picked along their path, and the blessed offering of thanksgiving, they are moving with a swiftness they lacked late yesterday.

"It can't be far from here," Adam estimates. He begins looking for a tall tree to climb to confirm their final course. Finding the tree he is looking for, he climbs steadily toward its highest perch, the effort becoming easier with each chin-up and thrust. Soon he is able to stand up on a secure limb and gaze ahead to see if he can solve the mystery of the object with the dancing light. From here, all he can see is the flickering light thereby confirming, only, that their course is right.

He climbs down, being careful not to lose the direction.

"Won't be long now," he says, as he grabs her hand. They continue their mission, their anticipation growing with each step.

Soon they are confronted by an arched gateway, adorned with branches and entangled, flowering vines. In the center of the opening stands the single object they'd seen which is about the height of the gateway. Embracing it are the same vines and branches defining the opening. Above it a small flame searches the wind.

Adam thinks, as they approach the mammoth opening, "This thing is huge. I guess it must be forty to fifty paces wide and at least half that tall."

The depth of the gateway looks to be a pace and a half and the attached walls of vines and leaves seem impenetrable. Their colors are the same as some of the plants he knows, but these have a different quality to them. It is almost as if they shimmer, while vibrating in a slightly off-key note, similar to one he has heard before. It appears to mimic the sounds sung by some of the birds that visit in the clearing around them, yet the frequency is not the same.

The view beyond the gateway is not much different from the various meadows, and rolling hills, they have seen in different parts of the Garden. They stand to the far right to see around the left edges of the opening, seeking to see all the different angles. If they get too close to the opening, it moves slightly farther away. As they back up, the opening moves toward them, finally returning to its original location. They repeat the investigation from the left side. While they ponder this mystery, several chipmunks and squirrels playfully scurry through the opening. Their two traveling companions join these small animals beyond the gate, just long enough to deepen the mystery, before returning.

Through the opening, the farther away they try to see, the more obscure the presented scenes before them become. They feel no threat or danger. *Yehovah* has never said they couldn't explore the full extent of the Garden, so they aren't doing anything contrary to what He has said they have the option to do.

The white symmetrical object engendering the flame appears beautiful within its raiment of branches and vines. There is no heat emanating from the small flame. Its pulsating light seems to have no source determining an increase or decrease in the brightness. Their impressions are those of joy and peace, and in no way are they feeling a threatening presence, though they do not understand why these things are so.

Adam does what he has always done with each new discovery, he gives it a name.

"I name you, *Passage Who Knows.*"

After a brief discussion about whether they should return to the clearing the way they came or seek another, less formidable, path, they decide upon the latter choice. Adam mentions he thinks he saw an easier route, along a river off somewhere on the right. They decide to travel that way, parallel to the thick vined wall which stands on either side of the gateway. They cannot see through the foliage. It's too thick. Nor can they feel anything when they try to reach into it. One such test only results in her becoming covered with a sticky substance that acts to attract a variety of flying insects.

None the worse for wear, they move forward, increasing their distance from the gateway. In a short time, they can't see it any longer. Not even a glow. It lingers, though, in their minds.

"What was that all about?" she asks.

"That was a gate, or opening, to another place. We could only see a part of it. I have the feeling that the land on the other side of the gateway is outside this Garden we inhabit. 'Passage Who Knows' is there to mark the authority of the Garden. The animals were able to go through the opening and yet the barrier moved away as we moved closer. I imagine the splendor within the Garden, that we so thoroughly enjoy, enlarges if we choose to go beyond where we are now."

As they walk, Adam is becoming increasingly lost in his thoughts. She walks beside him, speaking, more to herself, than to Adam. The leopard and the lamb are frolicking nearby.

"I wonder if we will ever come back here?" pausing briefly, she asks. She continues to ponder, "Why would *Yehovah* create such a place and not let us go out there like the animals can?"

For most of the time it takes to reach the river, they walk in subdued silence. It seems to take longer returning. There aren't new, wondrous sights to share, as there were when they began their adventure. Wishing to decrease the arduous nature of their return, Adam reaches down to pick a bundle of flowers and hands them to her. Her smile has the desired effect, and they join their swinging hands, and begin to sing a duet of thanks to *Yehovah*. They talk about how much they miss His teaching. After all, it has been two days, since they left the clearing and that is where He visits with them.

Tantzer stands and stretches his arms and wings. The scene he and Lairn`r have been witnessing makes fuel for an animated conversation. They know that the angel, who is guarding the gateway, has revealed himself only as the lighted candlestick. Appearing in disguise has become a customary means of interacting with Adam and his life mate. This allows open engagement without compromising the law of freedom of choice. Time to time, various angels have revealed themselves as wind, a feathery light, a pleasant fragrance riding upon a breeze. Thus, they only allow themselves to appear, when they stand nearby, during the couple's sleep. Tantzer's faux pas is not repeated.

Adam has mentioned, more than once, that he thought he'd seen something unusual when one of the angels lingers too long. These startling manifestations occur, only on occasion, upon Adam unexpectedly awakening from sleep. These happenings titillate the man's senses and comprehension of reality.

With a bemused look upon his face, Tantzer begins entertaining a growing crowd of inquisitive angels, as he recreates Adam and the woman's exploration at the arched gateway. He's replaying, before the Viewing Window as a backdrop for his antics, Adam and his helpmate's mystified investigation. The exaggeration increases, as the crowd grows. He first leans to the right side, stretching and shielding his eyes with his hands, straining to see around the corners of the Window. Then he repeats the extravagant demonstration on the left side of the Window, all the time replicating their conversation.

Just when those in attendance think he is finished, a new audience of angels arrives, encouraging Tantzer to begin all over again.

As night is covering the last rays of light, they arrive back in the clearing. The long journey has reached an end. They have learned a lot and answered innumerable questions, only to discover that in each case an answer birthed more questions.

Adam is convinced that it will be a while before he wants to venture so far from the clearing, even though there is the other side of the Garden to investigate. That area is beyond the view from the bluff just explored, so it all remains a mystery. Maybe, one day.

Without taking on preparation of an evening meal, he decides they should settle in for a long rest. Now that they have returned to the clearing *Yehovah* should come for a teaching. He has, within, a longing to see Him. Adam wants to be alert and openhearted, but he hasn't decided, as yet, whether to discuss the journey with Him.

On the fringes of the clearing a clump of tall grass moves and the head of the serpent is exposed.

"They are back," he hisses. "I sense a new knowledge to probe for weakness. Maybe the woman will come near the tree tomorrow, or the day after. I can wait. The final encounter there is yet to be determined."

REVELATION OF THE LINEN KAFTAN[29]

The Observatory is buzzing. Angels are arriving in large and small groups, seeking suitable places of repose. Dvar HaElohim is going to make known an inspiring revelation. There are inquiring looks searching arriving faces for any scrap of information. The last such session was when Elohim began the creation spectacular.

Michael has not yet appeared up front. One of our novice messengers, Gabriel, is supposed to be with him. They are likely hidden by the flowing veil behind the platform over there. That is where Michael usually makes his entrance. A rich green color fills the room. There is a delightful fragrance riding upon that hue. The intense color is saturated with the scent.

All the doors, except those used for egress, are closed and sealed. The curtains on the Viewing Windows are also closed. The one exception is the Window showing the created expanse. Even the curtain over the Window from which we watch the Garden is closed, and that has remained open, since Elohim placed Adam there.

I check, again, to see if I have the correct number of places reserved for Tantzer, Komodo`r, Lairn`r, Shtitsen, and, of course, Lez`n and Sryyab`r. Dāwīd, Gershom, Alexis and Mehgen` who would normally be sitting around us are fulfilling their commissions as guardians. I haven't run into Klalish, so I don't know if he expects me to reserve a place for him. This group sitting together during training sessions has become a practice I started soon after I completed the assignment of assembling the troupe.

My mind drifts back to the pleasurable experience of putting my troupe together. My first choice was Komodo`r, whose strength of focus seemed essential. I then selected Lairn`r and Tantzer. Lairn`r was chosen because we needed an inquisitor. Tantzer, a novice, I chose because of his energy. Klalish, a warrior angel, was added later, since it has become de rigueur to have a couple of these extra-large protectors interspersed in the troupes, following Lucifer's rebellion. Troupes number 100 angels, the number of which will vary from time to time. It depends on the need for services required outside troupe oversight.

The four angels I mention here have become a part of my inner circle and they share with me an intimate camaraderie. However, I know all 100 of them well. When needed, it falls upon me to recommend those most suited to perform requested functions, outside my jurisdiction.

Troupes are usually formed for a specific purpose. The members chosen have a common proficiency, although may reflect different facets, and therefore justly fulfill that single purpose. When it was organized, ours was planned to follow a different pattern designed by Michael, made up of disparate talents and interests. I was instructed to have only a single duplicate of any proficiency, with each of the two chosen from a different troupe, thus providing greater diversity.

It wasn't until Michael informed me of our intended mission, prior to the creation of Adam, that the reason for these instructions became clear.

Komodo`r rises from his chair. While stretching across Lairn`r, looking befuddled, Komodo`r asks me, "Do you have any new information about this session?" He has to talk loudly because of the other discussions going on around him.

With a frown, Lairn`r sits there with his face wedged between Komodo`r's right leg and my left thigh.

"No, nothing. We'll know shortly!" I shout back. He isn't the only one wondering.

Komodo`r sits back down, making his apologies to Lairn`r, who just shrugs and goes on fiddling with something he's carried in with him.

Tantzer volunteers a question, while pointing with his chin, "Any idea what is under the sparkling veil over there?"

"No. I have no idea. It surely is huge, isn't it! I guess it is about sixteen square cubits." I had noticed it before, but had forgotten about it, as I greeted the other members of our troupe. "It can't be long now. The hue is changing. It has a greater brilliance. The moment is about to…"

My voice trails off as a trumpet report interrupts further explanation. It announces the beginning and everyone quiets down. The trumpet echoes in our ears as Michael, followed by Gabriel, enters from behind the veil. Michael, arms held high above his head, gestures for attention.

"We have been given a great honor. Dvar HaElohim is coming to make known a revelation about the created wonder that has captured our attention."

"So Michael, too, is reacting to the magnetism of the created wonder!" I think, as I rise joining the celebration as Michael's announcement brings all the angels to their feet, shouting, "Hallelujah."

On the platform we see a single figure, slowly entering from a side door that just appears from nowhere. The figure is like that of a man. He has long white hair that rests low over his ears. His face is furrowed and kind. I focus my eyes to see more and recognize that his hands, too, are wrinkled. His hands are practiced hands. His eyes are narrow and bright. He wears a weathered gown that almost touches the floor. His feet are strapped in worn sandals. The man inches forward, without looking toward us. Rather he seems to look only toward the sparkling veil that Tantzer had been asking about.

As he slowly walks across the platform, I see that he carries a chest. I lean forward trying to see what is inside. I resist the impulse to stand, and remain seated, so those behind me can see. The man walks, covering and protecting the chest, as if trying to prevent someone from removing what is inside.

When he is near the veil, still holding the container, he shifts it, placing it under one arm. He then turns, points and speaks to the veil. I can't understand what he is saying, but the sparkles disappear into the fabric. Reaching with his empty hand, he then lifts the veil, tossing it aside.

It is then that an angel appears from behind the man. Quickly, catching a small edge of the fabric, he prevents any part of it from touching the floor. Carefully the angel folds it into a smaller and smaller roll. The folding continues until the roll disappears and is as nothing. From the floor an image begins to appear.

A shadowy figure moves at the feet of the white haired man. The shadow is about to slip past when, deftly, the man stomps upon its head, pinning the form to the floor. The shadow struggles to get free, moving this way and that, but remains subdued by the heel of the man. Seeming to resign itself to defeat, it settles there, motionless. After a season of stillness, the man then, picks up his foot. He begins shaking his foot, as one would after stepping in something unpleasant, until the mashed form falls off behind him and soon disappears, leaving behind three keys.

I wonder what it all means and look around at Komodo`r, Lairn`r, and Tantzer to see if, perhaps, they know. I notice that the late arriving Klalish has taken a seat next to Tantzer. Looking at me, with his lips pursed, he mouths something. He exaggerates the formed words to be sure I understand the sentence his lips are conveying. "I – understand – that - part. The – shadow – is - satan!"

The object that had been beneath the lifted veil now stands in full view before the awestruck angels. It is made of wood and metal. The wood forms a frame. There are pins of metal all around the edges. It is held together with long strands of metal strung between the edges. Above, below, and on both sides of the frame, are cone-shaped spindles with strands of fine thread stretched from the spindles through and around the pins. In front of the frame is a wooden stool.

134

Almost in unison, the audience says, "It's a loom, a weaver's loom."

The weathered face smiles. It is the only evidence that he hears anything that we say, or, that he is aware of us, at all. The man moves his legs around the stool, settling his weight upon it. As he lifts his hands he begins to hum. As he hums, the loom comes to life. He breaks into song. While singing contentedly, he occasionally speaks to the loom and the spindles, which obey his command.

The gracefully forming linen grows in beauty as the spindles empty with a starting, and halting, fashion. Thread by thread the elegant cloth comes to life.

Lairn`r digs his elbow into my rib as, ignoring my flinch, he points toward four baskets filled with heaping collections of spindles of fine thread, just like those arrayed around the edges of the loom. Hovering over each collection is an angel clothed in white.

Arching high, over all the hovering angels, is a rainbow of many colors. Each angel reads a scroll as they lift and examine a spindle selected from one of the baskets. I see about two in five examined spindles carefully placed into a river that flows between the angels. About three in five examined spindles are tossed into a smoldering pit of coals and consumed.

When a loomed spindle becomes empty, the weaver reaches into the flowing river to retrieve its replacement. Before placing it on the loom, he first examines the candidate for flaws. One in five, thusly examined spindles, has its threads tenderly pulled, mended, and groomed by the weaver. When a spindle is found worthy, the weaver places it upon the still laboring loom. The rest are placed in a bag that is hanging at his side. The bag is transparent and has no bottom.

One of the hovering angels speaks, "I am he who, by the hand of the One who framed the Highest Heaven, is a watcher and a governor of a kingdom. The threads on the spindles you see are those found worthy by the Framing Hand to give the light of governance to the Highest Heaven. This area of governance provides the law of boundaries to the omnipotence, omnipresence and omniscience."

I look into the basket filled with spindles and try to read the names thereon. I see the names "Love of Elohim," "Faith of Elohim," "Hope of Elohim," "Fear of Elohim," "True Worship," and "Divine Order."

The second hovering angel speaks, "I am he who, by the hand of the One who framed the expanding heaven, is a watcher and a governor of a kingdom. The threads on the spindles you see are those proven and found worthy by the Framing Hand to give the light of governance to the expanding heaven. This area of governance provides the law of boundaries to the light of the expanding heaven. Only by the flawlessness of the governance of the first angel does the Framing Hand exercise governance over the light of the expanding universe."

I read the names on the spindles in the second basket, and see "Law of Time," "Law of Space," "Law of Mass," and "Law of Motion."

The third hovering angel speaks, "I am he who, by the hand of the One who framed the expanding heaven, is a watcher and a governor of a kingdom. The threads on the spindles you see are those proven and found worthy by the Framing Hand to give the light of governance to the Earth and sky. This area of governance provides the law of boundaries to the light of the Earth and sky. Only by the flawlessness of the governance of the first and second angels does the Framing Hand exercise governance over the light of the Earth and sky."

I read the names on the spindles in the third basket and see "Law of the Sun," "Law of the Moon," "Law of Wind," "Law of the Sea," and "Law of Regeneration."

The fourth hovering angel speaks, "I am he who, by the hand of the One who framed the expanding heaven, is a watcher and a governor of a kingdom. The threads on the spindles you see are those proven and found worthy by the Framing Hand to give the light of governance to mankind. This area of governance provides the law of boundaries to the light of mankind. Only by the flawlessness of the governance of the first, second, and third angels does the Framing Hand exercise governance over the light of mankind."

I read the many names on the spindles in the fourth basket and see "Law of Faith," "Law of Truth," "Law of Sin," "Law of the Mind," "Law of Liberty," "Law of Expression," and "Law of Life."

We sit transfixed as the weaver tells his tale. The four angels respond on cue. A supporting cast of whirling spindles round out the drama of the exquisite linen that is riding upon the loom, though the plot remains a mystery. Michael also stands motionless, observing the spectacle. The significance of his presence decreases as the drama before us unfolds. One part becomes two and two parts become three, three parts become four, while between the parts, the weaver stands, examines the linen and says, "It is good."

"How many parts do you think there are in this composition?" I ask Lairn`r, as, engrossed, he rests his chin on his hands, his elbows on the ledge in front of us.

"No telling really. I have counted four so far, and he has begun a fifth," he offers, but remains focused on the action before him. Then he asks his own question, "Can you see any of the images within the linen?"

Very softly, so as not to display a lack of respect for the performance, I whisper, "I see a dark blue, almost black, field of emptiness with twinkling points of light scattered throughout the field. The points of light could be the star fields of the expanding heaven mentioned by the second and third angels. Have you met the four hovering angels before? I don't recognize any of them, do you?"

Komodo`r doesn't wait for Lairn`r to reply, "Wisdom suggests this demonstration is far from over. They might offer explanations later and ask questions of us. We had better pay close attention, in case we are called upon by Michael."

Turning to me, and whispering across Lairn`r again, he says, "I see the star field you mentioned, and I think you are right." He then sits forward and places his chin on his hands, mimicking Lairn`r.

We watch as, for the fifth time, the weaver stands, raising his arm over the newly spun linen, and speaks, "It is good."

This time he doesn't sit back down, but remains holding his arm over the exquisite fabric. He motions with his other arm to the hovering angels to remain calm as they wait, with their arms still at their sides, and their wings beating only enough to stay in place. With the loom still, the sounds of innovation cease. There is now peace, as those watching hold a communal breath.

This continues for a season, when the weaver steps from behind the stool, and approaches the front edge of the platform. He speaks to us in an elegant tone and the voice of many waters. "I Am...the weaver. By my hand all things came to be. I Am...the framer. By my hand was framed all things mentioned. I Am...the spoken word. Nothing exists that I did not speak into existence. I Am...the way, the truth, and the life. Nothing was, is, or shall be except I first desire it to be. You marvel at the things you see before you. Greater things than these shall you see. Blessed are you, for you shall see, hear, and understand these greater things, because in the time of temptation you were not found wanting."

A scribe, an angel tasked with giving perception and discernment of mysteries to ministering angels, stands up to speak. He unseals a scroll and interprets what we have seen unfolding before us.

"The Highest Heavens, mentioned by the first angel, is the perfection where Elohim dwells. The expanding universe, mentioned by the second angel, is the created heavens within which Earth dwells. The Earth and sky, mentioned by the third angel, is the place where man dwells. Man, mentioned by the fourth angel, is the place that Elohim hopes to dwell."

With this revelation, I wonder, "Will this circle be unbroken?"

EDEN'S ENIGMA

Lairn`r looks puzzled. The quizzical expression he usually wears is presently eclipsed by a look of bewilderment.

"Got a problem?" I question the questioner.

"No. Just wrestling with the mystery and meanings of the Tree of Life and the Tree of the Knowledge of Good and Evil!" he confesses.

I know my companion well enough to recognize that he's pleased to have someone with whom he can talk about this. Lairn`r sometimes chooses to vocalizes his thoughts, without a filter, which clarifies his thinking.

"You notice the waves of color emanating from the Throne?" he asks. Without waiting for a reply, he continues, "They appear predominantly orange with traces of several varieties of blue hues, wafting throughout. Right now, they appear particularly rich and inviting. Sometimes, though, they are translucent, other times, opaque, and then returning back to transparent over and over again."

Lairn`r and I are standing near the entrance to the Throne Room, which is full of worshipping angels, fulfilling their deepest longings. I dropped by to retrieve Lairn`r from his time of voluntary worship.

In explanation, I respond to his pondering, "The Seven Spirits, the name of the ministry manifestations of HaRuach, moves throughout Earth and simultaneously moves through the avenues of Heaven. His is a rich and powerful expression of One of the Three, which are Elohim, and He arcs over the Throne." I offer this while engaging my memory, and drawing upon lessons and understanding, I already have.

"What is the connection of The Seven Spirits and the Trees?" I ask, failing to connect the two seemingly divergent spheres of thought.

"We know that each of the ministries of HaRuach manifests itself as a rich field of base colors. See there, the rainbow arc over the Throne. Then, there are also the pleasant musical tones or copious fragrances, sometimes all these bathing the Throne at the same time. Sometimes He is the colors, tones, or fragrances," Lairn`r states the common understanding and continues, "Well, when the circuits of HaRuach find the Tree of Life, planted in the court outside the Citadel, or when He wills to visit the image of the same tree, planted in the Garden, the hues are predominantly green indicating the ministry of the Ruach of Life. Although, on occasion, there are wisps of royal blue and magenta that nuzzle the semi-transparent greens."

"Yes, I noticed that." I grant that I can see the visual scene he's describing.

"When the circuit finds its way to the Tree of the Knowledge of Good and Evil, it boils as all the colors manifest the seven ministries of HaRuach. These wrestle each other for prominence. One color squeezing into view, seeking a hearing, only to be covered once again by a different ministering color, whose presence is insisted upon.

"HaRuach, though, doesn't venture as close to that tree as He does the Tree of Life, where He plays hide and seek among the branches. At the Tree of the Knowledge of Good and Evil, He seems to be shielding more than embracing the tree." Lairn`r puts his mental images into words, trying to explain the poetry in motion, that HaRuach personifies.

"I was observing the most recent performance when it struck me that we have been missing the obvious. HaRuach is leaving clues as to the meaning of the trees with these performances," Lairn`r says, completing the link for me.

The Tree of Life and the Tree of Knowledge, two trees, singled out, unique in the Garden. Each has significance; each has a story to tell; and each has a representative image which occupies a place in a chamber of the Hall of Mysteries. The Tree of Life, as Lairn`r often points out to me, stands prominently central to the Garden and rates its own Viewing Window. It, therefore, falls into the category of "most intriguing."

"I come here from time to time and I just stare at it," Lairn`r says. "I guess I'm hoping to absorb some portion of understanding by just looking at it. It is a beautiful creation. Along with a lovely form and inviting presence, it has a distinctive appeal. There is an abundance of fully ripe fruit arrayed among its branches."

Tantzer is quick to point out, "The Tree of Life has another characteristic that makes it unique. Have you taken note of its fruit? At sunset the fruit recedes or just disappears. It doesn't spoil. It is just gone. Nothing of it is wasted or goes to rot. All night the tree is dormant and then when the sun's first rays grace the upper lush leaves, and the dew is on its petals, the fruit begins to appear, once more. Ripe and juicy, the fruit seems exceedingly delicious. We know this because the roots of the tree are planted in Heaven's soil and they drink from the waters flowing in the River of Life. The source of the river, of course, is deep within the Temple Mount."

"The fruit of the tree is of the same nourishment we, the angels, enjoy. It is of the Sovereign's meat," Lairn`r says, expounding further on the essence of the tree. "Various species of birds and animals enjoy this fruit and the benevolence of its branches."

He goes on, "They gather there frequently, chirping and singing all manner of pleasant melodies. Many of the tunes and melodies mimic those offered by angels, worshipping Elohim.

"The angels are curious as to why Adam and his helpmate have not yet sampled the fruit, so abundant on its branches. They have freedom to eat of everything in the Garden, except the Tree of the Knowledge of

Good and Evil, but so far they have ventured to the pleasant avenues leading to the Tree of Life, only once.

"And that is the other distinctive tree that is alone in the universe. The Tree of the Knowledge of Good and Evil is the one attracting the attention of the woman," Lairn`r rests his case, hitting at the heart of the mystery that is the enigma of the Garden.

Komodo`r begins his often repeated rendition regarding the trees, "When Elohim created the Garden and placed Adam there, the presence of these two trees raised questions in the minds of the easily inspired angels."

The smile across his face betrays his personal approval of his own cleverness…the last part of his opening line.

Komodo`r has the best understanding of mysteries of any of the angels in our troupe. It is natural for us to include him, when we finally decide to quit delving for understanding on our own, and actually become contributors to a solution.

Reflecting on how we became familiar with Lairn`r's preoccupation with the Garden trees, I add, "I suppose the real genesis, of what has led to a serious effort, was just after the Season of Trumpets.

"Lairn`r asked me one day, 'Do you want to gain deep understanding about the Garden trees?' He was catching me at a time when I couldn't possibly start something new. I told him that, although I would truly have loved to get involved, he and I had Heaven's missions to perform. After all, so much depends on our faithfulness to our covenant partners and Elohim."

During this recitation of what had transpired between Lairn`r and me, I am making every effort to be even toned. I rarely need to exhort correction and certainly did not want to be reminding Lairn`r of an uncomfortable moment.

Returning to that conversation, only in memory, and not aloud, I recall Lairn`r saying, "My apologies, Zukher. I do have a lot of missions to complete, before starting another project, no matter how important it might be. We seem to be jumping into so many different and unusual things since man was created. It is logical that we have to take time to catch up. Thank you for reminding me."

I responded, "Michael hasn't said anything because part of our troupe's responsibilities is focusing on these mysteries, but a proper balance is also wise and needful, just as long as man's shield is not compromised as a result of our choices." With that parting assurance, I went off to finish my own tasks that required immediate attention.

My reports to Michael completed, and my preparations for advancing some novice angels to the estate of trustee complete, I have time to prioritize the troupe's individual assignments. Komodo`r's duties are progressing sufficiently well and so are Lairn`r's, even though he usually is of a willing mind to tackle too many things at once. It seems to me it would regularly take a miracle to complete what he's started, however, I know One who performs such miracles. As I review the list, it seems only a couple of angels need help to get caught up, so I ask Komodo`r to tutor the stragglers. I want to quickly return to the process of, once again, seeking the understanding of things not yet understood.

What has been a series of interrupting interludes has now become a troupe assignation. We gather in one of the rooms on the Mezzanine.

"Komodo`r was saying that the two trees in the Garden raise questions," I begin.

"I want to see if the timing is right to seek understanding, or at least, make some progress."

"I have a few thoughts for us to consider," Lairn`r jumps in, speaking up before the more timid in our troupe have an opportunity to collect cohesive thoughts.

"Of the two trees, only one has a consequence for man. I suggest we begin with that tree, since increasing our understanding will enhance our ministry to them," Lairn`r suggests, while looking around for any dissent.

"I am in agreement with Lairn'r's suggestion, however, I take exception. It is not certain that only one tree has a consequence for man. That is a possibility we need to keep in mind, but absent any certainty that there are other consequences for man, let's have the scribe correct the record and move on," Komodo`r declares.

"I stand corrected," Lairn`r confirms.

Lez`n confirms, "So it is corrected."

Lairn`r, our legal conscience, continues, "Let's move on then to the Tree of the Knowledge of Good and Evil and the warning, as set forth by Dvar HaElohim. What is meant by *death* is not *ceasing to exist*. Its meaning, rather, is going from an estate of eternal communion of life with Elohim to an estate of eternal separation from Elohim. An example is His judgment of satan and those who are forever lost. So if man, or his helpmate, chooses to eat of the fruit of that tree, they will, in fact, be joining in satan's rebellion. They will thus be, eternally, in an estate of non-communion with Elohim."

"Since man is in the image of Elohim, does that apply to man's body, as well as, the soul and spirit?" Tantzer asks.

"They are physical. Therefore they are, at least in part, subject to the laws of that realm," Komodo`r confirms our previous conjecture.

"Yes, because his body is of Earth, it would return there. Thus the body would be separated from the spirit. The spirit is life, because of the righteousness within. Since the spirit is the means by which man is in communion with Elohim, the body experiences death, but the spirit would return to Elohim. It is of His essence and cannot be separate from Elohim.

"That leaves the soul and the personhood of man resides in the soul. Death, then, would mean that it could not continue to have communion with Elohim. It would, then, have to go to a place of separation from Elohim. Logically, this would be the place of torment within Sheol. That is where certain of those involved in the rebellion are chained. Therefore, I must conclude that the soul of the offender would go there," Komodo`r states with great assurance. He seems to expect no dissenting interpretation of the consequences of disobedience regarding eating the fruit of the tree and death.

"Excuse me, please. I have a question." It is Lairn`r. It appears he has a follow up.

"Yes," I say. "To whom are you addressing this?"

"Komodo`r, or anyone else, who might have a response."

"Then please proceed." We are looking for answers. While I believe the interpretation presented by Komodo`r is sound, we should examine many different angles to prove his theorem.

"I actually have a series of questions, if I may," Lairn`r speaks up and looks at me. I nod affirmatively.

"Komodo`r, does the acquisition of knowledge result in sin?" Lairn`r asks, looking steadily into Komodo`r's eyes.

"No. Not in and of itself," Komodo`r replies.

"Is the knowledge of good and evil sin?" Lairn`r quickly asks, picking up the inquisitor's cadence.

A pause from Komodo`r indicates a careful answer will be forthcoming.

"I am compelled to answer that I don't know, because we constantly acquire greater knowledge of many things, including good and evil. The knowledge of good and evil, as exhibited by the rebellion, is but a single example.

"Now that I have made that statement, I change my answer. No! Knowledge of good and evil is not a sin, in and of itself. There must be something else involved."

Tantzer stands with an arm raised for attention. "May I ask Lairn`r a question for clarification?"

"Certainly!" Lairn`r, Komodo`r and I say in unison. Not one of us is offended by his breach of protocol.

"Is it considered to be a sin to attain sovereign knowledge while in direct disobedience to His word, time or purpose?" Tantzer queries his teachers.

"Yes! Any action in direct disobedience to Elohim, His word, time or purpose, is a sin," Komodo`r jumps in.

"Yes, yes, that must be it," Lairn`r interjects. "If man acts in disobedience to Elohim's command, and acquires knowledge, he declares by his actions that Elohim is capable of mendacity, which, therefore, is sin."

With that added nuance, there is conviction in the room and we are all of one accord.

"If man eats of the fruit of the tree, then he will have sinned and will die. The body would return to the Earth. The spirit would return to Elohim to be united with the life giver. And the soul will be separated from Elohim forever," Lairn`r declares, to which we all voice unanimous assent.

Surely, part of the image of the Mystery of the Tree of the Knowledge of Good and Evil has become opaque, since the resisting seal has been opened. The name of our troupe will be recorded as opening this seal, unless another troupe has reached this understanding before us.

The Tree of Life remains a mystery and not one of Heaven's troupes has a modicum of logic on which to launch an investigation. We know that Adam, and the woman, were created to live forever. Tantzer, fresh from his helpful input regarding the forbidden tree, suggests the Tree of Life isn't presently needed, unless man sins.

After some pondering, we conclude that his theory isn't logical. Why would Elohim plant the tree in the Garden and say, "Freely eat of it," if it is for no purpose. The man and woman, having eternal life, do not have need of the fruit of this tree named the Tree of Life. The other part of this enigma is that the luscious fruit it produces doesn't attract man's consideration, not even out of curiosity. This is surely another puzzle in the Garden.

An angel named Chayim, a keeper of knowledge, drops by during one of our conclaves. He is a member of another troupe and he is, also, seeking understanding of this mystery. Angels who belong to various troupes often join in when they know a discussion is enticing, especially when there is much to learn. Drop-ins like this are always welcome. We soon learn this angel, in particular, has much to add. We are not yet aware he will be the one to break our speculators' stalemate.

Chayim's record in The Book of Citizens is known to Lairn`r. They greet each other warmly. After suitable introductions, Lairn`r asks Chayim the reason for his presence.

Chayim replies, "In our recent past, I was blessed to have a commission of honor. My commission was acting as one of the never-ending worshippers before the Throne."

Worship of Elohim is eternally manifested by an angelic multitude so commissioned. This is a handpicked choir, whom Elohim has awarded with this greatly coveted honor. They offer up continual, unrestrained praise and worship.

Chayim continues, "That honor affords those so exercised an opportunity to witness all things about the Throne. The intimate acknowledgements there are revelations that are not exposed anywhere else within Heaven.

"After my commission expired, as you are aware, all of them do, I had a deeper knowledge of so many things. Such worship transports one's senses to heights that can only be recognized as a promise of glories that words cannot describe. Intrinsic in being continuously in

His presence is a hope that the state achieved during that worship will become a retained reality. A new normal.

"As Eternity distances one from the last chord of our collective worship, so are we increasingly distant from the magnitude of what that reality promised. In conclusion, I find that my being, my senses, are now more alive than before I began the commission. A remnant, of the glories that were experienced, continues. I am both fully satisfied and famished! I am filled with abundance and yet, suffer from a great hunger for more. I am not the same as I once was.

"I understand that the Tree of Life is many things. It is meat for Adam. Like the Bread of Life we have here, it is sustenance. The River of Life, from which it receives nourishing waters, is a restorative balm that promises healing that the angels need, but Adam seems not to require now."

Chayim is referring to the injury to his person that an angel may experience during an encounter with the rebellious ones. Wounds inflicted upon these angels are healed by an immersion in the River of Life.

"Also, as is the Tree of Life planted here in Heaven, it is a source of abundance of life beyond any present norm." We all know that Chayim is speaking with authority, because of what he experienced during and after the commission.

"If eating of the Tree of the Knowledge of Good and Evil brings death, then eating of the Tree of Life brings life to life in the same way," he says, sitting down in the center of our troupe.

"Please repeat that and expand upon your line of thinking," I encourage, motioning for everyone to sit down to listen.

Chayim's earnestness is obvious as he relates, "If eating of the forbidden tree brings death, then eating of the Tree of Life increases life within life. Each emersion in Heaven's abundance, while remaining and abiding in Him, adds more of His life to the measure of life we already have, or the normalcy of life we accept.

"Man was created to never cease to exist or give up self-consciousness. Life flows from him to those around him. Elohim calls it virtue. Someday life will pass from them to a child. By eating the fruit of the Tree of Life, newer, greater life passes into the spirt, and from the spirit, into the soul of Adam. Thus, he is elevated into a greater man," Chayim amplifies his earlier revelation.

Gradually, one by one, the angels listening begin to grasp what Chayim is saying. The last one is Tantzer. Finally this final holdout sees the light.

Chayim stands to take his leave. We continue to sit, mulling over these revelations. When the last of the power of Chayim's presence is gone, the questions start.

"So what happens if man eats of the Tree of the Knowledge of Good and Evil, before eating of the Tree of Life?" Komodo`r asks.

"What if Adam eats of the Tree of Life and the woman doesn't?" Tantzer asks.

"What if Adam eats of the Tree of Life and the woman doesn't, but she eats of the Tree of the Knowledge of Good and Evil? Where will the new children come from? Will Elohim have to take another rib?" Lairn`r chimes in.

"Yes, what indeed! Elohim's battle plan is resting on what man does next," I use this as my closing argument. "With that I declare this meeting over."

THE WIND SONG

"It is beginning," I whisper to my woman, lying next to me. We had decided to sleep here in the clearing in anticipation of our day of rest. This day is the seventh since our last day of rest, something the Lord impressed on us to enjoy. He said the same thing about the pleasant fruits he's given us to eat. "Ahhh," I sigh with my mouth wide open, as I yawn. "Every seventh day is our day of rest. We should spend the day…

"Oh, I must have dozed off," I say to my woman. When I get no response, I reach out and turn toward her, but she has already arisen, and is nowhere in sight. I can't help smiling, when I think of her. When she looks up at me, and she gazes into my eyes, I get these strange feelings that seem to fill me up from within! And because of all of this, I have not been able to name her.

I've had no problem naming all the animals and birds. With the trees and flowers and fruits, I've had no trouble at all. When I do think of a name, it sounds either too simple because she's so grand, or too harsh because she is so gentle. Other names sound too intense because she's so delightful and playful. She weaves flowers and leaves into head rings, or necklaces, for me. I know I'm smiling again, and decide to keep on calling her "my woman," until the right name that is respectful enough, comes into my mind. Like the names for everything else did.

I have no idea how long I've been thinking about her and seeing her in my mind.

Looking over my shoulder I see her returning to the clearing. She is carrying a basket woven from grape vines and branches from olive trees. She has something in the basket that is covered with large banana leaves. When she reaches me I can't keep from smiling, she pleases me so. I lift an edge of the covering leaf. The sweet scent of the bananas, which she has already peeled, the figs she has skinned and the pungent, yet delicate, aroma of the freshly skinned orange wedges, greet my nostrils. She sits beside me and we share the morsels she has prepared. There is a mischievous and alluring smile, playing on her lips.

Meanwhile, the breath of *HaRuach* has begun to make circuits around the clearing and so our attention is drawn to the movement. Nearby, the breath persuades some foliage to shiver with excitement. All living things in the clearing are graced by His breath.

The tender stir of this breath seems to randomly skip some plants while embracing others. Sometimes it skips vast distances, pausing here and there, nudging a blossom here, and a leaf there. Blades of grass and wild thistles are troubled by the near misses, as the light breeze places a cat's paw upon a low riding limb of a nearby cedar. Then it is off with a whoosh, moving as an updraft, redirecting its amorous attention toward an errant lily.

As we watch this ballet, we feel it kissing us as it rushes by, enjoying the dance, swaying this way and that to the melody of the birds, who are now singing in harmony to the rhythms of the many vortexes left behind. *HaRuach's* zephyr orchestrates, the brilliant colors filling the scene, and choreographs the undulating motions of life aroused within the clearing. Each artist seems to know exactly what to do once the gentle waft of breath ruffles their coats or brushes their cheeks.

The varying shades, too, become excited, bursting forth in newly created pigments, the changing patterns, with their naked colors awash in brilliance. Each hue begins to blush with tawny waves, unique and fascinating. We are soon intoxicated by the fragrances of the rich perfumes drifting on the elevated drafts of air.

The jealous butterflies begin chasing the whispering wind. It sings to all, while playing the tree branches like stringed harps and organs of

Heaven. To our ears it sounds like some of the animals are laughing, rejoicing with the celebrating chorus. Each crescendo reached is surpassed by the next, reaching new heights and exploring greater depths, while carrying our spirits on a ride of pure joy.

"How wonderful it is to be alive and one with all creation," I marvel.

Then an offshoot of the breeze separates from the river of wind, as it is about to begin another circuit of the clearing. The arm of the wind that has separated swoops down to embrace the lamb, who is dancing nearby. The lamb bleats joyously and nuzzles the arm embracing him. Before our eyes, the hitherto transparent wind, now streaked with purples and gold, seems to change form and becomes one with the lamb.

"Now, I see. I am so blessed to be in this place," I whisper, as the woman slips her hand in mine in a practiced gesture of closeness and affection.

Soon, the lamb and the wind pirouette and begin cuddling with us. We become enthralled by this display and by our oneness, one with their joy. And it is perfect. In a blink, I look again at the scene before me. The panorama has now transformed into unrecognizable imagery. The beauty that had been before us has become so wondrous that it defies description. The majesty of what we see is almost painful to contain. I feel like bursting. My arms receive strength. They rise by themselves, reaching toward the heavens. My voice trembles with vibrant praise and an earnest desire to express the discovered splendor of that which had once been a shrouded uncertainty.

An involuntary intermission is imposed upon this phenomenon, when we are momentarily distracted by several late arriving birds. These well-plumed and multi-colored fancies need to find their perches on one, or two, of the limbs of nearby trees. As is their custom, several of these choose to search for perches down front, expecting everyone who arrived early to now focus on them. Even the winds and the lamb pause in their exuberance. Upstaging all, they begin preening and adjusting their plumes, as if examining themselves for a secret sin or two. Having successfully interrupted the performance, they settle in and assume the appearance of interested viewers.

The intermission over, my woman, the lamb, and I turn again into the wind. Once again, the wind increases in strength, heading to complete one of several more circuits of the fading clearing. I venture a glance at my woman, who has her face turned toward heaven. There is a look of complete joy and fulfillment radiating from her. As she seems to push her face toward Heaven her arms brush her raven hair and she bursts forth into worshipful song.

I join in immediately, somehow knowing the words before she sings them. I am able to pick up the melody she's singing as it, simultaneously, comes to her and to me. We share this rapturous worship, the lamb, my woman, and me, swaying from the force of the powerful wind, now pressing upon us. Then suddenly, we hear singing coming from the rapidly evaporating clearing before us. Looking everywhere, though, we see nothing, yet our paradise becomes filled with a multitude of voices, coming from mouths we cannot see, reaching pitches we cannot reach. Oh, wonderful!

Tantzer and I are in the Observatory, gazing through the Window at the Garden, in the land of Eden. We have arrived early, trying to catch the twosome as they awaken from the past night's sleep. Both of us notice the woman has placed a basket near them.

"Do you see that Zukher?" Tantzer whispers to me.

"Yes, I see it, but why are you whispering?" I reply and ask.

"Ah, I guess I don't need to. They can't hear us, can they," Tantzer replies, smiling.

Our timing is impeccable. They soon prepare to enjoy their seventh day. The day Elohim has provided, during the days of creation, as the day of rest.

As the courting continues in the Garden, others join us. All seem drawn to the blessedness of the moment. Komodo`r and Lairn`r are among the first. Not all of them are from our troupe. This congregation reveals that a mixed company of angels share equally in our fascination.

We become further immersed in the episode unfolding before us. Together we watch, we listen, and we wonder. When the Suitor envelopes the lamb with a swirl I hear, or rather, feel, a musical note that fills my being. I soon notice that the congregation is independently humming, or singing, in rapturous impromptu harmony. Our chorus before the Window is worshipping in Heaven, following a musical score written by HaRuach. Note by note, our corporate worship increases in splendor. Pleasant fragrances swarm around us, vibrant colors invade our senses, and where we are gathered seems to fade from view.

Now my attention changes for an instant to focus on the Observatory, and I realize it has filled to capacity. How, or when, the rest of these angels crowded in here, I do not know. Yet here we are, as a single chorus, worshipping with Adam, his woman, and the creatures who are frolicking within the clearing.

The sounds of praise and worship suddenly cease. Silent expectation ensues. "It is so quiet I can hear my heartbeat," Adam thinks, entertaining a strong urge to look around. He wants to reach out to his woman, but dares not, for fear that any movement will shatter the moment. He feels suspended in reverential awe.

"Oh, my! What's this?" runs through his mind as he feels a moist, cool touch in the palm of his hand. He turns and looks down, and sees that it is the lamb that is nuzzling!

"This is so delightful!" He smiles as he watches the lamb move to his woman, where it repeats the gesture, both seeking and giving affection.

After a while, the clearing returns to our view. The birds resume warbling and the crickets chirping. A gentle breeze is all that is left of the grand spectacle. "Did you hear other voices?" his woman asks.

"Yes! I heard a multitude of them. Any idea where they were coming from?" Adam answers her question, with one of a thousand of his own. "There is no one here now, but the familiar creatures we know," Adam continues, noticing that the lamb has returned to his contented grazing.

THE ANONYMOUS STONES

After the intromission of Dvar HaElohim, the recent events in the Garden, and needing a period of reflection, I petition Michael for sabbatical. I feel persuaded to take the opportunity of considering all the volumes of new knowledge accompanying the creation of man. Michael readily grants my request, instructing me to stand down, but first asks me who is going to lead my troupe in my absence. I know there are many qualified leaders among us and any of them can lead a troupe of this caliber. I hesitate before giving my reply, as he waits.

With a grin, he says, "I have just come from a meeting with Dvar HaElohim. While there, He mentioned that you would be asking for a sabbatical and He recommended that I pass to you a name for consideration. He also clarified that even though He made a recommendation, you still have complete freedom to choose whomever you think best.

His recommendation surprises me.

"He suggested Tantzer."

Michael, quoting Dvar HaElohim, says, "'The choice of a leader is not about their qualifications when chosen, but the promise fulfilled when the responsibility is fulfilled. The potential of fruitfulness, when chosen, is sufficient for unimaginable results at the end, provided it is mixed with faith…My faith. The present qualifications correctly reflect the past and present, but not the promise of the future.'

"He also said to reveal to you that when you were chosen to lead this troupe your selection was not because of your qualifications demonstrated in the past, but because of suggested qualifications, based upon the law of promise from seasons yet to be."

I thank Michael after confirming that I would indeed choose Tantzer. The promise of Dvar HaElohim's faith is enough. Leaving immediately, I rush to inform Tantzer. I don't know how he will respond, but fully trust in the wisdom of Dvar HaElohim, His foreknowledge, and His faith. Having demonstrated His foreknowledge of my petition for a sabbatical is just one more example of so many we've seen, proving His prescience.

I find Tantzer in the Observatory, gazing through the Window focusing on the Garden.

"Tantzer, I have an assignment for you," I begin. "Of course, as always, you have the liberty to choose not to accept this."

He nods that he understands. He stands so that he is able to continue to view the Garden, with his peripheral vision. Tantzer always has a ready mind, though sometimes not quite as serious as circumstances warrant, I'm afraid.

"I have received permission to take a sabbatical for a period of contemplation. I am passing the scroll of leadership, which Michael gave to me, into your hand." Having announced his assignment, I reach into my cloak and pull out the scroll of leadership, extending it toward Tantzer.

The unintentional blink of the eyes is all that betrays any surprise, as he thrusts his hand forward, accepting the scroll.

"How long will you be gone?" is his only response.

"I don't know, Tantzer, but I am considering a short season, measured in four or five Earth cycles of seven. Dvar HaElohim, Michael, and I, know you will do well. Thank you for your willingness," I toss a parting word of encouragement. He might need it.

There is no need for me to inform the troupe. The first act of a new leader is to do the informing. I know he will handle the leadership duties well, since Dvar HaElohim recommended him, as a demonstration of His foreknowledge and faith.

Immediately, upon returning from the sabbatical, I meet with Tantzer. With a nod of appreciation, he returns the scroll of leadership into my hand, just as protocol requires. He informs me that nothing of any consequence has occurred during my absence. In anticipation of my return, he already has had everything recorded in the Book of Remembrance. With that, he pivots on his right heel and speeds away.

I am thankful for the opportunity to stop and reflect upon all the knowledge I have gained since the creation. This includes some insight into several matters I am planning to present to our troupe for review, when we gather shortly. The rest and relaxation is over and it's time to engage, but a review of the provisional leader's notes is in proper order.

Leaving my residence, I notice Komodo`r walking across the clearing out front, just as he is reaching to pick up a stone resting in his path. It looks like a sapphire. I quicken my leisurely pace to catch up.

"You are completely satisfied with the results from the symposium and the adoption of your theorem?" I ask. "I didn't have a chance to talk to you about it before."

From Tantzer's notes I'd learned that, during my sabbatical, Komodo`r had proposed a theory about the universe. In it, he explained how everything in the universe, and not just the stars, influences happenings on Earth, and events on Earth can change the universe.

"Yes, completely. In some aspects it was most successful," Komodo`r replies with a broad smile. He is obviously pleased.

"The effect and acceptance was what you expected then?" I know Komodo`r isn't willing to dwell upon the effect and acceptance. He is already applying his considerable strategic skills to the next complexity that dares to cross his path. As he reaches down to pick up a particularly appealing topaz, I ask, "If you don't mind my asking, why are you collecting those precious stones?"

"While you were on leave, Tantzer gave me the duty of collecting precious stones for Shtitsen's troupe. I wasn't told what they were going to use them for."

"Yes, I read that Tantzer has agreed to have you do that. It is quite an honor, since the troupe Shtitsen leads is working on something planned for the future," I say affirming Tantzer's instructions to Komodo`r.

"May I see the list of stones you are supposed to collect? Here let me help you," I say, reaching out to offer a helping hand.

Komodo`r seems reluctant, but hands me the list. Glancing at it, I read, "gold, silver, sardius, topaz, emerald, turquoise, sapphire, diamond, jacinth, agate, amethyst, beryl, onyx, and jasper."

"Which ones do you already have?" I ask.

"I have several of the sapphire, topaz, gold and silver," he says, removing handfuls pulled from a pocket below his sleeve. As he does so, I see him quickly look them over, to be certain he's remembered, correctly.

"Ok. I know where there are turquoise and emerald stones," I tell him, "along with plenty of the jacinth, agate, and beryl. Would you like me to gather them for you?" I say this, over my shoulder, already headed in the direction where I recall I can find them.

His reply is, "Yes, thank you." And he returns to the grounds in front of the residence.

Returning a while later with my collection, I wait until Komodo`r has an opportunity to empty his whole pile of stones into a larger pocket.

"There, these are the jacinth, agate, beryl, turquoise and emerald stones. What do you have left?" I ask, expecting he has the rest. I am surprised to learn he still hasn't picked up a single diamond or a jasper stone.

"The diamonds and jasper don't seem to be anywhere around the mansion. I'll have to look elsewhere. I'll check outside Lairn`r's mansion.

I seem to recall once seeing some of those stones outside his place," Komodo`r says, walking away, offering a "thank you" as he goes. His pockets are bulging, changing his usual fastidious appearance.

I think about the list, searching my memory for any significance it might have. I can recall nothing, so I decide to wait and look into this later.

The stones that Komodo`r is collecting puzzles me. After a diligent search, I can find no mention or trace of them in the records of Heaven, nor in the Hall of Mysteries.

The basis of my puzzlement is that the absence of any mention of the stones appears to be inconsistent with one of Elohim's precepts. It is one that has always been reliable. It is a foundation of our quest for knowledge and understanding of all truth, even truth whose source is Elohim's faith. That precept is, "knowledge and understanding comes line upon line, precept upon precept, here a little, there a little."

My conclusion, then, is that truth doesn't just appear out of nothing. Creation does, but truth does not. It has to have a foundational origin, even if that origin is microscopic. There was the argument, once postulated by an inquisitor angel, who was very much like Lairn`r, that Elohim is the origin of all things. Therefore, He can just declare an understanding He has as truth, based solely upon Himself as the origin. The concept was that this would not contradict the precept. That is a logic only an inquisitor angel would make, in defense of a truth. That logic, though, has a flaw, which only Dvar HaElohim is worthy to reveal. Many have tried, in vain, to use this reasoning, during various seasons of inquiry.

Occasional periods of complex debate occur, regarding this question, particularly between inquisitor angels. These periods are called "seasons of inquiry." Such events are well attended and sharpen one's warrior skills for battling the consequential enemy. It was during one of these periods, when this unnamed inquisitor was, once again, taking all comers and making his point. Soon all had acquiesced. There was no opposition. Assuming he had once again won the day, he turned around to find a figure standing behind him. It was the figure of a man, in the likeness of fire from the waist down and from the waist up, full of brightness and glory, as the color of amber.

It was Dvar HaElohim!

We all fell on our faces before Him, offering praise and worship.

When He spoke, He spoke as the sound of the many waters, like those of the singing river outside the Citadel and He said, "Arise, arise. I have come to join in the debate. I have been observing the proceedings and have come to challenge the inquisitor."

With a kind smile, He turned to the inquisitor and asked, "Will you yield the lectern and take the stand?"

With a gesture of Dvar HaElohim's hand, the inquisitor sat on the throne that his most recently vanquished protagonist had just vacated. A look of calm and caution, replacing the surprised look he had evidenced.

It wasn't unusual for this One, of the Three-in-One, to attend our tests of reasoning. What is rare is for Him to take the scepter of the inquisitor.

Dvar HaElohim proceeded to prove His finer lines of reason, by asking the unnamed inquisitor, "So, you say, the precept upon which truth is established is, 'line upon line, precept upon precept, here a little there a little.' Is that so?"

"Yes," the witness said, with great confidence, comfortable with the opening gambit.

"If that is so, then upon which line, which precept, or which 'little' was the truth established?" Dvar HaElohim asked.

"Upon the law of truth itself, Adonai, upon the law of truth," the inquisitor answered, using the affectionate plurality reference for the Three-Who-Are-One, reassured by the common understanding of the most novice of angels.

"What does that truth say then, bold one?" Dvar HaElohim asked.

"All truth is established by two or three witnesses, Adonai, two or three witnesses." The inquisitor's answer was one of the greatest of all precepts, because all truth is established, at least partially, upon that principal.

Dvar HaElohim sparred with this inquisitor using a familiar sequence of logical rationale.

"Who, or what, were the witnesses upon which the precept, itself, was established? What line? What precept? On what 'little' does this rest?" Dvar HaElohim asked, His voice peaceful and full of purpose.

The inquisitor replied, with his most successful closing argument. It was the one that no one had been able to crack, or beyond which the attack had never been moved.

"Adonai, it is You. For You are the three witnesses. Yehovah, You, Dvar HaElohim and HaRuach. You are three and each of You has borne witness that the precept is true.

"Where would He go next?" I wondered. Many had tried to discover a crease in the inquisitor's analysis. We all knew that all things were created by Him, and for Him.

Dvar HaElohim went on, "You have answered well, bold one, for We have borne witness to the precept. I have a new question. What precept did I base My witness on? Do you suppose I would risk My name and Heaven's throne on just My will or power?"

"I don't understand the question," the inquisitor replied.

I couldn't tell if he was stalling for time or really meant it. I knew I couldn't answer Dvar HaElohim's question, but I did think I understood it.

"I am asking you if you are reasoning that We have not based our witness upon a line, precept, or 'little,' but We are solely basing Our witness upon Us being Elohim," Dvar HaElohim restated the question.

"You are Elohim, and there is no greater witness than You for You are holy and righteous," was the reply. I thought it weak since by the very question, I now understood Dvar HaElohim was explaining a greater revelation of Elohim. Still, no answer, just sparring.

"Which is greater, inquisitor, titled holiness and titled righteousness or demonstrative holiness and demonstrative righteousness?" Dvar HaElohim asked.

"That would be demonstrative, certainly demonstrative," the inquisitor declared, brightly. He was glad to be past the risky line of reasoning, examining the inner personhood of Elohim.

"When We had borne witness to the precept in question, were We doing so by titled, or demonstrative, holiness and righteousness?"

"I cannot answer that question, Adonai. No angel can."

"I perceive, inquisitor, you are limiting Us. You are persuaded that all that We do and say is good only because there is none greater and none more powerful, and not because Our inner self is demonstratively perfect and sinless, therefore, holy," Dvar HaElohim said, piercing the heart of the matter.

With this iteration, Dvar HaElohim was asking if Elohim was only holy and righteous, because He said so, and not because He actually demonstrated He was.

"I cannot answer that, Adonai. No angel can. Only Eternity knows the answer, only Eternity," the inquisitor said. His confidence gone, his boldness diminished. He leaned forward, anticipating his defeat.

Dvar HaElohim declared, "Inquisitor, you have done well. You have risen above many of your equals and thought to honor your creator by returning unto Us four fold more than you received when you were created. I will answer the question and conclude by asking a final question, one question, which the angels will ponder.

"Let all Heaven and Earth know and understand. Elohim is righteous, because His deeds are righteous. Elohim is holy, because He is holy

164

in all things, as well as, within His inner personhood. In Him is no shadow or turning, no claim to power or correctness that has not been demonstrated and earned.

"I now ask you, and all who hear My voice, does Elohim sin if He bases his witness on precepts that are yet to be revealed? Do future demonstrations of Elohim's righteousness and holiness justify establishing precepts, and bearing witness, in the present?"

With a nod to the just honored inquisitor, Dvar HaElohim departed the season. No one had anything to say. We just left quietly.

Aha! The mystery of the stones will have to wait! I conclude that mystery is based upon future precepts, just as that to which Dvar HaElohim had referred.

THE NETHER REGIONS OF EARTH

A shudder breaches the serenity of our ensemble, as we wait the moment of our descent. We rejoice over all the responsibilities proving Elohim's trust in us. All, that is, except one. The exception is the responsibility that is now looming. It is the anticipation of what is ahead that brings such trembling.

We will be leaving here, the splendor of Heaven, to serve a season in the bowels of the Earth. We refer to this place as the "nether regions." We will be guards, protecting the Earth from those abandoned by Elohim and imprisoned there. These, to whom I am referring, are kept in chains while awaiting their eternal destiny. We will be preventing their marauding ways from repeating the havoc and destruction they inflicted upon Earth, following their fall from Heaven.

After the fall, Elohim chose Earth as a place of imprisonment for Lucifer and those who had chosen to follow him into eternal darkness. Deep below the surface, in the heart of Earth, a place of separation called Sheol was created. This place is made up of two compartments separated by a great chasm. One of the compartments is dark. It is a bottomless pit, called *"torment."* The other, the one called "Paradise," is a wondrous place of continuous light. Those who inhabit the dark side are our former compatriots, all of whom belong in just such devastation. It is impossible for those on one side of the abyss to reach the other, but they can see the other side and witness what the opposite offers. We are not yet aware of who will be residing in the wonderland. We know, only, that it is being prepared for others who do not warrant *torment*. We will be leaving shortly from the Observatory, through one of the Windows. The one we will use is huge, framed in gleaming silver. The black curtain, which hangs over the Window looking upon *torment*, is sealed. The sights and smells, of that compartment of Sheol, are never permitted to reach Heaven's grandeur. The glistening aqua curtain, covering the Window looking upon Paradise, is drawn back on either side, framing the view. The two draped sides are held open by golden chords, tied in graceful knots, adorned by scarlet tassels.

Komodo`r looks formidable standing over there, leaning next to the Window. He's clothed in warrior's armor, as are all who will be leaving, including Lairn`r, Tantzer, and me. Each of our heads is covered by a helmet and our feet shod. Each of us carries a sword and a shield. We are a celestial force, equipped for war of great proportions and eternal consequences. Although the angels of darkness are chained in the pit, the fabric of Eternity, which, in fact, includes Heaven itself, is still vulnerable to attack from this horde. We will counter every probe and defend every foray.

Distasteful as it is, we are fully cognizant of the necessity of our service. Those we guard against were once just like us. They were like us, but not of us. Their rebellion clearly revealed that. Many here, in our expedition, know the angels of darkness by name. The name by which we knew them is vastly different from what it is now.

In Eternity past, before the fall, I served with several of those whom I will be guarding. Komodo`r knows some of them, too, and so does Lairn`r. I don't know if Tantzer knows any of them. There was a season when Lairn`r served alongside satan, then called Lucifer. Other than Komodo`r, I cannot recall if anyone else did, who is assembled here. When he is asked about it, Lairn`r says that Lucifer remained aloof and apart from those who served at his side.

So many serving with Lucifer were driven into the vortex of the rebellion. Some of those who did not follow, however, were held under suspicion for a while, until Elohim cleared them of any duplicity.

Lairn`r, though, was never under any suspicion, even though he knew Lucifer well. He understood Lucifer's persona, and he was not seduced by it. In fact, the opposite is true. As I said before, Lairn`r was the first to question things that Lucifer was expressing to those huddled around him. Lairn`r's cross examination caused a rift between them. After presenting his apprehension to Michael, they never served together again.

Not all the angels we guard are as powerful as Lucifer. Many are rather weak, when compared to the angels of light. These, a single angel of light can easily vanquish. However, some of the hordes are extremely powerful and several angels, like Klalish, are required to subdue them. These powerful strongholds are named after their essence, such as, Death, Hatred, Error, and Slumber.

We hold no compassion or sympathy for any of them, despite their plight. All of them are a twisted lot. Together, they chose to abide in a darkness that is limitless. For any of us to have the slightest compassion, or even sympathy, for them would mean that they have some virtue. They have not. Their value rests solely in performing as mere minions before the tidal winds of Eternity. The light that they rejected repels the darkness they chose. All wounds they suffer are self-inflicted.

The distasteful experience we suffer during our service is not rooted in any yearning we have for their reconciliation. There is not a single hint of any of that within us. Rather it is simply because we are there in Sheol, and in their proximity, that causes a root of repugnance in us. All the while we are there, we long for the glories of Heaven, and to be rescued from this emptiness that describes absence of Elohim.

Their misery washes over the conscious and subconscious minds of those guarding them, like waves of filth, despite wearing the helmet. The dearth of any joy or peace, any beauty or light, is pervasive. It feels like it saturates our being, and vexes us in ways we do not identify nor experience, anywhere else. That vexation, aggravated by the distance from Elohim, is the reason that these ensembles are rotated.

Those imprisoned in *torment* rarely try to approach us. The darkness, with which they are now one, has twisted their very appearance. So much so, that they are mostly unrecognizable. One of the threads, in the linen woven by the Ancient of Days, is that darkness begets darkness, just as light begets light.

"What will it be like?" Tantzer asks Komodo`r, Lairn`r, and me. He wants to see which one will try to explain the unexplainable.

"Your first time in an ensemble like this, Tantzer?" Lairn`r asks, already knowing the answer.

"Yes, and I would like to know what to expect."

"Well..." Komodo`r begins, with a mere flicker of a smile. "You have been through warrior training, right?"

"Yes," Tantzer says, turning quickly to focus on Komodo`r.

Komodo`r proceeds to explain the differences between *torment* and Paradise and what is expected to be quite an experience for this novice. Then he pauses to see if the question is genuine, or just an exercise to release stress.

"*Torment* is dark and has no bottom. There is no light there," Lairn`r says, taking over. Meanwhile, he's looking toward Komodo`r to be sure he isn't out of bounds.

"The other area, Paradise, is full of light, certainly not as bright as Heaven, but glorious. When I went there on my first tour, I was posted along the edge of the gorge on the *torment* side. To reach there it was necessary to wing it from Paradise. While I never saw any of the fallen angels, I could feel their revulsion and hatred. I was definitely uncomfortable, I must say," Lairn`r hesitates for a second, remembering the season of which he speaks, recollecting the awful blackness of the compartment. He, instantaneously, conjures up the feeling of void, the sight of nothingness, when he attempted to look down into the chasm to see the bottom.

Lairn`r's hesitation gives Komodo`r his opening, "The agony and suffering is beyond imagination. The hatred of one infects those around him, while the collective inflicts additional anguish upon some condemned shadow, standing nearby. It is nothing, nothing like Heaven, just the opposite. One incredible thing that I learned then, is that because they abide in darkness, they are unable to see any reflection of themselves. Nor does any one of them know exactly what the others really look like. They exist in a vacuity of complete deception, even with each other. Each one seeks only to satisfy his own desire, titillating and thrilling himself by tormenting the shadows around him."

Komodo`r, who has served on several other ensembles, has the most experience of the four of us regarding tours of this nether region.

"While they would prefer inflicting misery on the guarding angels, when that isn't possible, they turn readily upon each other," he recollects, speaking of the vile images in his memory.

"They are able to deceive other shadows and hide exactly what they look like from them, but you will be able to see them as they really are because you abide in the light. Nothing will be hidden from you. It is their inner ugliness that reveals itself in their grotesque appearance. Inside, and out, they are altogether given up to fulfilling all manner of abomination. That was a surprise to learn, although now it is common knowledge. Even the soil of Earth beneath them is ugly and infected by their corruptness. The light around them is but deeper darkness unto them. They express no regret for their sentence, only hatred and contempt for Elohim, for us, and now for man."

Komodo`r turns his attention toward the Window, where the angel leading us stands up to adjust his armor. When he sits back down again, Komodo`r shrugs and returns to the discussion.

"Zukher, how many times have you served this duty?" Komodo`r tosses the baton to me, with a knowing smile.

"This is my fifth ensemble," I answer, smiling back in gratitude. "Each time, the post to which I was assigned, was in a different place. The compartments assigned me, in which I've served, have alternated."

I decide to go over the protocol once again, primarily for Tantzer, and for anyone else within earshot that might be unsure of what lies ahead.

"The angels of darkness…" I barely begin.

171

"You mean the AOD!" Tantzer interjects lightly.

"The AOD," sternly, I begin again, "are in great pain. The armor of light you are wearing repels them and reinforces that pain. They will not, actually cannot, approach you physically. However, they can and will, try to communicate with you in any way possible and may try to entice you. Each one is still trying to fend off the consequences of his defeat. Their goal is to draw us in with them. I encountered a powerfully deceptive one, during my last assignment there. I had to get some help from Michael.

You must rebuke every attempt, not just ignore it. Your armor, helmet, and covering for the feet are of great help, but your mind must be willing to battle against them, as well. To indulge such communication for any time longer than it takes to tell them 'no' is not only risky, but dangerous. Nothing worthwhile can be accomplished by such communication.

"They cannot be redeemed. They are eternally unable to commune with you, as light cannot have fellowship with darkness. You will likely feel them, more than see them. The sensation that will visit you, in the depth of your being, is one of uncomfortable groaning. You are in every way clean and they are in every way unclean. Just command them to cease. End it at once. If there are any problems, contact me, or one of the roving protectors. We will come immediately."

"What is Paradise for?" Tantzer asks of anyone.

"It is a place filled with a measure of the light and glory of Heaven. There are beautiful buildings, much like the ones you live in, here. It is a pleasant place and very comfortable to be in, not at all like the *torment* side," I reply.

"But, until now, Elohim has not provided us its purpose. Those posted in Paradise will be acting as guards. They are there to protect the angels who are completing the construction of facilities there. Those building the facilities belong to another entirely different expedition. They are also rotated, as are we."

"There are several other differences between the two compartments. The smells are different. The stench of *torment* is overpowering, while the fragrances coming from Paradise are breathtaking and uplifting," Lairn`r explains, picking up the dialogue again.

"There is, also, the gorge or chasm to contend with. It is impossible for someone chained or sentenced to the *torment* side to get to Paradise. The AOD continues trying to draw in the AOL, anyway, not accepting the insurmountable barrier the chasm really is."

It looks like we are about to start on our expedition, so I wrap it up, "Finally, you will always be able to recognize our voices, when compared to the voices of the AOD." I find Tantzer's acronym more and more appealing. I really have to hand it to him. These rays of joyous light seem to dance in his imagination.

"The voices may be expressed audibly, or inwardly, but recognizable they are, just the same. Remember, exercise your authority, use your shield, and stop any and every attempt to communicate. Are there any other questions? We are about to leave," I conclude, anticipating no more questions cropping up to keep us from getting on with this.

A quick look toward Tantzer and I see no sign indicating further questions. I turn and move away, while taking up the silent vigil, interrupted by Tantzer and Komodo`r. Tantzer will do fine. The first tour to the nether regions is not easy. This will be a big challenge, but Elohim wouldn't permit Tantzer to go along, if he weren't up to the challenge.

Actually, I was a bit rattled my first foray into the bowels. What I purposely didn't tell Tantzer is that incursion was the very first ensemble that was sent there, just after the fall. Komodo`r was along, but we were in different troupes back then. That expedition was a challenge that I will always remember.

The rebellion didn't last long. The battle was short, but intense. Lucifer left the throne of Tsuwr,[30] where he was king,[31] and made a direct assault on the Kingdom of Heaven. He demanded the keys to the Throne, the keys to creation, and the keys to Eternity. He anticipated taking the kingdom from our Sovereign, Yehovah. Prepared by His foreknowledge, Yehovah didn't hesitate to act. He didn't indulge Lucifer for an eternal instant. Rather, He commanded the legions of angels of light to fall upon Lucifer, bind him, and bring him to the Throne Room where, before Yehovah seated on the White Throne of Judgment, he was sentenced.

Lucifer had, what he thought was, a surprise for us, although Elohim, the one who knows all ends from the beginning, was not surprised. We, though, the angels of light, were. What caused utter astonishment in the ranks was that one angel in three had chosen to follow Lucifer and contest the Thrones of Eternity and of Heaven. Of course, Lucifer was expecting an even greater number. The battle raged, yet the outcome was never in doubt.

Armed with Elohim's knowledge, Michael, under the command of Dvar HaElohim, rallied the astounded angels of light. The defeat turned into a route. The angels of darkness were chained and, together with Lucifer, cast down from Heaven.[32]

Angered, Lucifer threw a hate-filled tantrum, raining destruction upon his kingdom of Tsuwr and Earth. Thus it came to be that "the Earth was without form and void and darkness was upon the face of the deep." His kingdom of Tsuwr was destroyed.

It was he who, on the day he was created, had every precious stone adorning him: rubies, topaz, emerald, chrysolite, onyx, jasper, sapphire, turquoise and beryl, whose settings and mountings were made of gold. Lucifer, who had been the model of perfection, had been full of wisdom and perfect in beauty. He who became an anointed cherub, and walked among brilliant stones, and was blameless in Eternity past, was now the model of corruption. He had become distorted, had become the father of lies. Wickedness was at the core of him. He now had nothing, but an army chained in the bowels of Earth, and a tenuous future.

With the fall, Lucifer was filled with violence and destruction causing the loss of his beauty and splendor. Darkness alone inhabits the footprints he makes.

For now, he remains the lord of Earth. The righteous Elohim obeys the boundaries of the threads which say that the ways, the gifts and callings of Elohim are without repentance. Satan is, therefore, allowed to exercise a tyrannical lordship over the Earth. He will continue to do so, until someone comes who is mightier than he. One who is exceedingly worthy, who will take away from him the three keys of that kingdom.

When Lucifer was cast down, Yehovah commanded a multitude of the AOL to take the fallen AOD, to the place of *torment*. As a front guard they remained there, to prevent escape, until relieved. Immediately following their departure, Michael formed the first ensemble to establish the maintenance of a permanent vigil. Klalish and I were selected. Klalish was a great choice, since he was one of the first angels to engage the enemy, once they launched, what they thought was, a surprise attack. Why Michael selected me, I do not know. I was just a novice in issues pertaining to warfare, having served in a troupe specializing in organizational matters.

There was quite a mixed bag of experience when we assembled. Each of us arrayed in the armor of light, wearing the helmet and with feet covered just like the latest envoy. Michael gave the ensemble, then, directives similar to the ones I had just covered with Tantzer.

When we arrived, our leader gave each of us the post at which we were to stand watch. With a nod, he was off to post another guard, farther away. I couldn't see anyone else after he left me. My post was near the chasm that separates *torment* from Paradise.

I commanded an area two hundred cubits by four hundred cubits. I took to looking around, curious about this place to which I'd been detailed. As I did, I noticed a group hulking on the *torment* side directly across the chasm from me. If they hadn't moved, I would have missed them in the darkness that possesses them. As I watched, I guess I let my guard down a little. I thought that, while they looked somewhat like the angels of light, there was a discernible difference. It was their wings. They were shadowed and striking, but were without the graceful curves that define our wings. Theirs had been deformed into a shape I had not seen before. Theirs were bony, while ours are muscular and supple. Theirs were gaunt, projecting a fierce ominous character, while ours are soft and full. The contrast arrested my attention. They had changed so visibly from what they had been before their deeds were physically manifested.

After my eyes adjusted to the darkness over there, I had the thought that I recognized one of the miscreants, but I couldn't be sure. The distortion of its form was continuing, as I watched. With a lowered guard and without thinking, I whispered the name of the angel I thought I knew and whom I might have recognized.

"Silber Lo`shen?" I whispered, questioningly.

Too late! I had forgotten the directive from Michael. I flinched when one of the reprobates turned and looked my way. Without hesitation, he called to me, invitingly. I strained, but couldn't see his eyes. There was only blackness instead of his facial features. I was aware of being drawn toward the abyss between us, or at least, it felt that way. I shook myself and slapped my helmet. What good it did, I don't know. When I checked myself, I hadn't taken a step. Somehow, the dark presence was able to affect my sense of reality.

I staggered some. I was about to be ensnared by his appeal, when I felt a hand upon my shoulder. I gasped as I turned, and with a wave of relief, I saw Komodo`r standing there. How long he had been there, I didn't know. With a knowledgeable smile, he said, "Are you ok? You seem disoriented and confused. I thought I'd better check on you."

"Wow, I lost it for a bit," I confessed, still getting my thoughts together. "There is such force there, clutching and pulling. I should have kept quiet. Maybe I should not have looked over there." I felt like my mind needed a bathing in the River of Life.

Komodo`r didn't say anything else. With a wave he turned and swooshed away. Very soon he was out of sight. It was then I remembered. He was one of the protectors assigned to Paradise. I had seen him while waiting to leave that first staging area. I knew, then, why they are needed.

I turned back to my post. I resolved I would not repeat my mistake. Thereafter, I refused every overture from the AOD. The armor, helmet, foot covering, shield and sword were necessary, but so was watchfulness. I had the thought that being expectantly watchful would shut the door to their overtures. They are relentless, however. They never quit testing.

Standing there alone, I took an additional moment to carefully search my memory for what I remembered about Silber Lo`shen, in Eternity before the fall. He had been a skillful orator. He entertained great audiences with his gifts. I had been in the audience more than once when he performed and I appreciated his ability to sway the listener.

He had been accompanied by a troupe of musicians. He would speak swaying staccato words in rhythm with repetitive, melodious tones, emanating from instruments, provided him in the background. It was very affective. We even joined in, on occasion. Back then, I knew the name of everyone playing the instruments. Trying to remember their names, I stopped myself. Was he, or were they, pushing thoughts again into my mind, I wondered?

I decided that the answer to that question was "no." Then suddenly, I realized that every single name of those I'd seen perform was no longer recorded in the Book of Citizens! The hulks I had noticed, upon starting my first watch, must have been the troupe I enjoyed. As it was then, Silber Lo`shen was in the lead, swaying an audience. An audience of one. Me. I wanted to swoosh away and return to Heaven.

The announcement comes. We are told to get our things together and prepare to leave. I see Komodo`r, looking at me with a knowing smile. He must have been thinking about the first ensemble, as well. I nod and return the smile. That first ensemble, and the steadfastness that Komodo`r exhibited, was a major factor in his being my first choice, when I was directed to form a troupe.

Tantzer is fidgeting with some nothings. I step over to help him and offer one last word of wisdom, "You will do fine, Tantzer. I have been assigned the post of protector on the Paradise side. You have been assigned a post nearby, near the gulf. Did you know, I had that same post on my first ensemble?"

"I did hear that," he smiles at me, standing taller than his size.

We begin our songs of praise to Elohim, led by a gifted vocalist, accompanied by angels playing Heavenly instruments. This songster gives himself to the moment and lifts up the name, Elohim. Thus, we are strengthened for our expedition and we lift off. With a grim face, Tantzer falls in beside Komodo`r, and I join in on the other side.

A Temple in Eden

I believe the most interesting place in all of Heaven, besides the Throne Room, isn't the Citadel's Hearing Center with its magnificent columns. It isn't the Observatory with its high arched doorways opening to places that defy imagination. Nor is it the splendid courts and luscious gardens with their purposefully random placement, along Heaven's golden avenues, each scented to beguile the most discriminating nose. Komodo`r, Lairn`r, or Tantzer may have a differing opinion from mine, but I believe the most remarkable edifice is the Temple of Elohim. Elohim dwells there, spending great spans of Eternity, sending forth virtue to all His citizens.

The Temple is located high upon the most exquisite plateau Heaven has to offer and there are many of those mounts here. Resting on that plateau, it overlooks the Citadel and the pastoral regions which encircle the Citadel and Temple Mount. The Temple's full intent, and construction, remains an unsolved mystery, holding a place of prominence in the Hall of Mysteries.

The unworthy never trespass its courts, nor approach within close proximity, for fear of glimpsing its glorious porches. Satan is still allowed to seek, with success, an occasional audience with Elohim, if it is conducted during the Season of Trumpets. It is important to note, however, that not a single particle of dust from the sole of satan's feet dares drift into the vicinity of the Holy Gates of the Temple. The Holiness infusing the perimeter would instantaneously consume it.

Just as matter cannot continue to exist when colliding with antimatter, so the evil inherent in the very smallest particle satanic would suffer immediate destruction on this Holy of Holiness. Entering the presence of the Temple grounds, satan, or any part thereof, provokes the judgment of Elohim, which would curse its existence. It would, thereby, be condemned to damnation, which surely waits.

Holiness, the essence of Elohim, is the watch word on the Temple Mount. Although angels do stand a post, there is no need for angels to guard its welcoming gate. The steps ascending to the elegant portico at the gate is itself, Holiness. Holiness is, in fact, the only protector that is required. A significant detail is that this reality is what exposed Lucifer. Members of troupes, loyal to Elohim, recognized that certain angels, including Lucifer, refused to attend functions held on the Temple Mount.

If Lucifer had actually achieved his wicked ambition and had found a thread to successfully pull and unravel Eternity, he still would not have been able to approach, nor occupy, the Temple. He would have successfully ascended the Throne, but he could not have possessed the Temple. He would have had to try to destroy it, and success in that endeavor remains in doubt.

Gabriel and I are discussing the finer points of this observation. "The foundation of the Temple is bedrock-solid, one with the bedrock of Heaven. That bedrock is Holiness," I am emphasizing, when Lairn`r enters the Observatory. He is carrying a loose bundle of rolled up scrolls. They seemed to be sticking out everywhere.

He drops one of the larger ones, as he comes to rest in front of us, proclaiming, "The veil that covers the mystery of the Temple, is partially lifted. I was studying in the Hall of Mysteries and I glanced over at the image of the Temple. I saw that a seal there was broken. I never heard a trumpet alerting us to this. Did either of you hear it? Did I miss something?"

Stooping over to help Lairn'r by picking up the errant scroll, I reply, "I didn't hear a trumpet. Gabriel, did you?"

I decide, "Gabriel, please take a message to the troupe. Tell them to meet us in the Antechamber of the Hall."

Recognizing the urgency, Gabriel doesn't take the stairs. Instead, he flies off with the message. Lairn'r and I head for the Antechamber, dropping, and picking up scrolls along the way. We talk about the discovery, but realize that we don't understand anything more, now, than we had known previously.

The Antechamber is an oversized room, located deep within the Hall. This single level chamber boasts only one arched entry. A solid gold keystone holds the entrance together. On each side is a pillar of purest platinum. The floor of the chamber is the bedrock of Heaven just like the Temple.

Looking up as I walk in, I see the Viewing Window hanging from the ceiling. Its curtain is drawn. Gatherings in this chamber routinely use this Window during the frequent discussions held here.

I take a deep breath of Heaven's fragranced air as I mount the platform. Proceeding to exhale slowly, I move behind the podium. I haven't counted pairs of wings, but it looks like everyone is here.

Raising my hand for attention, I decide the best introduction would be direct and right to the point, "By now, you all have heard the news of what Lairn'r has discovered. Another of the seals of the Mystery of the Temple has been broken.

"Lairn'r, since you found the broken seal, please proceed to update us and oversee the discussion."

Stretching my right hand out as if to guide him into a place behind the podium, I wait for the burdened Lairn'r to climb onto the platform. Quickly, trading places with him, I sit down where he'd been sitting. Seating is certainly at a premium today. He pauses to look around the chamber, before beginning.

His gaze is broken when, once again, one of the scrolls falls from his grasp. It plunks on the platform. This breaks the stillness of everyone's rapt attention and at that moment he points toward the suspended

Window above us. The curtain, that had been covering the Window, simply disappears. The scene on the Window reveals a telescopic view of one of the most prized exhibits of the Hall of Mysteries: The Temple.

That exhibit hovers just above a waist high table prominently centered along a wall of the Hall. Only the seven pairs of the feet of the Temple are revealed and they look like the feet of a mighty creature. Using the unclouded feet as a guide, it appears to be made of opaque bedrock, although it is encapsulated by a cloud filled with flashing lightings and rumblings, slashing here and there. Upon each revealed pair of feet is a seal. We could see that the seals are broken on four pair of the feet. The remaining three are still sealed. Turning from the Window and the exhibit displayed there, Lairn`r is ready to begin.

"Before arriving, I had occasion to gather these scrolls. When, during Eternity past, we looked into the mystery, it has been essential to begin with these scrolls. They contain Elohim's architectural design for the Temple. Any revelation, knowledge and understanding we receive about the Temple will be confirmed here."

With that introduction, Lairn`r picks up one of the larger scrolls from those that are now piled on the platform at his feet. When he has the scroll unrolled across the vast podium, an image appears, rising from the scroll. It comes to rest upon its surface. It is the image of the Temple. Flying high over the portico at the entrance is a banner, with the inscription, "Holy, Holy, Holy." I whisper the words. They sing within my ears. As the image comes to a complete rest upon the scroll, we hear the voice of a resounding trumpet saying, "Let the worthy come into the presence of Elohim, for they are welcome here. Let the unworthy be forewarned to turn away, not looking upon the image before them."

From my vantage point, I can see the resting image of the Temple. All its walls are made of finest linen, inside and out. Its pillared entrance faces the west entrance to the Citadel. Five golden pillars guard the entrance. Their height is four times that of the tallest angels, and towers high over all who stand there. From the entrance one can see the colossal inner court, four times the size of the holy place, and shielded by its own pillared gate. Its walls facing the outer court, shield the sanctity within, from casual view. Eyes of those worthy to enter the holy place rest upon a curtain of purple bordered in braided gold. Within that tapestry is that which is most holy.

As my eyes absorb these sacred themes, Tantzer gently taps my shoulder and whispers, "Beautiful, isn't it? I guess you've seen this before. This is my first time, you know. This revelation is known and understood by you, right?"

"Yes," I whisper back, not diverting my eyes from the scene. "I remember my first time. I never get used to seeing this. You won't, either."

It is then that I see an angel appear in the inner court, glowing in white raiment. He floats into the air, high above.

"This is new," I think, as I try to comprehend the magnitude of what is transpiring before my eyes. "I have never seen this angel in the court-yard before."

I watch, as the angel lifts higher and higher and he grows as he ascends toward Lairn`r, who seems startled by the expanding, ascending seraph. The angel rises and grows until he rests, standing with his legs strad-dling the image of the Temple. With gentle authority, he thrusts his hand forward and takes an unopened scroll from a humbled Lairn`r, who is frozen in mid-motion.

Lairn'r's eyes grow wide when the angel says, "Don't be afraid. It is I." Lairn`r falls, prostrate, before the commanding angel hovering over him. Lairn`r declares, "It is the Lord! It is the Lord!"

It seems as if a great veil has been lifted from the eyes of this hum-bled assembly. When the angel before us transforms to reveal Dvar HaElohim, now standing before His citizens, we too, fall on our faces to pay respectful homage. All of us are silent. Not a muscle moves. He allows us to remain prostrate for only a moment, when we hear Him say, "Rise. Rise. Let us continue."

His inclusive use of the term "us" within His directive is most reas-suring and gratifying. The gathered body of citizens hesitantly rises to its feet, ever gazing upon Dvar HaElohim. Just being this close to Him satiates us with a calming, yet exciting, feeling of elation. I feel like I am having a private audience with my Sovereign.

"Oh, my!" I exhale. "This is like a seal of approval upon our seeking and searching. Not one of us is missing the significance of this moment."

"The Temple, you see, speaks of copious mysteries. Two of these have already been revealed. Behold, the revelation of two more mysteries," Dvar HaElohim articulates, great satisfaction ringing in His Voice. He points to the image with His forefinger, and holds the pose, His arm outstretched, and then, He is gone! Vanished!

The image, clothed in mystery, amends its shape. We watch mesmerized, as the Temple transforms into one that seems to have the limbs of Dvar HaElohim, standing erect, radiating an intensely, glorious light. The light is so bright it becomes difficult to see any of the details.

We are intoxicated by the light, losing ourselves in it. I turn my head and see others have also turned. I am trying to keep from losing my balance. We try, but we just cannot look upon the brilliant image without it affecting our equilibrium.

The image then speaks with the Voice of Dvar HaElohim saying, "Come and see. Come and see."

We start crowding closer to the platform, our gaze involuntarily returning to the image, whose brightness softens sufficiently for us to see that the form is resting upon the Throne of Elohim.

Then the chamber is filled with the Voice saying, "Behold, let it be known unto you and all who enter therein, and for all the rest of Eternity. The Temple and Elohim are one. Let those who are worthy understand. This is the revelation of the third mystery."

I ponder this. The third mystery is becoming clarified in my mind and to those around me. I question what it portends. Tantzer leans toward me and whispers, "Zukher? That means that the outer court of the Temple represents HaRuach. The Holy Place identifies Dvar HaElohim. And the Holy of Holies speaks of Yehovah. I do have this deciphered correctly, right?"

I smile at Tantzer. "You've got it!" I tell him, receiving a grin in acknowledgement.

Then the Antechamber becomes filled with a cloud of wonder, as a hand stretches forth from the form seated on the Throne and a scroll is selected from the open hand of Lairn`r, still on his knees, mouth open, eyes wet, not missing a thing. The hand of Dvar HaElohim then opens the scroll and tilts the scroll to show us the writings. As He does, a new image comes from the scroll. It is the image of a man. The man grows tall and stands erect. The image of the man reflects the shimmering glory of the image sitting upon the Throne of Elohim.

A wondrous river appears before us and flows from beneath the front wall of the chamber, curling gently across the platform, passing between the image of the Throne and the image of the man. Again we hear, "Come and see. Come and see."

Tightly crowded together, we are each in awe. Our eyes strain forward to look upon the splendid river. Its swift waters slow and run deep, becoming smooth and still like a mirror, reflecting the two majestic images as the river passes between them. We watch as the image upon the Throne becomes three, each radiating the brightness of the other and all three exercising power and dominion.

The still, reflecting waters become troubled. The ripples erase the reflection of the three bright images upon the Throne. They coalesce into one. There remains the one bright image on the Throne and next to it, stands the image of the man. As the waters calm once again, we watch intently. Each of us wants to catch every nuance. From the image on the Throne, a hand stretches toward the image of the man and fastens upon it, drawing it close. A great gust comes forth from the brightness and seems to fill the image of the man. We then see, in the river, only the image of the man which has the face of Adam, and the hands of Adam and the feet of Adam. He is clothed in a lesser brightness than the image we had seen on the Throne. While we are watching in approval, appreciating the conception of Adam, the river disappears. The man next to the Throne, standing upon the open scroll, now duplicates the image of Adam that was in the river.

With rapt attention we watch as Adam splits into three identical images. One image is the brightness of the image on the Throne. The second image radiates less significant brightness. And the third image, lesser, still.

The Voice comes forth, "Man is created in the image of Elohim, after His likeness. Just as Elohim is three Ones-in-One, so man is three ones-in-one, existing in harmony. This has already been revealed unto you."

We witness, breathlessly, vessels likened to deep cups, hovering over each of the three images of Adam. Five cups hover over the image of the body, which emanates the least brightness; five cups hover over the image of the soul; and five cups hover over the image of the spirit, which is the brightest of the three images. Each vessel has oil within.

The Voice then envelops us, as we watch. He speaks with great authority and says, "The vessels, you see floating over the image of the body, are ministries unto the body. They will serve as physical senses, or faculties. By these, and through these, the body is Earthly conscious."

The Guiding Hand that had opened the scroll, then moves and rests upon each of the five vessels suspended over the image of the body of Adam, and a voice speaks from each of the cups, saying, "I am the ministry of touch. Through me the body is able to know, and therefore, interact with Earthly things.

"I am the ministry of hearing. Through me the body is able to listen, and therefore, interact with Earthly things."

"I am the ministry of smell. Through me the body is able to detect the scent of pleasant and less than pleasant things of Earth, and therefore, interact with Earthly things."

"I am the ministry of sight. Through me the body is able to perceive the things of Earth, and therefore, act together with Earthly things."

"I am the ministry of taste. Through me the body is able to discriminate the things of Earth, bitter and sweet, and therefore, discern Earthly things."

"Through these five ministries, or senses, the body of Adam is able to minister to itself the things necessary for life upon Earth. To know it and subdue it."

I am momentarily distracted when I look at Lairn`r, still prostrate on the platform behind the podium, as he tries to gather his senses. Komodo`r is erect, as always, and he is seemingly unfazed by the magnitude of the unfolding revelation.

After these things, the image of the body of Adam kneels toward the image of the soul of Adam and submits unto it, placing his right hand beneath the heel of the image of the soul. The ministries of the body offer no complaint, paying homage unto the soul. As this occurs, the body grows in stature, becoming mighty and strong.

"What is that about?" Tantzer queries of Komodo`r and then locks his eyes on mine.

"Wait, there might be an explanation," Komodo`r tosses a cautionary, but quizzical, look. This momentarily subdues Tantzer, but with his face turned somewhat, Komodo`r winks at me.

All the angels now gathered in the chamber are of a willing mind, but at a loss for words, when the pervasive Voice asks, "Do you know the meaning of the mystery before you?"

Waiting to see if anyone is going to offer a response, I chance a look around the chamber, at the faces spilling out beyond the chamber into the corridors without.

The authoritative Voice brings my attention back to the revelation. "Just as the great expanse is an ordered creation, so man, too, is an ordered creation. The body of Adam, with its will and intents, is in submission to, though independent of, the will and intents of the soul of Adam. Be it understood that the ministries of the body, the vessels, are but loaned to the body by the soul, for the soul grants life unto them. If the soul is absent from the body, the soul can see, hear, taste, smell, and touch, though not touch Earthly things. However, the body, without the soul and spirit, is dead."

Komodo`r motions for my ear, while tugging on Tantzer's sleeve, drawing him close enough to join us. "We need to talk about this. What Dvar HaElohim is confirming is what we concluded early on. Man is not like us. Man is more like Elohim than he is like us. Though created a servant, man must actually be a joint heir to the Throne, whose end is greater than its beginning."

Nodding my head, affirming what Komodo`r has observed, I quickly turn, once again returning to the moment and the continuing revelation.

"The five vessels suspended above the image of the soul, containers of ministry to the soul, are soul senses or faculties," the Voice, beginning another thread of thought, wasting not a single moment.

Again, a voice within each vessel speaks.

"I am the ministry of emotion. Through me the soul is able to know the sensation of sentiment, excitement, and passion, and therefore, be moved by all living things on Earth, the angels, and Elohim."

"I am the ministry of reason. Through me the soul dispassionately wrestles with, and weighs, all matters: Heavenly; Earthly; and soulish; both mighty and small. Whatsoever the heart of Adam determines as necessary for judgment, I perform."

"I am the ministry of imagination. Through me freedom of choice attracts the soul to life's infinite possibilities: Real or unreal; pleasant or unpleasant; wise or foolish. The appetites within the heart of Adam, direct the path of my exploration."

"I am the ministry of memory. I am the book of man's soul. Through me the soul retains and recalls all that man feasts upon, with all the senses and faculties of his body, soul and spirit. Whatsoever Adam lives, I retain and recall."

"I am the ministry of conscience. By way of me the soul exercises discretion. I am a watchful beacon upon the pathway of man, whether it is Earthly; soulish; or Heavenly; real or imagined; pleasant or unpleasant. The weights of judgment of right and wrong, determined by the heart of Adam, I balance."

After this, the image of the soul kneels toward the image of the spirit of Adam, voluntarily placing its right hand beneath the heel of the spirit of Adam, thereby submitting unto it.

An image emanates from the soul. Two securely fastened doors, within an arched gateway, open before us. There we see a scroll upon which is written, "Law of the Mind," and a lamp whose wick is trimmed and ready. The guiding hand carries a ladle and methodically dips into each cup suspended over the image of the spirit of Adam, removing a measure of oil and adding it to the lamp. With each addition of oil, the lamp burns brighter until a glow fills the chamber.

The Voice of clarity and profundity speaks from within the open gateway, "Let all who are seekers come, see, hear, and comprehend the meaning of the mystery of the arch, the scroll, and the lamp. Just as the great expanse is an ordered creation, so man is an ordered creation. The body of Adam, its will and intents, are in submission to the will and intents of the soul of Adam. Also, the soul of Adam, its will and intents, are in submission to the will and intents of the spirit of Adam. This is all within the planned order.

The Voice grows in authority as each tier of Elohim's intricate ordered design of Adam is revealed.

"The gateway speaks of the heart within the soul of Adam. It is the final arbiter of all Adam's actions. Written upon tablets within the gateway are his intentions from which the arbiter draws guidance. Adam is consciously aware of some of these, while others are hidden, remaining subconscious.

"The scroll speaks of the mind within the soul of Adam. The writings upon this scroll are ever changing and subject to the governance of the Law of the Mind. Those judged unworthy of residence are erased; those, whose veracity remains undetermined, are held in abeyance; those found worthy, retain residency until replaced by those demonstrated to be of greater worthiness.

"The lamp speaks of the strength of the soul, its power and force, revealing the nature and measurement of the soul's character. That which influences the body, soul, and spirit influences the character of Adam's soul. When Elohim breathed into Adam and he became a living soul, that breath filled his soul with His character, goodness."

The Voice continues, "The vessels above the image of the spirit of Adam are ministries to the spirit of Adam. They are commonly known as senses or faculties. Just as the body and soul have senses, faculties or ministries, so the spirit of man has such ministries."

The guiding hand rests upon the first of the five vessels of ministry to the spirit. Again a voice emits from each cup, and says,

"I am the ministry of hope. I am the hope of Elohim. My expectations are anchored in the word of Elohim. My every desire is in accordance with His will. I drink from the River of Life. I remind Elohim of His promises and reveal them unto Adam. In so doing I fill man's soul with light and with an intrinsic hunger for Elohim."

"I am the ministry of faith. I am the faith of Elohim. I drink from the River of Life. My every desire is to take of the hope of Elohim and bring it to pass. I fill man's soul with life, which creates that which will be from that which is not."

"I am the ministry of intimacy. I am the intimacy the three Ones share. I drink from the River of Life. My ministry unto the three Ones and to man remains robed in mystery, but its fruit is abundant. When the intimacy of the Ones is joined in covenant with the intimacy of man, my secret will be revealed."

"I am the ministry of reverence. I am the reverence the three Ones share. I drink of the River of Life. My ministry unto the three Ones and to man is wisdom, knowledge and understanding. When the promises of the Ones are fulfilled in man, my ministry unto the Ones will become the inheritance of man."

"I am the ministry of true worship. I am the veneration the three Ones share. I drink of the River of Life. I join the worshipper with the worshipped and bathe them in delight."

The images and their voices disappear. Only Lairn`r and his scrolls remain.

The sonorous Voice rests.

Later, Michael, in private, says it best, "Man, indeed, is fearfully and wonderfully made. I wonder if we are sufficient to serve them."

INNOCENCE LOST

Michael summons me to meet with him immediately to discuss the budding crisis in the Garden. It soon becomes clear that we would accomplish more by seeing matters for ourselves.

On our way to the Viewing Window, he asks me to summarize the knowledge we presently have of man, looking for any indication that portends the situation that is currently developing. As we settle in at the Window we recognize that something is terribly awry. Gershom and Emunah, the woman's guardian angels, appear to be powerless to prevent a catastrophe.

Gershom, who had been looking for signs that he has an audience at the Window, is relieved to feel our presence, and says, "The woman is frequently making incursions near the center of the Garden. As you already know, she is talking with the serpent with more frequency and for longer periods."

Bathed in the innocence of Eden, and only from a distance, the woman gazes upon the tree *Yehovah* counseled about. It is a thing of beauty. Each time she comes to this area of the Garden, she comes a little closer and lingers a little longer. As she hesitates there, she plays the warning over and over in her head.

"Michael, we have tried distracting her," Gershom continues.

"We have reminded her of the command. We have nudged her conscience, but the effect on her is lessening. One time we sent a leopard, her favorite animal, to distract her. Still she talks with the serpent and her attention seems drawn, inexorably, to the Tree of the Knowledge of Good and Evil. Her spirit, the candle of *Yehovah*, conveys her reverence for Him, but she continues to return. Her spirit is starting to dim."

Klalish feels movement of the scroll within the bag he's carrying. Instinctively he reaches inside with his massive hand and touches its edges where the seals are. With a shudder, he pulls it out. The first seal on the scroll is broken. This must be the one Michael referred to regarding Gershom. He looks across the courtyard, toward the Citadel, wondering if he should seek an audience with Michael. A trumpet blasts the identifying notes calling our troupe to the Observatory. With this Klalish knows the answer.

Adam notices a change within the Garden. The birds are flying overhead, but there is no warbling. An expectant stillness hangs everywhere. The prancing deer are standing, heads cocked to one side, tails held high, not moving. The creeping things are not calling, one to another. At this time the bison usually graze along the river, while enjoying the afternoon sun. They are nowhere to be found. Adam, too, feels restlessness within. "What can this mean?" he asks aloud, but the woman is off somewhere, and cannot hear him.

"The serpent is such an important part of my day," she remarks to herself. "I look forward to hearing what he has to say. I could stop going into the center of the Garden and avoid him, but right now I want to learn what he is teaching. I'll surprise Adam. He will be so pleased with all I learn."

She has made a decision.

"There he is, over near the gnarled tree. I wonder what information he has for me today."

The anticipation of meeting with the serpent has become routine. She recognizes that her conscience no longer troubles her when the serpent is around. She still has questions, though, and her imagination is now popping with the wondrous possibilities this strange creature is about to reveal.

"Has Elohim said you shall not eat of every tree of the Garden?" the serpent asks her, as she approaches the clearing, a few paces from the gnarled tree.

The question surprises her. She knows the answer to the question. Adam has been telling her what *Yehovah* has said about the Tree of the Knowledge of Good and Evil. *Yehovah* has asked her, several times during their frequent walks, if she knew about the tree.

She answers, defiantly, "We may eat of the fruit of the trees of the Garden, but of the fruit of the Tree of the Knowledge of Good and Evil, which is in the midst of the Garden, *Yehovah* said, 'You shall not eat of it, neither shall you touch it, because you will die.'"

"There, that should settle it, once and for all," she thinks, happy to quote *Yehovah* and Adam. As she does, she notices her conviction regarding His command is not as strong as it used to be. With a start, she realizes her strength to resist the invitation of the serpent has waned significantly. There is, in fact, a yearning to be daring, here on her own with this strange creature.

The serpent hisses at her, "You shall not die! Elohim knows that when you eat thereof, then your eyes shall be opened, and you shall be as gods, knowing good and evil."

With her pulse racing, she turns from the serpent to look at the tree. The power of his argument is making her dizzy.

With the serpent behind her she decides to look at the tree one more time before leaving, resolving to never return to this part of the Garden again. However, she sees that the tree is good for food, and that it is pleasant to the eyes. She had seen this before, but today there is something new. Today she has a definite desire for what the serpent has just revealed to her. It is enticing. She wants to be wise. She wants the fruit. *Yehovah's* command, now, is but a faded echo that seems powerless and unimpressive.

With the thought, "If this is really wrong and I am found out, I will tell Adam that the serpent deceived me. I'll say that I was tricked into doing it."

With this breath of self-righteousness she reaches her hand out, plucks the fruit from the branch and bites into it.

As the pleasure of her new reality washes over her, she turns to see Adam standing behind her. Rising within her is a feeling of power she had never experienced. Impishly smiling at Adam, she stretches out her arm, and offers him a bite of the partially eaten fruit.

Adam sees she is different, as he looks past the serpent that is standing motionless between them. Approaching her, he sees with deep pain, the fruit she holds in her hand. His comprehension of what has happened causes him to catch his breath. His woman is in trouble. She has disobeyed *Yehovah*. Crushing in on him is a growing sense of loss. It is overwhelming him. He is torn by conflicting emotions.

First, the horror of discovering this woman shrouded in darkness. This woman he longs to hold, to protect. The naughty, mischievous look on her face. The unnatural smile.

"She is dying," he thinks. He feels the distance between them grow with each step he takes bringing him closer to her. He hears *Yehovah's* command replaying in his mind.

"So that is what it is to die," he thinks. "The woman didn't listen! She is in trouble. I can't think of that…nothing else matters…I have to find a way to rescue her from the death I see."

He makes his decision and reaches for the offered fruit.

"I can't risk losing her. She is part of me. She can't return to the light, but I can go to the darkness."

Klalish and I, and the rest of those called by the trumpet, are watching the drama in the Garden. We are drawn here as the critical moment arrives and she plucks the fruit from the tree. We witness the instant Adam first holds, and then eats, the forbidden fruit. When he does, Klalish feels the second seal open and the trumpet sounds once again. The angel who holds the trumpet, says, "Man has become like unto Elohim, intimately knowledgeable of both good and evil. Open the statutes of the Law of Sin and Death, that they may be judged by what is written therein."

"We have sinned against our Lord and eaten that which was forbidden."

Adam speaks his first words, after partaking of the fruit.

"Our eyes now see and we understand. We are worthy of death."

As the woman bows her head in homage to the declaration, she whispers, "So let it be."

Lying on their pallet, she buries her head in his chest as they try to sleep, but sleep doesn't come. The constriction in her chest tightens, the pain sharpens and she sobs! She doesn't recognize what that is!

She wonders, in panic, "Is this what it is to die?"

197

Adam turns toward her. They lay that way, wrapped in each other's arms, until first light, when they hear the sweet sounds of the familiar birds of morning. It is then they doze off into troubled sleep. Her last thought is how wonderful it is to hear the birds singing again.

They hadn't made a sound, not a rustle from their movements was heard, since she'd touched that fruit! That forbidden fruit! Why, oh why, had she succumbed to that ridiculous thing? She hadn't needed it, didn't even want it. She was just curious, that's all. The creature's laugh, when she had the bite of fruit in her mouth, made her feel ill, and so awfully afraid. And then she thrust it at Adam to get it out of her hands. And he'd bitten it, too!

She is afraid of these feelings that she's never had before. She is afraid that everything has changed!

"Oh, it has!"

This strained morning, as he and the woman arise from the discomfort of the night, there is a definite awkwardness standing between them. Their confusion is exacerbated by their lack of familiarity with each other. They'd grown so accustomed to each other, but now there is a feeling of strangeness that is new to them.

We watch with growing uncertainty as Dvar HaElohim enters the Garden. We had heard the trumpet sound and knew the second seal on the scroll in Klalish's possession had been opened by Adam.

"I regret the judgment that is to come," I whisper to Klalish. "Since they broke the Law of Elohim, they have no future."

The consequences of their disobedience are already manifesting. There is nothing we can do except continue to minister to Adam and the woman, but how long will these repercussions continue?

For a passing instant, I wonder why I feel distressed about what is happening to this created being. I have never reacted this way before.

Certainly, there was not a similar feeling of distress over the disobedience of the angels who followed Lucifer.

"I am troubled," I confess to Klalish. "This is a tragedy of eternal proportions."

With that, I see Dvar HaElohim in the Garden, calling out to Adam and the woman, "Where are you?"

Adam, holding the hand of the woman, while walking slightly in front of her, hesitantly appears from behind a stand of greenery.

"I heard your voice in the Garden, and I was afraid, because I was naked, and I hid myself," Adam responds to Dvar HaElohim's question.

Dvar HaElohim sees that each has a hastily entwined group of leaves covering the lower part of the body.

"Who told you that you were naked? Have you eaten of the tree that I commanded you not to eat?" Dvar HaElohim questions Adam again, sternly.

"The woman you gave to me gave me the fruit from the tree, and I ate it," Adam responds.

I listen more closely, as Dvar HaElohim turns His attention to the woman, "What is this that you have done?"

The woman, clearly shaken, replies, in a trembling voice, "The serpent deceived me, and I ate the fruit from that tree."

With wrathful eyes, but controlled voice, Dvar HaElohim now declares to the serpent, "Because you have done this, you are cursed above all cattle, and above every beast of the field; upon your belly you will go, and dust you will eat all the days of your life: and I will put enmity between you and the woman, and between your seed and her seed; it will bruise your head, and you shall bruise his heel."

At this rebuke the serpent changes and slithers away, hissing. It is fuming because Dvar HaElohim commands the winds of Eternity.

Dvar HaElohim now turns to the woman.

We, who are watching this interchange unfold, are filled with concern regarding how He will deal with the perpetrator of this irreverent deed that we've witnessed.

Dvar HaElohim is about to address the woman and we see His countenance change. Mercy now fills His eyes.

"What is this? I don't understand. Mercy?" I ask those who are watching with me. We've seen Yehovah mete out judgment with a firm, fair hand. He banished Lucifer from our midst and has, as we watch, transformed him to a new low. However, when He looks upon the woman, I recognize in His eyes, now filled with the distress I had been feeling, a combination of compassion, disappointment and sadness.

"I will greatly multiply your sorrow and your conception; in sorrow you will bring forth children; and your desire will be to your husband, and he will rule over you."

Adam and the woman now realize that, rather than ceasing to exist, they have been given a key to a path of redemption. She will not, immediately, cease to exist for her transgression.

Looking at one another, we realize this judgment, combined with the sentence spoken over satan, portends great loss, while unforeseen by us, great gain. I don't have time to think much beyond that, as Dvar HaElohim turns to Adam.

He looks at Adam with kind eyes, along with a smile I had only seen when Yehovah looks at Dvar HaElohim. Setting aside His divine right to judge as Sovereign, choosing to act in omnibenevolence, He speaks to Adam.

"Because you have hearkened unto the voice of your wife, and you've eaten of the tree, of which I commanded you, saying, 'You will not eat of it:' cursed is the ground for your sake; in sorrow you shall eat of it all the days of your life; Thorns and thistles it will bring forth to you; and you will eat the herb of the field; In the sweat of your face you will eat bread, until you return unto the ground; for out of it you were taken: for dust you are, and unto dust you will return."

The small assembly of angels that has joined me is shaken by these events, as Dvar HaElohim leaves the clearing in the Garden.

Exercising one of the few echoes of his original calling, not yet corrupted by his disobedience, Adam says to the woman, "You shall be called Eve, for you are the mother of all living."

Adam is so ashamed of what he and Eve had done. Perhaps he'd have been better off with only the animals to play and work with, instead of facing the complication of responsibility for Eve. However, that had not been *Yehovah's* plan. "She sure has messed things up, though," he thinks, regretting his duplicity.

Just then he hears the bleating of his companion, the cherished lamb. What a joy to have life simple again. He starts walking in the direction of what he hears when he detects a strange off-note. An off-sound. After a few steps he realizes it is the final sound of his favorite lamb. Adam walks more rapidly, while reflecting on the echoes of its life, which would be proven forever silent.

Yehovah returns with the lamb's skin for the skimpily swathed, essentially naked bodies of the two, waiting silently in the clearing of the beautiful Garden. Thus *Yehovah* provides a covering for the sin of Adam and Eve!

On the day following Dvar HaElohim's judgment visited upon Eve and Adam for their disobedience, I feel a powerful stirring within. In a moment there comes upon me a clarity that I had not experienced before. I had heard other angels speak of such things, but it had never happened to me. I know it to be one of the Seven Sprits acting upon me, and moving me, to do something. In pure obedience, I go to Michael.

"We must act quickly!" I tell him. "We must keep Adam and Eve from eating of the Tree of Life."

Michael immediately grasps the significance of what I am telling him and heads to the Throne Room.

Elohim says to the Heavenly host, "Behold, the man is become as one of us, to know good and evil: and now, lest he put forth his hand, and take also of the Tree of Life, and eat, and live forever: Therefore I send him forth from the Garden of Eden, to till the ground from where he was taken."

With that proclamation the third seal is opened and the third trumpet sounds. Upon hearing its resonance, Klalish reads aloud from the scroll to our troupe and to those, from other troupes, who have gathered around us. It is confirmation of my action in its undoing.

With his scroll now open and fully revealed, Klalish immediately departs. He joins another cherub, from a different troupe, and together they head toward Earth and the Garden gate. The flaming swords that they carry will protect man from entering Eden and eating of the Tree of Life. There they will remain as long as man walks the Earth, or man is once more worthy to access the Garden and then partake of the Tree of Life.

Lairn`r, Komodo`r, Tantzer, and I watch as Adam and Eve approach the gate they once explored, when they strained to see all that was beyond. Rapidly diminishing now, are most of their inner man's senses and a sense of Heaven's reality is fading. With each step man's spiritual senses fade and natural senses strengthen. Elohim's divine order for man's living becomes jumbled. They succumb to satan's seed, planted within.

That seed continues to grow, further crowding the inner man.

As we watch, a chorus of angels who formerly held a commission to worship continually before the Throne, gather impromptu, high over the courts in front of the Citadel. They break out into a new song and when I look at this choral group, I see Chayim boldly singing with all his might.

> "Thou clouded mystery, who made a covering,
> Great is the mystery of the Lamb.
> Thou clouded mystery, who's now a refuge,
> Great is the mystery of the Lamb.
> Thou clouded mystery, who reigns forever,
> Holy is the great I AM
> Our mighty king, who rules in justice,
> Great is your name.
> Our mighty king, who's conquered chaos,
> Great is your name. Great is your name.[33]"

The Sojourn Begins

Finding room at the Window is becoming more difficult as the word is spreading about satan's recent parry. We see the handiwork of the two guardian angels, Dāwīd and Gershom as Adam awakens from a deep slumber.

The unsteady feeling is so similar to the time he found Eve. As his mind clears, however, he panics. Yesterday's events have changed his sense of peacefulness to wariness. He now understands the feeling of fear. He sits up with a start and looks to see if Eve has disappeared.

She's still beside him. She doesn't stir. She, too, is unusually deep in sleep.

He looks around him and realizes that in the night they've been relocated. They're no longer in the clearing of the Garden. He recognizes that they are at the gateway that he named Passage Who Knows, but it looks different! The object that held the flickering flame is no longer there. Instead, he sees a flaming sword.

"How did we get here?"

He shakes Eve until she wakes. They know they must leave the Garden.

The flaming sword stops them as they approach the opening, but this time the opening is stationary. They cautiously move toward the gate and the flame moves aside to give them passage. Tentatively, Adam and Eve pass through. They turn and look back as the flaming sword moves in behind them.

They cannot go back.

We observe as Klalish fulfills his commission, thereby preventing their return. They travel about a Garden day's walk before the evening sun disappears over the horizon. Too far away to see the gateway, they no longer look back. We who watch understand how, with each step, they must ache for the life they have forfeited.

The next morning, arising from a troubled sleep, they lay there. They are lost in their own thoughts. Adam knows, instinctively, that he has to hunt for food to eat. Where to start? The few provisions they were able to take with them out of the Garden were consumed during last night's meal.

At first they didn't feel like eating, but later after satisfying themselves they realized they had consumed almost all of the food. The little bit of fruit, that is left over, is now spoiled and rotting.

"This is what it will be like from now on," he says.

He lifts his arms toward the heavens and thanks *Yehovah* for His mercy toward Eve and himself. He understands they disappointed *Yehovah*, yet He had preserved Eve from destruction when He found them. Of course, he couldn't be certain what His treatment of him would have been, if he hadn't eaten of the fruit, as well. However, his life without Eve was so empty, before he awakened from that strange sleep, and found her beside him. He had this powerful yearning that he couldn't readily describe, that seemed to be deep within his chest. He wanted her with him and couldn't conceive of existing without her presence.

"*Yehovah* is a just Sovereign," he whispers, looking up to the sky. It feels like no one is listening.

Those last few hours in the Garden were painful, but the walk from there to this place, yesterday, was severe. The flame guarding the gate terrorized both of them. He feels so far away from *Yehovah*.

Adam turns to Eve, and says, "I'll go and find us something to eat. I don't know how long it will take. I have no idea where I will find something edible. When I get back, you will have to prepare it."

With that, he turns away. Their relationship is forever altered. The idyllic camaraderie they'd shared, before the end of Eden, is a thing of the past.

I catch up with Komodo`r and Tantzer, walking across the beautiful courtyard which our residences surround. They are in deep discussion. As I approach, I learn it is about the recent events in the Garden.

"I have never..." Komodo`r begins. I am surprised by his tone

"Neither have I!" I interrupt. "When Dvar HaElohim returned from the Garden, just after excommunicating Adam and Eve, His eyes were wet. His face glowed with His everlasting glory, yet He looked as if He were suffering great anguish. He immediately entered into the Most Holy Place in the Temple. His shoulders were weighted with a yoke of sorrow. The angels ministering there say they could hear Him praying, interceding for Adam and Eve and the generations coming after them. He was praying for mercy, and deliverance and salvation."

"If I may," Komodo`r says firmly, with emphasis. "I – have – never – witnessed – such - unusual - events." Komodo`r speaks slowly and deliberately to strike home his point.

Gaining stride, his pace quickens, "When Lucifer was dealt with, there was certainty. The judgment of Yehovah was sound and unfailing. Now, with these terrestrials performing acts that are obviously disobedient, it seems impossible to measure the significance of their disobedience against the mercy of the judgment given."

I know what he means. The mercy Dvar HaElohim showed Adam and Eve is in stark contrast to the severity of sentence given to those cast from Heaven. Komodo`r and I are not questioning the righteousness of what has happened and is continuing to happen, but the basis of our understanding is grappling with equating the two calamities.

After concentrated deliberation, I conclude that comparing the misguided angels' disobedience, with Adam and Eve's disobedience, is like comparing the outer darkness with Elohim's glory. After all, Elohim is Lord, and everything He does is righteous. We, therefore, choose to wait to learn what is still hidden from our understanding.

Adam and Eve make their first home in a wilderness after walking a couple of days. It is not terribly far from the gateway in an area east of Eden.

Their first few hours in this world seem forbidding and strange. Gone are the deep blue skies that allowed Adam and Eve to see into the galaxies. The vibrant colors of the Garden have been replaced by similar species of created life, but their colors and fragrances are faded and dull, by comparison. Yet, Adam and Eve sense a hope deep within. A hope based upon a promise of *Yehovah*. That promise was not spoken using verbal words, as was the case before, but words, no less.

They have no knowledge of what is available outside the Garden, or what other areas have to offer. They know not of any other gateways to something better. Nor do they know if they're closing in on something worse. They are lost, and will be, until they explore the different possibilities that may be available to them. Adam is aware that he must be able to work the soil and search for food to sustain them. Where that would be best is not known. They decide that, for the foreseeable future, they will have to be wanderers.

"Maybe there is a place somewhere that has some of the same vegetation that we had in such abundance in the Garden," Adam thinks to himself.

To Eve he says, "We will have to do some exploring to find the best place to grow what we need to survive. It will be alright. We will find some place pleasant to live."

She has become so quiet. The playfulness that he enjoyed in her is now absent. He determines that showing her that he is not suffering anxiety will give her a measure of confidence and she will recognize that he can be in charge.

"Just as *Yehovah* had told us, I will rule over her and she will turn to me." Thus Adam has made the first of many independent decisions.

As they survey their surroundings they see some animal life not too far away. It should be simple enough to corral them.

"We can use them for clothing, like *Yehovah* has given us, and for sacrifice," Adam announces, while pointing off into the distance.

Without asking her, he picks up some twines he has twisted together and heads in the direction of the animals they see. All the while, he is thinking, "How does one kill a living thing? I know He did." Recognition of the knowledge that the need to slaughter an innocent animal is necessary to their survival, through sacrifice, causes him to gag.

Dāwīd and Gershom, along with the other two angels assigned to guard them, joined the traveling party when Adam and Eve left the Garden. Without them to minister, satan and his minions will see that Adam and Eve don't survive the first week outside the Garden.

"What new constraints are to be placed upon them?" I ask Michael the most urgent question I can think of regarding the duties of these four guardians.

"They are forbidden to do anything that inhibits the law of man's freedom to choose. Adam and Eve, and all that is in the world around them, are governed by the Law of Sin and Death. This will make life perilous. All this is true and just. However, Elohim is full of mercy and benevolence toward them. He says that He wants to bestow upon them unconditional compassion. This, Elohim told me, is the first precept revealing 'grace.' Where they prove to have a willing heart, even though they are destined to walk a way of their own choosing, their guardians are commanded to show them favor and kindness.

"Of them, will come One who will purchase back what they, freely, just gave away. The lamb who was slain will buy them back."

From now forward, these four, Mehgen' and Dāwīd, Gershom and Emunah, will be vanguards of man's future and the promised purchase.

Dāwīd and Mehgen' check the horizon for signs of the enemy. Noticing nothing, they conspire to help Adam gather the animals he needs. Dāwīd enjoys singing and creates poetry, as he works. Mehgen' on the other hand shouts and waves his arms when the few predator animals show an interest in Adam's growing flock. To Adam it looks like the animals are listening to his every thought, while they are only moving to the herding skills of Dāwīd and Mehgen'. By guiding the few animals that he's gathered, thus far, Adam's meager flock goes where it is necessary for them to go. The angels, therefore, show favor to Adam and Eve. Dāwīd and Adam aren't having much trouble, except for one rebellious lamb, who insists on straying away from the main flock.

It takes most of the day, but with some satisfaction, Adam finally herds the last of the sheep he's decided on keeping. He recalls giving them that name. It seems so very long ago. He selects a semi-enclosed canyon, one that is closed on three sides by ridges. The walls formed are so steep the sheep could not possibly climb out of their safe haven. He then places clumps of thorny bushes at the only way of escape. He feels sure that this allows him enough time to return to Eve and, with her help, quickly move their things to set up a new camp near the opening to the canyon.

Still new to the ways of this foreign world, he doesn't think about predators coming after the corralled sheep. He hurries, estimating that the camp they're about to abandon isn't very far away. It seems, however, to be farther away with each step.

"I don't remember it being so distant to that gorge. I hope Eve didn't move that camp after I left this morning," Adam worries. Unnatural fear seeks an entrance to his mind, clutching at his innards.

Trying as hard as he can, he cannot shake this feeling that Eve must have done something wrong. This is becoming a familiar impression. They disagreed last night. They were each so heated in defending their individual viewpoints. Yet, it makes no sense in the light of day. The argument last night begins replaying in his mind. He is so unfamiliar with the feeling of anger. Yet he did feel angry at her last night. He decides that, regardless of his feelings, he will be so glad to see her.

He pushes these thoughts away when finally, he sees, off in the distance, the top of their shelter. To his relief and surprise, it is right where he had left it this morning. Herding the sheep had taken him farther from the camp than he'd imagined. He is about to enter the area, when he catches a whiff of the meal she is preparing. It smells delicious, but those sheep need protecting.

"Eve, the food smells great, but I don't have time to eat now. I have the sheep in a closed canyon quite a distance from here. We have to move, and quickly," Adam says forcefully, and sounds scolding.

Eve, hurt by Adam's lack of patience, and full of last evening's disappointment, suddenly breaks into tears. The pain is too much. She's been alone all day, rather than spending the day as they used to, exploring, holding hands, playing with the animals that frolicked with them. Then, without his help and as a surprise for him, she gathers and makes the fire, prepares this food, and when he returns, he's so cold and demanding.

"Where did my friend go? Was he left back in the Garden?" she thinks, but doesn't make a sound. Pursing her lips, she just turns and begins packing. There is no one else to turn to. So there it is. Her mind flashes to that fruit! She swallows, as a bitter taste fills her mouth.

When Adam enters the camp Dāwīd and Mehgen' join the perplexed pair. All they can do is shake their heads. This wasn't covered when the troupe looked into the mysteries of man. When the two were in the Garden, there was never a problem like this.

The foursome can sense the tension. Dāwīd motions for Gershom to call on the wind, to begin a playful song by brushing and nudging some hanging ornaments fashioned after some reeds and shells, dug up along the stream. The sounds are musical notes to Adam and Eve and cause each of them to remember the music of the Garden. Instead of causing the guilt they suffered earlier, the music nurtures tears of remorse. Soon they are holding onto each other in a sweet embrace, whispering man's first apologies.

Dāwīd, Mehgen', Gershom and Emunah smile at each other, recognizing man has to learn what angels already know. Relationships hold importance which is very close to worshipping Elohim. Apologies are essential to maintaining relationships. Angels make mistakes and man does, too.

Off in a distance, but within ear shot, a couple of shadows listen. One is prince of the power of the air and with him is an underling. Adam and Eve have stumbled into the prince's territory. Underlings of this prince had succeeded in their attempt at causing discord between Adam and Eve the night before, but this time, their success lasted only a little while.

"Man has the same weakness as the Sovereign of Light. It is as Lucifer taught," the prince complains to the night. "We have learned a lesson this time. It seems that sometimes that weakness is capable of defeating me and the darkness I hold in my hand."

He turns, motioning to the smaller shadow that is lagging behind. Together they head toward Adam's unattended sheep. "If I can't steal their peace by acting through each of them, I'll destroy it another way."

Hearing HaRuach speak within him, Mehgen' shares with his three covenant partners the direction he is getting. Standing, he lifts and stretches his powerful wings and with a single down stroke lifts off Earth and into the heavens. All Adam and Eve sense is a brief gust of wind that quickly comes and goes. The closing night breeze is still warm, but Adam feels a chill or tingle run down his thigh.

"Eve, do you feel that?" he asks, the sensation reminding him of a feeling he's had before. A couple of times, when *Yehovah* said something that moved him, deeply, he'd experienced that same stirring. He looks at Eve as she nods her head, yes, but all he can say is, "Hmmmm."

A small band of jackals, cackle their sickening sound and sniff the night air. They are looking for prey. They don't react to the shadows hovering invisibly, overhead. The smaller shadow though touches the alpha jackal and it heads off toward the canyon. The hungry band he leads, slouches along.

They had become one of the first animals to recognize other animals as prey. It wasn't that long ago their instinct would never tell them that other animals were food. Then they were herbivores.

As they approach the ridge guarding Adams' sheep, they begin to creep and circle, their cackles unsettling the flock. Their hope is to stampede the sheep, so they can pick them off at will, thus filling their hungry bellies and their lust for blood.

When that doesn't work a predator instinct moves them to isolate a small lamb, frightening it into bolting. Finding a likely victim, they begin to move in. It won't be long.

Mehgen' must act quickly. Adam hasn't learned, yet, to protect his flocks from predators. It is as HaRuach revealed. He wants the flock protected.

"I mustn't do anything to frighten the sheep, while I protect them from harm," Mehgen' mumbles.

The solution seems obvious once it comes to him and he heads for the shadows and their servants. Swooping down, he declares to the waiting shadows, "Elohim rebukes you. You are to do no harm to Adam's sheep. These empty animals may do your bidding, but the sheep will not."

Suddenly, the shadows launch to attack Mehgen'. The three celestial beings begin twisting and tumbling, as they wrestle for dominion. As the standoff, between Elohim's scout and satan's forces continues, the jackals halt their advance and swallow their cackles. They can advance no further. They turn, moving off to look for prey elsewhere. For there before them, surrounding the flock is a band of angels with wings unfurled. The host of angels who will stand post, until Adam and Eve come to relieve them.

REVELATION OF ELOHIM

"The stars overhead are unusually bright tonight," Adam says to Eve. They begin to gaze upon the starry heavens. Maybe because Adam's calling was to name everything in the Garden, they have started giving names to some of the familiar patterns of stars. It has become an evening ritual that they enjoy.

Pointing here and there, they take turns identifying the patterns by name. Occasionally, they need to stop, because they can't recall a name. Although they recall having recently named a star, or constellation, one upon which they'd both agreed, sometimes they just can't remember what it was. A frustrated Adam realizes this is in obvious contrast to the total recall they had possessed in the Garden.

When this happens, they attempt recalling the names, using various techniques, such as associating the pattern with how they think the star clusters are shaped. Sometimes, it helps. Sometimes, it doesn't. They realize that by imagining lines connecting the various stars, forms appear that help them to reconcile the name with the pattern.

A few star groupings are accidently named twice, only to be reconsidered when the first name is actually recalled. These they vote on. A flipped stone deciding a split vote.

Suddenly, from somewhere outside the camp, Eve hears a new sound. It isn't the bleating of the sheep, so it's not a warning of impending danger. It is more like the sound of a gust of wind worrying a clump of bushes, as it rushes along the gullies that are scattered around the low lands.

"Just the wind," she thinks.

Mehgen' and Gershom settle in, coming to rest, squatting on their muscular thighs, as Omán and Boneh slowly rise beside them. A tour of duty, for the present, is over. Moving around their outpost, they stretch, preparing to return to Heaven's richness.

"Omán and Boneh, thank you for faithfully relieving us. It was wonderful to return to Heaven for a season of refilling," Mehgen' articulates their sincere appreciation, as Gershom smiles in agreement, and nods.

"I guess our arrival didn't disturb them much. Only Eve showed signs of being aware of us flying in. We don't seem to be able to completely hide from them. We seem to always leave a trace of evidence of our presence," Mehgen' announces, showing no concern. "After all, Adam and Eve were vaguely aware of our existence and attending presence, when they were in the Garden. They haven't, totally, lost that part of their spiritual senses, although their acuity isn't as sharp."

With that Omán and Boneh lift off. From this higher vantage point, they wave a goodbye and are instantly gone. The departure completed, Mehgen' and Gershom quickly give each other a knowing look, agreeing on the task at hand, and move swiftly toward the corral. They perceive a celestial predator, probing for an entry, is hoping for a moment of weakness during the change of the guard. Dāwīd and Emunah are hovering near Adam and Eve, which is their assignment. Man's working animals, the ones Adam and Eve have trained, are also alerted to the strangeness of the presence in their midst. Their restlessness remains, until the threat is gone.

"They never give up," Gershom says, bemoaning the persistence of the dark forces, aligned against the forces of light.

Turning, after the distraction caused by the restless dogs, Adam once again recites, from memory, the list of images. The largest pattern, they decide, is the image of a woman. They have named it, "The Maiden."

From an earlier campsite vantage point, it seemed to look a lot like Eve. The resemblance to Eve is the reason that Adam first noticed that constellation. He had been thinking a lot about Eve, and how much she agonized over the part she'd played in the drastic change in their lives. Their departure from the Garden has been devastating, but now, bereft of their spiritual vision, their suffering is greater, by far. The independence they now have, while frightening, can be considered freedom. However, there is undeniable pain, as a result of their altered relationship with *Yehovah*.

In a moment of despair Adam looks up and experiences an epiphany, when he sees the outline of Eve's shape above him, there in the sky overhead.

In addition to "The Maiden," they now also see other groupings of stars. The shapes of a lion, a scorpion, a lamb, a river, a goat, a fish. There are several images shaped like Adam, or *Yehovah*, performing different actions. They have developed quite a list, vocally blessing *Yehovah* for these awesome creations. They are content.

This moment of simple joy is enhanced by a feeling they recognize and in which they take much delight. *Yehovah* is listening.

They bow their heads, this first family, paying humble homage to *Yehovah*, recognizing His presence. Eve quietly weeps with fulfill-ment, while Adam's eyes fill with tears, as well. Any sounds he makes are muted, though, by the rapture he feels.

"Oh, *Yehovah*, we worship you, and offer praise and thanksgiving, because You have shown us mercy. Your presence chases the authority of our wickedness away. What do you ask of us?" Adam prays, while Eve lies prostrate before Him.

217

His voice is that of the rivers of Eden, bubbling and bursting with gladness. It comes from everywhere and yet nowhere, in this picturesque surrounding. For they hear it, not with their ears, but with their hearts. And it is wonderful.

"Children," He begins. "I am what you see with your eyes and now hear with your hearts. For, I am from the beginning, and have made a way for you and for your seed. As I told you in the Garden, My promise of this is written above.

"You see them afar off, and so it is for a time that is far off. See the words I have written to you, and your seed, for in them you have eternal life. They are My words for they speak of Me and My plan for you. They are My gift of life. Though you have sinned, yet you shall be white as lamb's wool."

With that, His presence is gone, but the aura of that encounter lingers.

They join hands and together gaze with fresh eyes at the patterns with which they've been amusing themselves. As before, they stare skyward, only this time, as one, they see and understand the word of *Yehovah* as written by Him.

"A young maiden will have a child," Adam begins.

"It says, 'Her child will be filled with glory, wisdom, and the majesty of *Yehovah*'," she continues, brushing the skies with her hand, as she points to various images.

"There, that one says her child will destroy the works of the serpent," Adam relates and smiles, knowingly. He turns and looks into Eve's eyes, which are now peaceful. The last time Adam saw her at peace, as she is now, was the evening before they ate the fruit.

They hold each other's eyes. At the same time, they ask, "Is it talking about us? Is that going to be our child?"

Together, Dāwīd, Mehgen', Gershom, and Emunah, rise from their hastily assumed position. They fell on their faces at Dvar HaElohim's surprise visit. Michael hadn't alerted them that Dvar HaElohim was going to manifest Himself here.

They watch and listen as Adam and Eve read the word of Dvar HaElohim, written in the skies above. The same skies they traveled to get here and the same skies that Omán and Boneh are now traversing on their return to Heaven.

"This doesn't change anything for us, does it?" Mehgen' asks.

There are no answers.

"Listen," Lairn`r commands those who are present. "Adam and Eve are able to read the star patterns, the ones Elohim tossed into the heavens. We haven't been able to do that. It looks like, through them, we will have a revealed understanding of the mystery of the stars. Listen!"

There is a shuffle as everyone finds a place to rest, hanging on Adam's and Eve's every word.

Komodo`r turns to me and points at the lower right of the screen, almost off the edge of the Window, where there is a hand and part of an arm. "There! There is someone, or something, hiding behind that rock. Can we move the Window to see who, or what, it is?"

The approaching "ear" does not go unnoticed by Dāwīd and Mehgen'. They have perceived satan's arrival. He would have been immediately aware of the epiphany and the presence of Dvar HaElohim. He lost no time in coming to investigate.

Lifting his eyes toward Heaven, Dāwīd quietly asks, "What should we do?"

Mehgen' replies, "He has a measured right to be here. The Law of Free Will and the Law of Sin and Death permit it, as long as he remains invisible and complies with those laws. We cannot prevent him, unless attacked directly."

Dāwīd, Mehgen', Gershom, and Emunah move to place themselves between the oblivious couple and satan. Their drawn swords held tightly, they move to intercept any doubts or unbelief that satan may be supporting within his seed-of-sin which inhabits them.

Adam and Eve stay awake all night reading the word. Just as the sun's rays penetrate the clefts high upon the distant mountains, Adam bows his head and offers thanksgiving to *Yehovah* for the word they have read. During the night, they decide to stay awake no matter how tired they become. They had sinned once. They aren't going to let this opportunity slip from their grasp, like the Garden did.

They think they understand the whole thing. "*Yehovah* spoke that a maiden is going to give birth to a son. That son will grow to be a man and will suffer, so that man can be redeemed. *Yehovah* promises to pay the death price hanging over our heads, and all mankind, because of the choice we made in the Garden. This sojourn isn't going to last forever. *Yehovah* has a plan."

"Maybe, someday, we will go back to live in the Garden. Then my guilt will be lifted," Eve says to Adam.

"So man has a role to play, as well as, looking into the knowledge of Elohim. This is so, although they have sinned, and satan has planted his seed within them. How extraordinary is that? Man is the means, chosen by Dvar HaElohim, to reveal much of the hidden elements of

Elohim's plan to fulfill His judgment upon satan and his followers," Komodo`r declares with an unexpected tiredness.

It is very unusual for angels of light to require a respite. This usually happens after some prolonged encounter with vestiges of darkness. My first personal encounter with that experience was prior to my sabbatical. It was quite unexpected that Komodo'r would reach a point of exhaustion after a prolonged observation of man. Following a sustained session before the Viewing Window, it becomes evident that each of us is ready to return to our quarters for some rest.

It seems we have been given a great gift by Elohim and man. Fallen man, at that. Even in a fallen condition, man is a vessel through whom Elohim reveals, therefore unseals, some of Heaven's long standing mysteries. Now seals have been broken by this created, fallen man.

"I must take this to Michael," I say, excusing myself.

I realize I am looking forward to this season with Michael. Any fatigue I might have had is gone.

Michael listens to my narrative about what Lairn`r, Komodo`r, Tantzer and I, have just witnessed. Carefully, I present the sequence of events, leaving out nothing. Studying his face as I do so, I don't see any surprise until I mention Dvar HaElohim's visitation. It is then that Michael first learns the details of the grace He has bestowed upon fallen man.

We sit there silently for a while. His head is slightly bowed, propped upon his right hand, while his right elbow rests on the table in front of him. His index and middle fingers are extended along his cheek. His other two fingers run beneath his nose. It is Michael's familiar pose when his mind is off somewhere for an extended period of time. Where he acquired that pose, no one knows.

We sit there like statues. Finally he speaks, "I concur with your findings and the findings of your troupe. It will be recorded as such. As to the revelation that one of the purposes of man is to be a vessel through which Elohim will reveal mysteries, I can only say at this time, that it is true. Elohim has spoken and it is written, that in His foreknowledge He knew before the foundation of the heavens was laid, that Adam and Eve would fall."

As I leave Michael's chambers, I whisper to myself, "I wonder what he didn't tell me?"

UNTO US A CHILD IS BORN

"Oh, my!" Eve exclaims, as she raises her hand to cover her face. "That sun is bright."

Standing in the becalmed, cool river, after her morning cleansing, she feels refreshed, clean, and beautiful. Adam says she is beautiful. A small, playful smile tickles her lips as she thinks how pleasing that is to her. Looking at the river she notices her nude reflection. In these private baths she has a chance to think back to the Garden. The memories of that bliss still remain, though the emotion of the loss is no longer as starkly painful. The promises of the written word have assuaged her guilt.

She ponders the melting of those first awful days, moving her hand absentmindedly down her body. She looks again at her reflection on the surface of the water. There is a difference! There is a rounding to her abdomen that she hadn't noticed before. It is then she remembers! It has been 11 or 12 weeks since she last experienced the cycle common to her. Her heart jumps! She is with child. She is going to have a baby. Adam will be overjoyed when she tells him.

"I wonder. Can it be he is the promised child written in the Word above?" she speculates.

Adam is watching the sheep and goats. Every so often he has to find a new grazing area, since sheep and goats eat everything growing, down to the roots. Today he is the farthest he's ever been from where he and

Eve pitch their tent. Every so often they have to move the campsite. Each time they move farther from the gate of Eden. Adam knows the flame is there still, guarding the entrance. That sword, glinting and deadly, would be there, too.

As the evening sun begins to settle in the west, Adam grabs the leading sheep by the collar he'd invented to aid in directing him. He pulls it toward the campsite. He's hungry and knows Eve will have prepared something delicious for them to eat, before they settle in for the evening. It is different here. Gone are the lush green pastures he had found so close to the gate. Now, there are vast patches of dry brush to contend with. There's a greater distance between watering holes, too.

"I guess, great *Yehovah*, this is what you meant," Adam prays out loud, just as He taught them, while they walked in the Garden together.

He is now accustomed to the hardships. The greatest challenge is the serpent's seed, which is still increasing in influence, instilling ugly, unclean thoughts. Then there are those voices jumping in, from who knows where. It isn't the voice of *Yehovah*. He and Eve know what that voice is like. This voice causes pain and crested feelings of oppressive guilt. Feelings of accusation are accompanied by a stifling presence that tries to constantly remind him of what he and Eve had done.

It is always a mixture of feelings and contradicting thoughts, each competing for the forefront of his conscious mind. He knows whence they come because these distasteful, unbidden contemplations started just after eating the fruit. That serpent must, somehow, still be around. He will have to take time this evening, to wrestle these, the ones troubling him today, into submission.

In the distance, he can see the tops of the tent poles. There, kneeling outside one of the flaps is Eve. His feelings for her are clear and continue to grow. He feels a swell in his chest, when he comes upon her as he returns from tending the sheep each evening, or as he nears her with fruit or tender leaves from the pickings each day.

They share everything. They have a bond that he couldn't have imagined, before *Yehovah* gave her to him. She is a part of him to share his life. Their mutual knowledge of Eden, *Yehovah*, sin, and the recent challenges, birthed a oneness, greater than that they'd known in the Garden.

For that, Adam is thankful and says so, "Lord *Yehovah*, my King and shield. Thank you for Eve, and that you found a way, so we didn't have to be destroyed like the lamb." With these words, the heaviness of his prior thoughts disappear.

"Were there any problems today?" she asks. "That leopard. You know, the one you told me about. The one stalking the flock. Did he come any closer?" She knows a leopard places the flock in danger, but it places Adam in danger, too. That anything untoward could happen to him is unthinkable. What, then, would she do?

"No, I didn't see anything of it, today. I think it ran off. I found a fresh kill though. A wild hen of some kind. If it gets hungry enough, it might make a try again. I think I will take a couple of the dogs with me tomorrow, if they will follow. I still need to train them some more, but just having them around should deter any predator."

She wonders whatever happened to the leopard, she was so fond of, in the Garden. Talking about one here brings back some bitter-sweet memories.

Adam notices something different about Eve. He is not sure what, but something, some kind of secret. Just as he is about to ask, she smiles up at him.

"Adam," she says with a playful coyness, "how long has it been since we left the Garden?"

"About 15 years, by the seasons and the stars. Just about 15 years." He knows this by counting the passage of growing seasons, and that they are into a new one. 15 years is about right.

"Why do you ask?"

"Well, *Yehovah* commanded us to be fruitful and multiply, right?" a smile fills her lovely face. It is the only hint of her surprise. Taking his hand, she gently places it on her mounding belly.

"We are going to have a baby!!!"

Several thoughts of "what, when, how" erupt in his mind. It is all that Adam can think of, his mind racing with a rush of pleasant thoughts. All Eve can do is continue to smile.

"This confirms the prophetic word I spoke over you, while we were still in the Garden. You are the mother of all living!" With that he tenderly takes her into his arms. This evening is one of the best, since leaving the Garden. Together they wonder if this child is the one referred to in the word, written above.

"We are witnessing another 'first,' Komodo`r."

Komodo`r and I were walking past the Citadel, when something impressed us to drop by the Observatory to see what Adam and Eve were up to. Our troupe's fascination with man has not abated, even after their departure from the Garden. Angels in most troupes don't understand how the Garden's events have enhanced Elohim's mysterious plan, but somehow they have. Of that, we, in my troupe, are certain. Now, because we obeyed an unheard of Heavenly prompt, we are the first angels to learn that Adam and Eve are going to have their first child. The "created beings" are now instruments doing the creating of another human being. In this, once again, Elohim has distinguished man from the angels. Angels cannot reproduce. Elohim has invested, in man, the power to procreate.

I proceed to solicit our scribe, Lez`n, to record these events, and place them in the Book of Remembrance.

"Amazing!" Komodo`r says, shaking his head as he retreats toward the exit from the Observatory. "Amazing!" he repeats, and then he turns and disappears from view, going toward the Steps of Ascension.

It isn't that Adam and Eve are reproducing that places Komodo`r into a twist. When Elohim created Adam and Eve, He said, "Be fruitful and multiply." Komodo`r knows this. It is that Elohim, in His wisdom, has waited 15 years after the sin, before Eve has been able to conceive.

"We now have another mystery in the Hall of Mysteries." With that Komodo`r is down the Steps of Ascension and presumably, out the door, leaving me to wonder what this speedy exit is all about.

After a few more glances, I, too, leave. But, of course, I am in no hurry. Still wondering what precipitated Komodo'r's reaction, I leave to find Gabriel. He can get a message to Michael about Eve's news. Michael has left standing directives with us to let him know, immediately, if there are any significant changes involving the pair.

"Eve's news draws warmth into the tent this evening," Adam thinks. "I wonder if this event portends good or evil. *Yehovah* mentioned that by her actions, Eve had introduced pain into the birthing of a child. What that means, specifically, we will now learn. One thing remains true. Every new happening brings with it a fear that was absent in the Garden. It is the dread of the unknown. *Yehovah* mentioned that these fears could be overcome.

"He said, 'You will conquer the paralyzing anxiety by an unfailing faith in Me and My word, written in the heavens above. And by encouraging yourselves by what you learn daily about Me and My promises.' I'm sure that He is with us." Adam continues to extract some solace from these remembrances.

"We seem unable to prevent negative thoughts from creeping into our minds, though these are unbidden. *Yehovah* says, 'This thing is the seed of the serpent, a result of your weakness. The venomous unease you will feel was placed within you by the serpent, at the instant you ate.'

"How this phenomenon occurs is perplexing. By exercising our choice over *Yehovah's*, we invited or planted a seed just like I do each growing season, and which we have done within Eve.

227

"For now, I must defeat this feeling, and comfort Eve. Hers is the difficult part, enduring what lies ahead. While yet in the Garden, we learned
that birthing for man takes about nine moon cycles, beginning when
the seed is planted within."

Adam, then, muses aloud, "I am not so sure when the birthing
time began."

"No, Adam, I am not sure, either. All I know is I haven't had the issue
in about three moon cycles. So I am thinking it means we have about
six more to go," Eve responds to his reflections.

"Do you have any idea what it will be like? Our life is one of constant
discovery. It's so different, living without the shield and protection of
the Garden. Anything can happen. I miss *Yehovah's* presence. I know
we have His presence. I know that He is always with us, but seeing
Him, and walking with Him as we did, was wonderful. I miss that,"
she adds, verbalizing thoughts they'd been sharing ever since that day.

"Reminiscing is an evening routine. Life was not just easier, but also
more abundant. There is a lack of a sense of purpose. A 'knowing'
that is now missing. There, in the Garden, there was closeness with
Yehovah and His physical presence, daily. Now, here, there are times
when we feel Him, almost like it was. But there are also times when
we feel so all alone."

Adam needs to talk about the coming event, "I expect you'll give birth
like the animals. We are different from the sheep, but they birth their
young, and nurture them until the lambs are old enough to take care
of themselves. The animals nurse for different lengths of time. Some
animals take only a few days, while others take months. It seems the
larger and more intelligent they are, the longer it takes."

They had noticed and talked about the similarities before. It is a way
of learning, and mastering, the world in which they find themselves.
Sometimes, making a comparison has failed them, and there have been
consequences, as a result.

"You know, Eve, I was just thinking about how we've learned some things. Do you remember after we left the Garden, we crossed a swollen river? That day, our desired path was blocked by that river. As it turned out, it was wide and deep in several places. We saw cattle crossing the deep areas, without any trouble. Remember, we tried, and sank. The fear seemed to choke us. We flailed around for a while, splashing in panic. And, then, seemingly out of nowhere, my foot touched the bottom and while standing on the tip of my toes, I grabbed you and we waded ashore."

They often remind each other of such things. It is a way of keeping track. This time it is Adam's turn.

Listening in, I remember the day that Adam is talking about. We have often prevented harm to Adam and Eve, as they migrated farther away from the Garden, obeying the directive of Elohim. Sometimes circumstances have warranted increasing the number of protective angels, as when we prevented the slaughter of the first flock of sheep.

If princes of satan marshal an attack, Michael sends Adam and Eve a company whom he has formed as a rescue sortie. Their numbers vary, depending upon what the prince powers bring to the front lines of battle. Forewarned by Michael, who anticipated a problem, I sent two extra angels, Omán and Boneh, who joined Dāwīd, Mehgen', Gershom and Emunah. When Adam and Eve waded into the river and began to panic, fear clouded their thinking. The added backup afforded by Omán and Boneh proved essential. They stood watch while Dāwīd and Mehgen' dove into the river and, below Adam and Eve's kicking feet, they used their wings to fan the rough muddy bottom, developing a ledge on which they could stand.

As in the Garden, the angels cannot counter man's use of the freedom of choice. They could not stop them from going into the river.

If Michael had directed one of the ministering angels to appear before Eve at the critical decisive moment, she wouldn't have touched the fruit. By using that route to try to prevent a sin, the angel, himself, would have sinned and in so doing, would have violated the law of freedom of choice. At the river, it wasn't a chosen act of denying Elohim, so an overt act performed by the angels was permissible.

"To provide for Eve and me is a difficult juggling act. Our lot today is so different from what it was," Adam ruefully remembers.

"Before we left there, *Yehovah* promised to provide our needs, though cautioning us that it would not be in the same manner as in the Garden. Yet, He would be here. His written word promises that. The need to remain long enough in one place to plant, cultivate and harvest the few crops we grow, along with the need to move the flock of sheep to have adequate grazing for them, are conflicting. We balance these opposing requirements, while avoiding predators like the leopard.

"So far, we haven't come upon any other of our kind. We didn't expect to, but unknowns are such a common thing here."

I see Komodo`r heading toward the Citadel. His pace is more like a half-run than a walk.

"Komodo'r, where are you off to?" I have to shout, quickening my pace to try to catch up. Angels do not lumber, even though they are twice the size of man. Their motion is one of ease and rhythm, producing great speed with very little effort.

"Zukher, you haven't heard? Didn't you get Gabriel's message?" Komodo`r answers my question with one of his own, never looking to see if I hear.

"I heard the message, and headed right over, but why the quickstep?" I know why, but a little playfulness might lighten the moment.

"It could happen any time and I don't want to miss it. Come on! Keep up, or get left behind!" Komodo`r isn't playing, and soon we disappear within the Citadel. As we reach the foot of the Steps of Ascension, he floats up, taking three steps to my one.

Once I reach the top and head toward the Window in the Observatory focused on Adam's campsite, I notice we are not to be alone. Gabriel, Lairn'r, Tantzer, Shtitsen, Sryyab`r, and, of course, Lez`n, are already here, waiting and watching. Michael, too, is here. He's yielding to the urgency of the novel event.

Lairn`r turns to me as I settle in behind his shoulder, "Where is Adam, has anyone seen Adam?" It is the first I understand what the real urgency is about. Adam is not anywhere around the campsite. I decide to check other Windows, with no idea which one will offer a sign of Adam.

"I found him. He is over by the bluff, about a half day's journey from the campsite. A lamb wandered away during the night and he is hunting for it!" an angel, from a different troupe, exclaims.

Michael solves the momentary mystery, "We dispatched a group of angels to assist Eve with the delivery. She is going to need it."

No one asks Michael what he means by Eve "needing help" as she begins to pace around the campsite. Her arms are wrapped around her mid-section and her face is full of anguish.

As the others watch, Michael slips quietly away, heading up the Steps toward the Throne Room. Elohim must have summoned him.

"Great Lord *Yehovah*!" she exclaims, "Hear the voice of this hand-maiden. You have promised to help us when we are in need and I do not have Adam around me now. I am about to deliver this child into your kingdom. Help me for the spasms of birth envelop me, and I am anxious to be delivered of this child."

From our vantage point we can see several angels massaging her abdomen, while others encircle her, forward and backward, over and under.

A shout comes from Tantzer, "Look, over there!" He points, "In the distance around those rocks, the ones near the bushes! A pack of hyenas is moving close, sensing a quick kill, I guess."

"She sees them, I think. She has grabbed a staff, but that will be no defense against a pack," Komodo`r resolutely states.

"Michael?" Lairn`r inquires. But Michael is nowhere in sight.

"No time to hunt for him," he mumbles, turning back to the Window.

Just then, we watch as three of the angels attending Eve suddenly turn as they become aware of the evil hyenas, edging closer to the tents. They fly toward them, swooping and flapping, creating a dust storm, until the leader dashes away, followed by the pack. The incident avoided, the unrelenting storm, precipitated by the angels' wings, pursues the pack to keep them at bay.

"So little one, with eyes so wide, I hope you learned your lesson and will not run off again," Adam says, cuddling the lamb who continues to struggle to be free. "I have you."

Adam is tired and wants to sit down to rest for a while, before heading back. As he turns, he notices a panting leopard sitting high above on a group of piled rocks, watching. His tongue is hanging from his semi-open mouth, showing his deadly teeth. It seems intent on waiting for a meal.

"Me, or the lamb?" Adam questions, as he heads back to the campsite. Eve will have the child any time now, and he wants to be there to help deliver the baby. With that thought, a chill runs through his body, and fear clutches his throat.

"I need to get back!"

As he leaves the Throne Room, following his audience with Elohim, Michael knows what needs to be done.

"Gabriel," he says without looking to see if Gabriel is anywhere around. He is usually found waiting, at the ready. "Take a message to Adam. Without revealing yourself, prompt him to get back to Eve, but he must not leave the lamb to do so. Take Tantzer and a few warrior angels with you, more than enough to break through the enemy's defenses. Don't delay, Gabriel!"

Returning to the Observatory, Gabriel approaches Tantzer, touching him on the shoulder, nodding for Tantzer to join him. While they combine forces, a group of warrior angels joins them, and they disappear through the Window leading to Adam's location.

Gabriel finds Adam, exhausted, just starting to stretch out on the ground. Without revealing himself, as Michael commanded, Gabriel reaches his hand forward, placing it upon the small of Adam's back. The other hand he places upon the stomach of Adam, while whispering to his spirit, "You must return immediately and not wait. Eve needs you, now."

When Gabriel sees Adam react to his prompting, he grabs Tantzer and races to join Dāwīd and Mehgen' already shielding Adam. The rest of Gabriel's party leave to help Gershom and Emunah, and the others gathered around Eve. Some will break off to shield the child, soon to be born.

Adam stands and picks up the staff he has carved from a twisted limb that he found outside Eden's gate. He then lifts the offending lamb and heads back to camp.

Behind Adam, Tantzer, invisible, sees a shadowy figure approaching from the left of Adam and points it out to Gabriel. In a flash, other shadows appear. Together, they head for Adam. Soon Adam is surrounded by angels battling imposing forces. Their pitched invisible battle rages on, as Adam struggles to get home.

"I am exhausted," Adam thinks. "I searched all day for this lamb. It would be nice to rest a little before heading back. The voice inside my head tells me to return immediately and not to wait. I just can't rid myself of this feeling that Eve needs me, now!"

Adam has heard voices like this many times here in the wilderness. Briefly, he remembers other times when the feeling has been slightly different. He has been concentrating on trying to discern which are from *Yehovah* and feels this is one of those times. It's a force he feels deep in his abdomen. He's learned to trust it.

Aloud, he says, "Little lamb, little lamb, you are so cute. How did you wander so far, so fast? *Yehovah*, hear the prayer of Your servant. Help me to not give in to how tired I am. Help Eve until I can get back to her. You are our defender. My hope is in You, for there is no one else to help us." Adam stumbles, as the last words of his prayer leave his lips. He almost drops the lamb, his fatigue is so great.

"If I had stayed in the camp, I would be there to help. Is this lamb worth losing Eve?" he questions himself. "If Eve had not eaten the fruit I wouldn't have eaten it. I know it, I just know it. Now we struggle so, just to stay alive! Maybe I should just drop the lamb, and run, instead."

At this thought, the lamb strains in his arms, bleating as if to say, please don't leave me. Remembering the lamb in the Garden, Adam wills himself to press on. His mind begins filling again with fearful thoughts and self-recrimination. Each new thought is worse than the last.

"What if *Yehovah* decides to now punish us for our sin and the child is born, but not alive?"

Adam knows their sin means death. Elohim told him so when he was warned not to eat of the fruit of the tree or touch it. He understood, then, what death meant.

"I recall I understood that death meant separation from *Yehovah*, a distance from all that is lovely and pure. Since leaving the Garden, that sense of distance seems to ebb and flow, ever changing. When the starry word was revealed He was close, now He is far away," Adam thinks, confused by all that's changed. He hasn't been able to understand yet, why or how this is happening.

The death that worries him now, though, is physical death. Like what happens when a baby lamb is born, still, or one beast kills another for food. Every time he comes upon a kill like that, it reminds him that he and Eve were the cause of the slaughter. Sometimes the darkness of guilt is almost impossible to contend with. It is then he hears the voice, telling him to go. It says, "Be at peace and encourage yourself in *Yehovah*, Adam. I will make a way for you and Eve."

At this time, a melody springs up from within. Very soon, with it come words that speak a message.

"There is a way over the mountain; there's a way through the sea.
There is a way in the desert," sayeth the Lord, "It's in me.
I'll conquer death's destruction; I will set the captive free.
There is a way over the mountain," sayeth the Lord, "It's in thee.[34]*"*

Gabriel and the angels battle the powers of darkness. It is a full scale engagement. Some are trying to hinder Adam, and steal his peace and joy. If possible, they will try to kill Adam outright, ending the lineage of Adam. As Adam gives in to doubt, the defending angels of light are weakened. As Adam overcomes the doubts, the angels of light are strengthened. Adam's faith and belief become the final arbiter, deciding the outcome of the invisible battle raging around him, vacillating darkness and faith, wrestling for dominance of his mind.

During the battle, Gabriel and Mehgen' are able to secure a place in the attackers' front lines. This affords an opportunity for Tantzer to free himself from the entangled mass, and minister directly to Adam. It is Tantzer, who gives Adam the melody and the words of the song.

The battle continues unabated, until Adam begins to sing. As he sings, the dark attackers grow weaker and their thrusts splinter. By the time

Adam sings the song a third time, the shadows just disappear into the hills and shrubs.

Tantzer smiles as he returns to the front lines, arriving at about the time the last attacker turns away.

"The words just appeared within my mind," he says. "Dvar HaElohim must have sent them. I remember hearing the melody earlier, just before we left Heaven. Outside the Citadel, a group of angels was vocalizing a melody by imitating some of the instruments of worship. Elohim had this covered all the time. His foreknowledge is awesome!"

Adam begins to feel *Yehovah's* peace wash over him as he continues to sing. The more he does, the louder he gets. The louder and longer he sings, the more peace he feels. Soon, he is so full of faith. He thinks he can take on a lion bare-handed and easily come out the winner. The distance seems somehow shortened and then he sees the top of their tents. After setting the rebellious lamb down next to the flock of sheep, he heads toward the tent.

Eve looks ahead, seeking solace from anything within her sight. The birth pains grow in their intensity with each spasm. She places a soft wool blanket over a small patch of sand, and waits. She understands giving birth. She has helped Adam deliver several lambs and goats. Grabbing a limb with both hands, she sits over the blanketed patch of sand, bending forward, and straining, as the pains come upon her. She can feel the baby's movement within and the pressure as the head bears down.

"Lord *Yehovah*, hear the voice of your handmaiden. Be my strength and ever present help in the hour of my need. Do not delay, dear Lord. The hour of my delivery has come."

Eve lifts her head and looks into the distant hills. It is then that she sees the panting leopard, lounging upon a mound of rocks that overlooks the camp. It stares into her eyes. How long it has been there, she doesn't know. It is strange, though. She has never seen a leopard this close to the camp because of the dogs. This one just sits there watching, occasionally raising its head sniffing the air. The leopard is downwind of the camp site, the predator's preferred place of attack, in order to remain undetected by the dogs.

"Is he here for me? Or my child?" she wonders, while panic develops. "How shall I defend myself?"

Just as the final agony consumes her concentration, the leopard springs forward, sensing a gap in Eve's defenses. She wants, desperately, to give up. Through the painful haze, from somewhere, she hears a loud yell.

"Heeeyyyeeee!"

"Is that the Leopard?" she thinks as she shuts her eyes, waiting to feel his teeth rip into her, and wondering if this wouldn't be a relief.

As she reaches to catch the dropping child, she again hears a yell, "Geeettttt oooouuuuttta here!"

At that, the startled leopard turns and bolts off, into the underbrush. It will have to find a meal somewhere else tonight. Lifting the newborn child to see its face, she turns to see what could have made the awful noise. It is Adam, running, waving, and tossing stones at the place where the leopard had been.

With a sigh, shaking his head, Adam slows to a jog and heads toward Eve. Bending over, trying to catch his breath, he finds her crying and laughing, all the while cuddling a crying infant.

All the angels gather around Adam, Eve and the child. Duplicating the example set by years of watching Adam perform his ministry, she

237

names the little boy, Cain. The forces protecting Eve and the child are joined by Gabriel, Tantzer and those who surrounded Adam, as he made his trek with the lost lamb. Together, the angels stand a careful guard over the newly enlarged family. For now, a crisis has been averted. The enemy lured the lamb away from the flock to lead Adam to the chase, so that Eve would be alone. He planned to send the hyenas to disrupt the protection around Eve with the purpose of preparing an opening for the leopard's attack.

Gabriel knows that Adam, Eve, and Cain will never realize the full measure of protection the assigned angels had provided.

In the distance, Gabriel sees the outline of a shadow lurking and watching. Slowly the shadow, in the shape of a grotesque creature, turns away as Adam falls to his knees, and hugs Eve and the child.

That night Adam builds an altar and names the place, "*Yehovah Who Knows*."

EDEN LOST

Added to joyful anticipation of their first child's birth was the question whether he would be the promised child, they read about, written in the stars.

Promised child or not, with the birth of Cain, adjustments had to be made to the established order of the first family. The first several years, most of the new burden fell upon Eve. During those early years, Adam's added responsibilities consisted, only, of frolicking with Cain when he had time. All of this impacted upon the couple's private moments.

Through some trial and error, they've divided up the work. Besides Cain and his demands, Eve continues doing the chores and tending to the small garden of greens and vegetables, which she prepares for their meals, along with whatever Adam is able to gather. Adam prods the flock of sheep, and hunts for food.

Complicating this arrangement is his flock's need for fresh grazing land and its conflict with her garden. Relocating the camp must always wait until the garden crop is harvested. Adam's concern regarding leaving Eve with Cain alone at night complicates matters ever so much more.

Day after day, the new order is repeated. Each spring begins a new growing season. If they've moved, the area selected for the garden is cleared, rocks removed, the soil tilled, and then planted. Fifteen years after leaving the Garden, Adam introduced a new custom. When the garden is planted, he pulls a knotted rope from a special sack he made from sheep skin. It is usually kept inside the tent. With the rope in his hand, he thanks *Yehovah* for His mercy and provision, and then ties another knot in the rope, thus keeping track of years. A knot for a year.

They hadn't seen the hyenas or the leopard again, since the day of Cain's birth. There has been an occasional predator, but not those. Predators are a constant threat. Training the dogs has been accomplished and they are working well. They always alert Adam and Eve whenever a predatory animal is nearby, although this means there are many more mouths to feed.

Balancing time for *Yehovah*, and overcoming the curse, takes so much time. It seems to make doing it all, impossible. As Cain grows older, he too, demands more of their time, but he is also a source of amusement and satisfaction. They remember their own early efforts at learning, as they watch him grow. Their very own child! What stories they plan to tell Cain when he is older. Adam smiles, joyously, when he thinks of the things they will do together. Cain is a strong sprout in a forest clearing. How large and how fruitful he will be remains a family mystery.

Adam and Eve have several such mysteries for which they anxiously await illumination. Right here and now, safety, provisions, and raising Cain are most important. Like his father, Cain is handsome and muscular. The older he gets, the more he demonstrates his own interests. Like his father, Cain prefers exploring over other chores. He is fearless, resourceful, and very determined.

"It won't take many more years and he will be frustrated by limiting his exploration to the outer edges of our camp," Eve often says. The only unsettling characteristic that she perceives is an exaggerated resistance to authority.

While still in the Garden, they felt a prompting, later confirmed by *Yehovah*, to establish an annual commemoration. It seemed vital to continue it, when they had been expelled. Just as with everything else, they've decided it is important to include Cain in the commemoration tradition.

Just after planting the garden and the sheep are sheared and new lambs are born, it is the time for remembering. Though they certainly hadn't planned it this way, it turns out to also coincide with Cain's birth. Each year, Eve makes cakes from some of the last measures of flour she has saved from the previous harvest, and pours some wild honey over them. It is a treat Adam has loved. Now that he is older, Cain, too, loves the cakes, refusing to share more than one small cake with Adam and a smaller cake for Eve.

This year is the fourth planting after Cain's birth. Adam has decided Cain is old enough to understand what it means and should, there-fore, join them. As before, Adam and Eve begin their day of rest after watering and bedding the flock of sheep. They sit together around a fire, singing some songs of praise and thanksgiving, still remembering tones from their time in Eden. Their favorite is a melody remembered from that one windy, blissful day. It was so special they even gave it a name. They call it, "The Wind Song."

Adam and Eve have beautiful singing voices. In spite of the persistent difficulties each year, they are learning to trust *Yehovah* for more than what is provided for their sustenance. They are thankful for so many things. Most of all, they are thankful that the measure of death, they are now experiencing, still permits a relationship with *Yehovah*. They are also thankful for the promise in, and of, Cain.

The commemorative is a festive meal, punctuated by a liturgy, and honored by the offering, unto *Yehovah*, of an unblemished lamb. The meal is a banquet of food, a time of celebration, rejoicing, and delight in being alive.

The liturgy is one they recite by heart. Its fundamental questions and answers create a different kind of banquet. Each subsequent season, after the bowls that Adam has fashioned have been cleared, the prayers are offered. It begins just as it did in the initial season. The first time, Adam asked the question that is now the question of invocation.

"*Yehovah*, how did we come to be and how did this world and garden come to be?"

Before Cain's birth, and until he was old enough, it was Eve's honor to ask it, "Please tell me again. How did we come to be?"

This year is the first for Cain to have this honor and he asks, "Father, tell me please. How did we come to be?"

Whereupon, Adam now recites the liturgy he memorized while in the Garden, "In the beginning, each growing season, I asked, '*Yehovah*, how did we come to be and how did this world and garden come to be?'

"His reply was in the form of two questions, 'My son, my daughter, which account would you like me to tell you? Would you like to hear My testimony as *The Creator* or My testimony as *The First Witness*?'

"To which we reply, '*Yehovah*, You know all things, please choose for us!'

"And so, He chose. When *Yehovah* chose to testify as *The Creator,* He would begin his testimony with, 'This is the generation of the *heavens and the Earth*, as I created them...'

"When He testified as *The First Witness,* He would begin His testimony with, 'This is the generation of the *heavens and the Garden,* for I was there. I am the first and true witness of all things coming to be.' These words, He would say, depending upon which beginning He chose. Each testimony of the beginning had a different emphasis and therefore a different beginning.

"He taught me the beginnings of all things. So now, I tell you His testimony, just as He taught me.

"The word of *Yehovah* following these things was the same each time He testified, as it was the first season that He told me...and so this year, the first when Cain asks the invocation, I tell the rest of His testimony of the beginning."

Since leaving Eden, Adam and Eve felt they must add their part to the testimony of Yehovah. So beginning the first season after they left, Adam finished speaking the Word of Yehovah's testimony just as it was given unto them. So this season Cain asks the second question, "Papa, why then are we not in the Garden?"

Adam, with joy over Cain's words echoing in his heart, repeats the rest of the commemoration's liturgy, "This is our generation in the Garden. In the Garden, there appeared a serpent. It was more subtle than any beast in the Garden. In due time, the serpent said…"

When the benediction comes, together, the first family repeats, "This is a memorial unto all our people, even unto the end of time. It shall be told to those who come after, even when they return to the dust. Let this memorial be told so all may know and understand from whence they have come, and why the precepts of life are as they are. *Yehovah* did not cast us out without hope. For written in the skies above, He wrote a promise of One who shall come and save us from the deeds we have committed."

In the season when Cain is 8 years old, when the meal, liturgy and sacrifice come to a close, his mother says, with a smile, "Cain. You, my son, will soon have a brother. You will have someone to share this life with, to play with and to whom you will teach all that you have learned."

Cain, turning his eyes away from his mother's embrace, asks his own question, "Mother, what is a brother?"

He is only partially listening as she makes the explanation to him. He is speculating, "I wonder if this is something I am going to like, or not?"

Eve's announcement means adjustments have to be made to the order of things. Adam and Eve's limited, extra time, once exclusively devoted to Cain, has to be reduced. Clothes for an infant have to be made by Eve. The tent where Adam, Eve, and Cain sleep has to be expanded or a new one created, for the older child to sleep in, by himself. That requires planning. The number of sheep in the flock has to be increased, so the older sheep can provide wool for the additional tent.

Cain, reluctantly, is doing his part, but as time gets closer to the birth, he's spending a good deal of his time telling his parents how he thinks this expansion should be handled. The young lad's fancies, which had initially amused Adam and Eve, have now become unwanted and annoying. Cain doesn't seem to notice their displeasure, though, because he keeps on correcting Eve, when Adam ceases listening.

When Eve can, she tries ignoring him, but that simply leads to Cain teasing the working dogs. All in all, the news of someone else and the inherent need to compete for his parents' approval is not lost on Cain.

"Adam and his family have developed a new order to their lives, and, accordingly, we are going to have to make some adjustments," I alert the troupe.

"Lairn'r has noticed an increased presence of the powers of darkness, investigating our perimeter."

Adam and Eve are more practiced in their balanced walk with *Yehovah*. They readily welcome His presence, enjoy listening to His commands, and seek greater understanding of the Word of Elohim, as it is written in the skies.

Satan still tries, although it appears unsuccessful, to destroy Cain. The vigilance of Eve, no longer the serpent's accomplice, serves as the primary protector when Adam is away. She isn't conscious of the presence of Elohim's covenant partners, whose responsibility all three of them are. However, satan is.

"Now, with the arrival of another child, she might let her guard down," I muse.

"Where do you think the attack will come from?" questions Komodo`r. "Cain is the most vulnerable one, but because he hasn't matured enough yet to be accountable for his actions, we have added more than enough ministering angels to guard him. Even at this young age, there remains a measure of free will. That won't change just because there is another child. We will add as many angels, as needed."

Cain's birth was an adventure for Adam, Eve, and those responsible for protecting, and ministering, to the family of Adam. We all wonder what lies ahead.

In the fullness of time, in accordance with the law of man, once again, Eve will be the mother of life. She gives birth to another son, whom she names, "Abel." His name means, "breathing spirit." The baby is highly favored from birth. Thick, curly, dark hair and a glowing complexion combine for a handsome child. The birth, too, is uneventful. Adam stays close to the camp before the birth. As further protection, they've trained a dog to fetch Adam upon command. The problem of having Cain in the way is solved by Eve.

She tells Adam of an idea she has to keep Cain busy. Since he is now old enough to help his mother cook, and is oh, so careful around the camp fire, Eve thinks they should just ask Cain to boil some water, when the time comes.

So it is, when the time is close at hand, Adam says to Cain, "Son, we need some boiling water. Be so kind to take this vessel, go down to the stream nearby, get us some fresh clean water and boil it. Keep a close eye on it, so you can bring it to me, as soon as we call for it."

With a suspicious look upon his face, he leaves the birthing tent and does as he is told. By the time Cain has the water prepared, Eve has presented the family with a new male member. Abel.

Just as Cain enters the birthing tent, Adam takes the water and tells his firstborn, "Thank you, son. Well done."

While Cain watches with big eyes, Adam dips a woolen cloth into the hot water. He wrings it out and refreshes Eve's face and arms, washing her with the warm wet cloth.

Cain stands to the side, watching Adam, until Eve waves at Cain, and says, "Come son, come closer."

With some hesitation, Cain moves closer to his mother, and sees the bundled newborn in his mother's arms. He tries to lean into Eve for her reassuring embrace, but his mother says, "Not now Cain. Wait until I feed your brother."

There is much to do, now that a baby is in the camp. Adam and Eve remind Cain that he is expected to help take care of his brother and teach him what he has learned. Cain slowly nods his head up and down, but he thinks, "This is a lot of fuss over something so small. Lambs are born every year without this fuss. What makes this so special? And he doesn't do anything, except whimper, spit up or sleep."

His eyes stare at the infant occupying the arms in which, until now, he nestled. Adam, recognizing Cain's need, picks him up and together they head off to go wading in a nearby stream. Just when Cain begins to forget his feelings of rejection, the flocks need grazing and the garden must be weeded. Adam tries to take Cain along, but Cain shows little interest in tending the sheep. His interests are centered on improving things in camp. Adam's ideas aren't as good as his. Always staying within sight of the fancy baby, Cain does his own thing.

"Son, I will have to take the flock beyond the hills, off to the south today. Get my staff and bring one for yourself, and let's go," Adam says. This suggestion occurs many times. Adam is intent on involving his son in the work that he does.

"Papa," always, Cain replies. "The way you constructed the gate to the pen is not right. I've got an idea that will do it better. When I get done, then I will come and help you."

The problem is that Cain never comes to help. He starts, but never finishes, doing things in a different, "better" way. And, year by year, the knots in the rope increase. Cain and Abel grow older, increasing in stature and learning.

In the fourth year after Abel's birth, following the planting of the crops, the sheep shearing, and delivering the baby lambs, Eve prepares a large mound of honey cakes. Adam calls for a day of rest. Once preparations have been made, Adam, Eve, Cain, and Abel gather around the fire. With the songs and the prayers offered, Eve gently pokes Cain in the ribs, and whispers, "Ok son, it is now time to ask the questions."

Cain has been asking the questions for the past eight growing seasons, since Eve passed the honor to him. This time, though, he pouts. He surprises everyone when he asks, instead, "Why do we do the same thing every growing season? I hear them every year and they don't make sense. The two stories disagree! Anyway, I'm tired of these old stories!"

The audacity of this question catches us off guard. A quick look around the area, surrounding the gathering at the fire, doesn't reveal any lurking shadows. The inability of angels to read man's mind isn't a liability, but it certainly isn't an asset either.

"Komodo`r, have you seen any princes of darkness around the campsite?" I ask. "That would explain this question."

"No, there aren't any dark spirits anywhere near the family. There haven't been any in over a week. Where do you think it came from?" he replies, answering my question, and asking a bigger one.

"It is the seed of satan. The seed that infected man, and has been within him, since the Garden," Lairn'r ruminates, his posture fixed in an aggressive pose.

"That seed isn't always so apparent, but it seems to have grown within Cain into a rebellious sprout. It is manifested when Adam and Eve quarrel, though they seldom do. I have been told that when the baby loses its temper, there is evidence of it, as well. This, from Cain, is rebellion!"

"So, you are saying that this impertinent attitude of Cain is satan's nature seed, becoming mature in Cain?" I direct my question to Lairn`r.

"Yes. The hedge of protection cannot protect Cain from something within him. That would break the law of free will. The same law we couldn't break in order to keep Eve from eating of the Tree of the Knowledge of Good and Evil," he explains. "We know foolishness is in the heart of a child. Only correction and discipline have a chance to alter his mind, or development of twinges within his soul sense, called, 'pangs of conscience.' If Cain continues to rebel, if he makes a lifestyle of it, that will breach our protection. Then the dark spirits can exploit that breach and minimize our power to protect him."

Tantzer arrives before the Viewing Window overlooking the camp, and wonders, "I hope Cain hasn't asked the questions yet. I like that part of their celebration."

"Cain refused!" declares Komodo`r.

"Refused! Did you say, 'Refused'?" Tantzer rejoins. "Why?"

"That is what we are discussing," I respond.

"Lairn'r says it is the seed of sin, or more accurately, seed of satan. The consequence of having eaten of that fruit."

"Oh, my!" Tantzer retorts. "Man seems determined to tempt Elohim, and be the cause of his own destruction.

"What is Adam, or Eve, doing about it?" Tantzer continues, totally perplexed.

It has been only a single second, since Cain voiced his defiance. Time enough for us to talk about it and for Tantzer to join us. Folding his wings, he settles beside Komodo`r, who is still looking through the Window.

"Son," Adam gently replies, "you are old enough to decide for yourself. If you don't want to ask the questions, you don't have to. You are, also, old enough to know that asking the questions is an important observance of who we are and a way of remembering from whence we come. As for what you have said about the two accounts disagreeing... they don't disagree, they agree. They are just different views of the same thing. Like when your Mother picks a gourd from the garden. If you look at it from one end, it looks almost round. If you look at it from the other end, it has several different sides with no two of them looking alike. Looking at it from the side, it has lines dividing it the long way, but those divisions are not always equal. That is the mystery of *Yehovah's* testimony, told to us, by Him, in the Garden."

"Cain, ask the questions," Adam insists firmly, "don't compound our foolishness with your own."

All Cain does is purse his lips and shake his head, no.

Adam, having no choice, turns to Abel and says, "Abel, my son, it is a few years, yet, that your brother is to do this, but are you ready to ask the questions?"

"Yes, my honored Father. I am ready to ask the questions," Abel gushes with great enthusiasm.

"I am so glad you asked me. Last year, I hoped you would ask me. Cain had the honor, but now, of a certainty, I am ready."

"Please be blessed and proceed," Adam says, with pride.

"Tell me again, Father. Tell me again, Papa. How did we come to be?" Abel asks, glowing with a proud smile.

Without further hesitation, or distraction, Adam repeats the memorized liturgy. For the first time in quite a while, it has increased meaning.

As Adam proceeds, Cain sits down, and politely waits until the commemoration is concluded. Then, Cain rises to his feet and walks into the dark of evening. He has much to think about.

Just before he disappears beyond the fire light, Adam calls out to him, "Cain, my son! We love you, and we want *Yehovah's* blessing to rest upon you." Adam's calling voice trails off, as Cain moves farther away, ignoring or not hearing, his father.

"So!" Komodo`r says, "Cain, too, is like a god, knowing good and evil. He has reached the age where he must answer to Elohim for his deeds."

"Yes," Lairn`r answers. "The candle light of his spirit is fading. This we recognized earlier, during the planting. Now he must answer to Yehovah, just like his parents. Sin stands at the opening to his tent. Its desire is toward Cain and the law of free will judges him."

Later, when other chronicles look back upon this time and write of things yet to be, they all will say, "It was a time of unstitching, unfaithfulness, antipathy, laced with perplexity."

A Son is Given

Cain has had enough.

The spring of his sixteenth year, Cain comes to Adam repeating a frequent complaint, "I don't understand it, Father. I work hard, tend the crops, pull the weeds, and still I lose half the crop to drought, or some wild animal eats the sprouts. Everything is against me.

"Mother's garden doesn't have the same problems as mine," he whines.

After Cain's miracle birth, Adam and Eve soon recognized that Cain wasn't the child promised in *Yehovah's* writing in the heavens. Cain is a handsome young man. He is highly favored with looks, strength, and knowledge. None of this helps grow crops, however. He can use a bow better than Abel, but not better, yet, than his father. He runs like the wind for great distances, without tiring.

Since he showed no interest in shepherding, Adam spent a great deal of his free time with Cain instructing him in the raising of crops. The method he taught was the one Adam learned in the Garden.

"When we were in the Garden there was never a drought, nor could there be. Water lifted every day as dew. Every morning the leaves were wet with moisture," Adam explains. "You've been so inventive when it comes to the advice you bestow upon your Mother and me, why don't you pray to *Yehovah* and ask for a solution."

Cain listens, but he has heard it all before.

When he is just over twenty-four years of age, his father says to him, "Cain, my son, you are not devoting your life to *Yehovah*. You understand, I cannot answer for your deeds…or your brother's." This is not the first time his father has stressed the need for him to connect his life to *Yehovah*.

Once again, Cain flips what he is told into an offensive response. "Abel isn't doing his share, Father. Can't he help me with the crops? You gave him a flock to shepherd. All he has to do is sit and watch. That gives him a lot of time to think about things," Cain complains. His criticism is foreign to Adam.

"How can someone, who sees the importance of life every day, complain about the effort it takes to nurture it?" Adam wonders.

"Son, as our firstborn, you were free to choose to tend sheep or raise food. You have mastered watering the crops, even if the dew fails to come during the night. The ditches you made, bringing water from the wells you have dug, speak highly of your ingenuity and hard work. Abel still has to wander, ever farther and farther, to find grazing for his flock. If I have failed to repeat it enough, I tell you again. I am proud of you and your skills," Adam reassures his struggling son.

Adam reaches to embrace his firstborn, surrounding him with his loving arms. Cain allows the embrace, but Adam feels little warmth returned. His lack of warmth has been apparent since Abel started asking the memorial questions.

It is common knowledge between his parents that Abel is a youth close to their hearts, even though they recognize that he is not, either, the child of promise. Eden feels further away every year.

"The strain between the two young men is growing," Tantzer senses and announces. It has been quite a long time, since he had visited the first family's camp sites.

"The family, as you describe them, Lairn`r, has placed a considerable footprint upon the pages of Eternity."

"It is troubling that four created beings live in such discord, when they depend upon each other so much," Lairn`r returns this unsettling revelation to Tantzer. "Ever since the candle of Yehovah was snuffed out within Cain, the discord has been an increasing influence upon the family, growing greater with every passing season. While reacting differently to the discord, each of them is forever choosing to avoid a resolution."

"And what resolution do you suggest, Lairn`r?" Komodo`r challenges, he has been listening silently to his covenant partners, as they watch the unfolding drama through the Window.

"They need Elohim to intercede. He always brings peace, but only Adam, Eve, and Abel pray for a solution. Cain, when he prays, only prays selfish things, ignoring the needs of the others. They have a threefold chord, yet Cain always chooses to go it alone!" Tantzer chimes in with great zeal.

"Dāwīd, Mehgen', Gershom, and Emunah have tried distraction, quickened memories, and songs, sung by the winds, to lay a foundation for reconciliation. These strategies move Adam, Eve and Abel. However, they only harden Cain. He is making so many wrong choices. He then complains, when he receives the fruit of those choices. The law of sowing and reaping always returns crops based upon the seed planted. Cain should know that. He sees it in the natural, yet is blind to it in the spiritual," Komodo`r sums up the obvious for the listeners.

The season for the memorial becomes the focus of the family. For a week, preparations are made. Eve serves triple duty...wife, mother of two competing children, and attending priest. Adam plays husband, referee, and high priest in this memorial scene. Cain is the reluctant observer. Abel has been the witness for years, now, asking the honored questions.

Adam has, until this year, selected the proper offering, from the family's flock, for them to offer to *Yehovah*. It was as He had taught them, by slaying the sacrificial lamb to cover their sin. Adam has remained faithful to explain to Eve, Cain, and Abel how sin separated them from *Yehovah*, and how it is necessary for a yearly blood sacrifice to cover the previous year's sins, if *Yehovah's* favor is to abide for another year.

"This we do in remembrance of our beginnings and the reason that the lamb was sacrificed in the Garden. We will do this until the child promised in the heavens is born, therefore removing our sin from us, so we can return to the Garden," Adam teaches each year.

Cain was tolerant of his father's efforts to prepare everything. When Abel was given the responsibility of a flock, Cain was caught between his feelings about his brother, and reluctance to perform the memorial, as his father has said it need be done.

As the year moves on, Cain is troubled because he cannot find an answer to his dilemma. He thinks of making a pilgrimage to the Garden gate. That might be enough for his father. When he hints of his idea to them, his mother says, no, fearing that he might be harmed by predators or the flame. Cain knows she fears the leopard, who, she has said, tried to kill him when he was born. He's thought about just leaving, but where could he go?

"Father," Cain asks, several weeks before the pending memorial, "what crops I have are almost harvested."

"Well done, son," Adam says, trying to encourage his firstborn, while hoping this conversation will end well. It seems that, of late, nothing involving Cain seems to work out right.

"Father," Cain interrupts Adam's efforts to shear a struggling sheep. "Sorry to interrupt you, but I want to prepare an offering for *Yehovah*."

"Okay, take a suitable portion of your crop and offer it to your brother, and ask him for a lamb to sacrifice. *Yehovah* has taught us, it must be without blemish or sickness. Remember, your offering must be a blood offering as a memorial covering for your sins this past year," Adam patiently repeats the proper sin offering.

"Father," Cain says, in his most persuading manner.

"Yes, son," Adam replies, giving up on shearing and letting the sheep go, for now.

"I don't believe that *Yehovah* only accepts a blood sacrifice. Why won't he accept one from the work I have done. Why does it have to be something from the work that Abel has done?" Cain questions. He is still trying to find another way around the problem.

"Well, my son. It isn't about us. The only thing we bring to the memorial is our sin. When your Mother and I sinned in the Garden, all we could bring was our dead selves. We had nothing to offer to remove our guilt and shame, except our lives. Life is in the blood. *Yehovah* slew an innocent lamb, so that our shame was covered. A lamb that had been my own constant companion was sacrificed, so that your Mother and I might have a chance at redemption. You know what redemption is, don't you?" Adam asks Cain.

"Yes, it is returning to the state you were in, in the Garden before you sinned, standing, innocent before *Yehovah*. It is as if you hadn't ever sinned," Cain says, reciting the lessons from his father's past.

"Very good!" Adam says, confirming, with a measure of relief, Cain's knowledge.

"The only atonement is blood...yours, mine, your Mother's, a lamb. Someday, as *Yehovah* has written in the heavens, there is the promise of a child born who will be the real living sacrifice. Until then, an innocent lamb must die so you can live, and live under *Yehovah's* favor and shield, another year."

The day celebrating the memorial has always been, until recently, a day of rejoicing. Abel leads his flock to a location he had picked out near the family camp, which he had intentionally preserved by preventing his flock from grazing there.

Abel selects a small lamb from his flock, being careful to choose one that has no blemish and isn't sickly. He has watched his father make this choice, since he was very young. He approaches the solemn occasion with reverence, for his father, and *Yehovah*. His father's accounts about the Garden, and their early days outside the Garden, always touch him, deeply. He knows *Yehovah* is real and is a rewarder of all those who seek Him. Abel is determined to, faithfully, do so.

In years past, Adam has undertaken to provide an acceptable sacrifice to *Yehovah* for the whole family. This year's memorial celebration will be different. Their plan is for Adam to offer his and Eve's offering first. As the head of the family gathered before *Yehovah* it is his responsibility to do so. This is as it has been.

There is a difference this year, however. Cain and Abel have each chosen to have their own individual campsites, a short distance from Adam and Eve's. Because of their age, Adam feels it is incumbent upon the two sons to individually provide an acceptable offering, at their individual camps, since they are now accountable for their sins.

At the proper time during the memorial, Adam picks up the lamb that has been lying on its side beside the stone altar he has built. Adam places it upon a nest of twigs and branches that have been ceremonially placed there.

"Such an innocent thing, you are," Adam thinks. "You must die that we might live and have intimacy with *Yehovah*."

In the normal course of the evening, Adam places his hands upon the lamb and prays. In an act of faith, all Adam's and Eve's sins of commission and omission are passed to the lamb. Adam then raises his right hand, while holding tightly to a knife that was crafted so long ago. It is one that is used only for the yearly memorial. Down Adam strikes, and slays, the innocent lamb.

Again, Adam prays, "*Yehovah, Yehovah*, righteous judge of Eternity. See the blood of the innocent lamb and cover our sin for another year."

Adam pauses, extends a flaming ember that was prepared earlier in the afternoon, and reaches into the twigs and branches. Quickly, they ignite and soon flames rise to consume the twigs and the branches, licking the dead lamb, turning it all into ashes.

Silently, Adam and Eve turn their faces to the Earth. In time, stillness engulfs the worshipping parents, whose thoughts begin to wander. Together, they reach out, searching for assurance that *Yehovah* has found their sons to be faithful.

Seated in front of the Viewing Window, a chorus of angels watches man's celebration. They gather here, yearly, to observe, along with man, the remembrance of what was and conviction in what is promised. As the years have come and gone, the divergent paths of Cain and Abel have added new drama to the plight of man's sojourn.

Adam and Eve have found sure footing, choosing to abide in *Yehovah's* mercy. The word, written in the heavens, encourages them. Each reading refreshes a hope of their return, someday, to the Garden. Sometimes, they wonder aloud, if *Yehovah* shares in the same hope.

"Elohim has accepted Adam and Eve's sacrifice. They have peace with Elohim and the Hedge remains around them for another year. And so, our ministry to them also continues. I know Dāwīd, Mehgen', Gershom, and Emunah are rejoicing over Elohim's acceptance. Their bond with these two seems to grow with each passing year. They take fewer furloughs, now, than when man first left Eden," Lairn'r says, summing up for the attending angels.

"It is as Elohim purposed it," I add.

With a wave of my hand, the scene changes from Adam and Eve's campsite to an inclusive view of Cain's camp and Abel's. I quickly apologize, since I've done so, without having inquired if anyone has an objection.

Before us, we now see both brothers preparing their individual sacrifices. Abel has a tied lamb, resting quietly at his feet. We see him making final adjustments to the brushwood which he has laid upon a stone altar. He had gathered them last evening, and carefully covered them, to protect them from the regular morning dew.

Cain, too, has his own cluster of branches. We watch him stack them upon a hastily assembled stone altar of his own. Beside his feet is a sampling of the crops he has raised.

"Cain's altar is a lot different from Abel's, don't you think?" Lairn`r asks us.

"Yes, but remember. It isn't in the beauty of the altar that matters to Elohim, but the heart. What matters is if Cain's heart is perfect toward Elohim." I adjust Lairn`r's point, "I think, the issue to concern ourselves with is the sacrifice."

Komodo`r adds, "The law of sin and death demands a blood covering for sin. It is a declared and demonstrated law. Dvar HaElohim slew the lamb when Adam and Eve sinned in the Garden. Each memorial, since then, there has been a blood sacrifice. A lamb, without spot or blemish is sacrificed, just as Adam and Eve, this year, have done. Each memorial, Dvar HaElohim demonstrates His acceptance by consuming the sacrifice with fire as He has this year."

"Every memorial the sacrifice has been accepted," Tantzer reminds us. He then asks, "Is it a sin if a substitute is offered?"

"Yes, it would be a sin of omission." Lairn`r states, "Although, it is a sin that can be covered by a proper blood offering, if there is true repentance of the disobedience."

Those angels in front lean over, totally engrossed, resting their heads upon closed hands.

We observe Ha-brit and Alexis, Abel's guardian angels, standing, alongside Abel, as he kneels before the altar and prays, "Great merciful *Yehovah*. *Yehovah* of my Father and my Mother, look upon this freely offered sacrifice. By your word, written in the heavens and from days of old, You alone are *Yehovah*. And You have promised to pass over my sin if it is covered by the blood. I pray that You reveal unto me Your acceptance, by consuming the sacrifice by fire."

At that moment, Abel reaches forth and sets a flame to the wood. As he does so, Ha-brit, Alexis, and those of us who are watching, see HaRuach rest upon the sacrifice in the form of a dove. With Dvar HaElohim's confirmation, Alexis touches the sacrifice and it bursts into flame, rapidly consuming that which is on the altar.

As we watch, there are many sets of eyes that witness this spectacle. While some look on approvingly, others watch with distain.

Fernez, Cain's probationary guardian angel, observes and recognizes Dvar HaElohim's acceptance of Abel's sacrifice. With waning hope, Fernez looks upon his charge, and sees fire ignite in Cain's eyes, eyes that have not yet looked favorably upon his brother's ministry unto Dvar HaElohim.

"*Yehovah*, this past year has been difficult for me. It is more than I can bear. My crops will barely sustain me through the next year. You told my Father and Mother, by the sweat of my brow, I would toil and labor. And, so I have. I labor night and day, cultivating the crops I have planted, and though morning dew rests upon the hills around me, very little rests upon my crops. So, accept my sacrifice, grown by my own hands. May it cover my sin, so this coming year my crops will be plentiful."

With these words, Cain reaches with a modestly burning limb, into the dry branches beneath his sacrifice. The flame ignites the branches, but before it reaches the stems of Cain's harvested sacrifice, the flame flickers, weakly, and dies.

We in the Observatory, and the three guardian angels encamped around Cain and Abel witness a new first upon Earth. Because HaRuach has rejected the memorial sacrifice, Fernez is constrained from lighting it. Cain stands there, frustrated, and tries again to ignite the branches. He even tears a piece of wool from his garment, attempting to ignite it, but nothing is able to sustain a flame. Finally, the embers of the limb he is using to light the branches simply die.

We witness Cain become uncontrollably angry, his features twisted in rage.

Suddenly, out of the heavens, we hear the voice of Adonai thunder, asking Cain, "Why are you angry? Why is your visage fallen? If you do what is right, you shall be accepted. If you do not do what is right, sin waits at the throne to your heart. Unto you is its desire."

Cain sits, his head down, before the altar he built. His sacrifice and branches are blowing in the chilling wind.

"Who cares!" he exclaims aloud.

"*Yehovah's* standards are too high," his heart speaks, thinking no one is listening.

With this, the last resistance to sin echoing in the ears of his guardian angel, Fernez, who is invisible to Cain, lifts his mighty wings. High over the head of Cain, with one powerful stroke, Fernez arches straight into the heavens above. He comes to an unneeded rest only once, long enough to take a final look at the created man beneath him. His commission over, a different set of angels will cover the post. And he is gone.

"Cain, I have another unblemished lamb nearby. Let me get it for you. Then your sacrifice will be accepted, too," Abel says, volunteering to help, when he sees Cain's fire has died.

That gesture is all that Cain can take. When Abel turns around to get the offered lamb, Cain acts swiftly. To the astonishment of both Ha-brit and Alexis, Cain strikes Abel on the head with a stone, just missing Ha-brit's hand that he reflexively extends.

Abel collapses to the ground, while angelic witnesses stare, shocked, and Cain dashes away.

Alexis hastily kneels beside Abel's motionless body. As the final glimmer of life leaves, Abel opens his eyes and sees Alexis in a glowing gown. A smile shines on Abel's face as, his physical eyes closing, he gives up his spirit.

All the appointed guardian angels watch, as the spirit of the first of man to die returns to Elohim, who gave it. Deep within, they know. Their understanding of man's makeup is correct. Man is a soul, who has the spirit of Elohim. While he lives in the physical realm, he inhabits a body Elohim created for him.

With life now gone from Abel's body, and simultaneously, with the spirit of Abel returned to Elohim, Alexis lifts Abel's soul from within his Earthly body, and looks into the wide eyes of a fully conscious, still smiling, Abel.

Immediately following his deed, Cain returns to his camp and has a visitation.

Adonai says to him, "What have you done? The voice of Abel cries out to me from the ground.

"Behold now you are cursed upon the Earth which has opened her mouth to receive your brother's blood; when you till the ground, from here forth, it shall not give you its strength; you will be a fugitive and a vagabond upon Earth."

Cain says unto Adonai, "My punishment is greater than I can bear. Behold, You have cast me out of the face of the Earth; from Your face I will be hid; I will be a fugitive and a vagabond in the Earth; and it shall come to pass, that every one that finds me will try to kill me."

Adonai responds, "Therefore whoever kills Cain, will receive vengeance that is seven times more grievous than the judgment upon Cain." With that judgment Adonai places a mark upon Cain.

Then Cain leaves the presence of Adonai, his father, Adam and his mother, Eve. His heart so hardened, he can think only of himself.

We watch the changes unfold as a group of angels, whose ministry is different from our own, take their leave of Heaven's beauty and pass through the Viewing Window. Their destination is the land of Nod. There they will stand their post. Their commission is to bring Elohim's judgment upon all Cain's labors.

THE BLOOD TESTIMONY

Mesmerized, we watch this tragedy visited upon Adam and Eve. Through their repentance, and in submission to Dvar HaElohim's unseen hand, they had formed a purposeful life. The genesis of this recent chaos was their disobedience. The reconciliation of this disobedience, Elohim's campaign against Lucifer, and man's redemption, can come only from Elohim.

I am troubled. So entrenched am I, within the confines of my limited understanding, that I am barely conscious of the foursome huddling around me. A touch on my shoulder brings me, unwillingly, back to the present.

"Zukher, what does all this mean?" Komodo`r asks me.

I am so surprised by the question, even more so by the one who is asking, I fumble the baton of leadership.

"It must mean we have failed to fulfill our assigned task. There, on the screen, a righteous young man is dead. We did not sufficiently antici-pate this. The idea that satan, or those of his legion, might try to commit this deed is conceivable, but not this! Perhaps we could have prevented this calamity!" Lairn`r proclaims in a loud voice, raising the specter of Eternity's gavel, delivering its sentence of judgment.

"Somehow, all of our endeavors and devoted preparation to the con-trary, we missed the mark. This catastrophe has occurred, despite our incorporation of man's fall into the equation. Because of that, Abel lies lifeless. It seems to us to be our failure. We never considered the possibility of such an untoward event, nor were we ready for the perpetration of such a dastardly act of destruction," Komodo`r laments, his broad shoulders noticeably drooping.

Tantzer says the most, by saying nothing. This moment's absence of his natural playfulness tells me just how much his reasoning is shaken by Abel's murder.

Gabriel, standing off to one side, is the only one exhibiting anything positive. He fidgets first on his left foot, and then on his right, while seeming to start saying something and then pulling back, reconsidering his notions.

"What do you have for us, Gabriel?" I ask, curious to learn what his eyes say is something important.

Before Gabriel can answer, he is called to an audience with Michael and our attention is drawn, once more, to the Window. The renewed motion there catches our interest and temporarily silences our self-inquisition.

Quietly, Ha-brit hovers at tree top level, along with Alexis, who is carrying Abel's fully conscious soul. These three hang there, just over the recently vacated lifeless body of Abel.

"If that is me, then who am I?" Abel asks, and quickly follows the first question with a second. "Who are you?" he continues, turning toward Alexis, his eyes growing wider.

Alexis says, "Well, Abel, son of Adam and Eve, the firstborn of the sons of Adonai, that is your body. That which is your body`, Abel, is of Earth and, in time, it will become Earth again. You are Abel, or the soul of Abel. Your spirit has rejoined Adonai. These are the three parts, making up the presence of Abel within Eternity.

"As for who we are...we are angels. We are part of the ministry of Adonai unto you. We have been your constant companions, since the instant you were conceived. You are about to take a short journey with us. Just as soon as your parents find your body, we will leave. Adonai has instructed us to allow you to see them, before we go."

The memorial sacrifice is over.

"We are covered once again," Adam says, always thankful that *Yehovah* is merciful. "He has made a way for life to spring forth from the curse of death that is hanging over our existence, even here."

"Yes," is Eve's reply. "His acceptance of our sacrifice brings such peace to me. I know it is difficult to have to slay a sweet, innocent lamb. Especially one you helped birth. It seems that the more important the sacrifice is to us, the greater our peace is when He accepts it. These are things we never asked about, while He walked with us in the Garden."

"When we finish packing the instruments of the memorial here, let's go visit Cain and Abel," Adam suggests. The couple still bears concern regarding the acceptance of their sons' sacrifice.

Their trek is short and they soon reach Abel's herd of sheep, but something is wrong. Abel isn't tending them and the animals are scattered, unprotected. None seem to be harmed, yet Adam feels a strange clutching at his chest.

"Eve, find Abel. See what is wrong. He wouldn't leave his sheep unattended like this, unless he is in trouble. I'll call the dogs and herd the sheep into the pen. You go see about Abel," Adam directs.

Eve finds Abel's lifeless body lying crumpled where Cain has left it. Streaks of dried blood stain his hair and run down the right side of his cheek.

"Oh, Abel!" Eve cries, falling to her knees to pick up her young son's head. She sobs uncontrollably, while hugging his head against her breast, stroking his arm. "Abel, oh Abel. My son, my son!"

Adam bellows, "What happened?" as he comes upon the agonizingly confused scene.

"Oh, *Yehovah*! This! This tragedy is impossible to bear! Why, oh why did this have to happen?"

Adam slumps to his knees next to Eve. Each of them is thinking, "All that future, destroyed. The promise, of someone who would finally live righteously, is gone."

Gathering the lifeless body into his arms, with Eve beside him, Adam carries Abel to the foothills, a day's journey closer to the Garden's gate. There they bury his body, with the faith contained in a promise, in the word of *Yehovah*, written in the heavens. One day, Abel will live again.

Alexis raises his huge arm, a grand gesture, accompanied by the spread of his wings.

Ha-brit and Abel swoop up alongside and gain speed as they pass, downward, through the surface of Earth.

"This will be another of many of a series of surprises in store for Abel this day," Alexis thinks, as the acceleration continues. Soon they break free of Earth's mantle and enter an opening into the heart of the Earth.

"What is this place?" Abel asks.

"A lot of questions, my young companion," Alexis replies.

Below, Abel is dazzled by beautiful buildings and a gathering of angels. Each of the angels is crowding around the intended landing spot of the three, hoping to be the first angel to talk with the first man in Paradise.

"So this is what this part of Sheol is for," an unnamed angel exclaims. The trio touches gently down in Paradise.

Eternity chooses Gabriel to deliver a message from Michael.

"Welcome, Abel. Your testimony of righteous deeds speaks loudly here. All who will be accepted by Adonai have a place of residence here. You are the first of many. You are the first man to live in the heart of the Earth. You are the first man to experience life after death. Those who will be brought here will have overcome the curse your father and mother brought upon man. One day, they will join you here."

"You mentioned my Father and Mother will come here. What about my brother Cain? You didn't mention him," Abel asks Alexis, sincerely concerned for his brother.

"We cannot speak of such things now. The path he has chosen is a dark one, filled with grief and emptiness. One day, he too, will be carried to Sheol. If he doesn't repent, and turn back to Elohim with a sincere heart, his residence will not be here with you.

"You are free to do as you please here, although this place is not your eternal home. You are free to choose which dwelling will be your abode, while you are here. Go and explore. We are here to minister to you, as we did on the surface of Earth. Here you will remain until the promises, written in the Word, have been fulfilled.

"The only restriction is that you must avoid contact with those on the other side of the great gulf. You are not to go near the chasm, and you are to stay within the boundaries of Paradise," Alexis proclaims.

The angels watch as Abel kneels on the ground of Paradise, and gives thanks to Adonai for his salvation. Soon the angels, already gathered around him, join in. Each one adds offerings of songs of praise and thanksgiving.

All those, gathered around and rejoicing with Abel, are so caught up in the moment that they fail to notice another crowd is also gathering. Pushing and striking one another as they seek dominance, they are eager to see the sights on the other side of the gulf, some hope for a reprieve...but none comes.

Adam and Eve return to their land after burying Abel. It is a somber journey, with no conversation.

"What happens now?" Eve asks.

"We will have more children, that is a certainty. We were instructed to multiply and replenish the Earth. It is the way of things. Living must go on until we join Abel, after passing from this realm into the next," Adam says. He is trying to offer Eve hope in the creation of new life, in order to replace the one they've just lost.

"I still don't see Cain, anywhere. He must have run off. He had to be the one who took Abel's life. No animal is capable of lifting such a stone and striking someone who is standing. You remember the bloodied stone there, beside Abel's body," Adam says, while wondering why their grief for Cain is different from that they feel for Abel. They have lost two sons this day, not one.

Their grief is so intense it leaves no room for anger. The need to mourn is overwhelming, crowding from their minds any other thought. Adam quickly joins Abel's flock to theirs to avoid a kill by the ever present predators. He then rejoins Eve and they turn to *Yehovah*.

Each speaks silently of the loss, the waste, and the feelings of failure. Food is not mentioned, nor any of the normal daily routine. Not now. This immersion in their sorrow and their prayers to *Yehovah*, to help them overcome their angst, are all they can sustain. After several days, Eve starts a fire and begins to prepare a meal. They must go on with their lives, once more.

Cain's meager crops are left to the winds.

Weeks have gone by since the death of Abel, and, yet, there is no sign of Cain. Adam takes Eve up to the top of a hill and stands before the presence of *Yehovah*. Lifting his hands toward heaven, he prays, "Great *Yehovah*, mighty creator, merciful to those who call upon You, hear us, we beseech You.

"Abel was a righteous soul and you have embraced him in your heart. Earth has swallowed him up. Earth, too, has taken Cain from us. He was born from us, but not with us, choosing to follow his own way. Be merciful to him and help him to find his way to peace, and to You.

"Now, creator *Yehovah*, hear the prayer of Your servant and Your hand-maiden and send us another son, that we might, again, have hope in Your promises. There is yet a redeemer that will wipe away our guilt before You, and return us to Your bosom."

That night Adam and Eve conceive a son. Once again, they share the hope that the Word of Promise will be fulfilled. Without a son, the promised redeemer cannot come and the Word of *Yehovah*, written in the heavens, cannot come to pass.

Komodo`r, Lairn`r, Tantzer and I, watch. Once again, a pair of angels, drawn from the ranks of another troupe, leaves Heaven's beauty. They take their post beside Eve and the child that forms within her being. Their commission is the same as the four angels from our troupe who have been guarding and ministering to Adam and Eve. All have a resolve even greater than they had before.

Gradually a new "normal" returns to the first family. They often remember, though, the two sons that are no longer in their prayers.

"Gabriel, you were about to share something with us before you left us to deliver Michael's message to Abel in Paradise!" I interject, so all eyes turn to hear what he has to say.

"Previous to my trip, I had been going on assorted errands, performing my increased responsibilities. These often brought me into Michael's presence, and occasionally, I've been privileged to witness a discourse between Elohim and Michael. Here is what I have learned.

"I heard Michael ask Elohim about the Cain and Abel matter. Looking at Their countenance, it was clear to me that Elohim was grieved by Cain's actions.

"Elohim said, 'Sin will never be satisfied, nor ever be filled up. As long as the heavens and Earth remain, it will never say, *it is enough*. Cain chose to walk in rebellion and the seeds of Adam's and Eve's disobedience[35] have found a fertile soil within his heart. Abel, a man of righteousness, chose to walk in My ways and precepts, fulfilling all that I purposed for him to do, long before Adam and Eve left the Garden. Those he has fulfilled, by being a living sacrifice. Though his life was cut short, it was not short of being a testimony, for his blood will be a testimony to the ages. It was needful that he should die, for in seasons yet to come, many righteous shall also take their place by facing death, to the end that My kingdom should testify to the world.'

"Elohim said, 'What others speculate on as a defeat, I know as a victory, for nothing can prevail against righteousness. All things, whatsoever they may be, work in concert to bring about good, and not evil, for those who are invited, according to My will.'"

Gabriel concludes, "We know Elohim did not kill Abel, but he permitted Cain to do so. Therefore, Abel's death is but the first of many who will pass from life into death, as a testimony against those who choose darkness over light, and death over life. Herein Elohim is well able to overcome what seems to be chaos, and create order from that which is intended as evil."

"This then did not happen as a result of any failing of the angels, but rather that the purposes of Elohim might be fulfilled," I speak to my companions.

"Yes, and so be it," Lairn`r says.

ANGEL FATIGUE

Privately, one by one, my closest covenant partners have expressed, or rather confessed to, a quandary. I am responsible for their leadership even though I, too, am beset by the same dilemma. If a resolution isn't soon forthcoming I will have to reach out to Michael lest my present double mindedness provide a foundation for serious chaos.

I'm grappling with a powerful urge to just do something. But what? Heaven's citizens don't waste energy needlessly pursuing dead works.[36] To give in, and simply seek resolution by my own energies, would clearly be such. Actually, our covenant with Elohim probably prevents it. Nonetheless, I have such an impulse to go ahead.

"Angel fatigue" is the name I've coined for an unprecedented condition that several angels of my troupe have been describing to me. Some of the details vary, but they all do seem to reflect a shared experience.

Komodo`r was the first to mention something about it, just after Adam and Eve were cast from the Garden. Then Lairn`r mentioned "his quandary" as he called it. Several others asked for time to privately discuss their concerns with me and I realized they, too, shared the phenomenon. Their secret-keeping is something unusual between angels, who are accustomed to operating transparently. It was after this that I realized I was also thinking thoughts I couldn't reconcile with our covenant.

In an effort to grasp a stream of understanding, I begin scribbling down a list of those I know to be infected. I soon become aware that there is a common exposure shared by every angel who has mentioned this fatigue. Each one regularly pursued the knowledge of, and empathy with, man. With that connection it becomes clear that the list needs to include, as well, all those who have regularly served commissions bringing them into personal contact with man.

Ah, epiphany! Though evidence is skimpy, I theorize that man has somehow infused us with something contagious.

Komodo`r's questions, the evidence of secrets being kept, the unusual instances when our decorum has failed, are all indicative of this infectious fatigue. I am now convinced, no convicted, that this fatigue is the probable source of our collective double-mindedness since the fall.

We seem to suffer a lack of sound judgment. In its place is a sense of consternation…in fact, sheer stupefaction. This is traceable to our unanticipated reactions to man's footprint upon Eternity, the world, and, in addition, before Elohim.

We, the angels of light, cannot conceive of dishonoring the covenant we entered into with Elohim. However, we are now troubled by the thought that we might be doing just that. Until man, such a thought seemed impossible to us.

We savor the invisible fellowship we have with this creation. His ever present sin nature doesn't keep us from relishing time ministering to them. Angels, in fact, covet the opportunity to do so. Why are we like this, when we abhor sin?

We recognize, privately, our increased vulnerability. There are so many unwelcome thoughts jumping into our minds. Elohim, who knows all things, must know of our dilemma. Should I seek an audience before Him? Should I petition for another Season of Trumpets to cleanse us from our collective error of judgment? Is this the path of Lucifer?

Elohim's response to Adam's and Eve's sin was merciful, not the crushing judgment we had expected. Instead, we saw Yehovah kill the lamb, in order to cover the sin. He knew the hearts of Adam and Eve would pursue Him, even after they sinned, explaining Elohim's actions toward Adam, Eve, and those in their direct line.

Likewise, Elohim rejected Cain's sacrifice because of Cain's heart. Cain enjoyed the privileges of the firstborn, and was the heir of the promises, yet chose rebellion and turned away. The curse and judgment followed his obvious unwillingness to offer a sacrifice that would be acceptable.

This knowledge doesn't justify our actions and hasn't silenced our nagging self-doubt.

Our present disorientation is energized by our two seemingly polarizing and involuntary responses to man's deeds, Grace notwithstanding. These have established the roots of our consternation. The first is our revulsion to man's deeds, even those deeds under the covering of Elohim's mercy. These actions insult Elohim and Heaven's citizenry.

The second is the irresistible power that fills us with great joy whenever we think about, or anticipate, invisible fellowship with him. This increasingly draws us toward man. Sadly, there is man's lack of conviction regarding righteousness. It acts concurrently as a deterrent to our enjoyment of our covert relationship with these perpetrators of sin. This predicament has frayed our composure at times. It causes us to question if we are drifting into the territory of disobedience. If we are, then will we be cast out? Will we be reprobates like satan, suffering, without a future?

Catching a whiff of what man calls, despair, I start to reflect on this possible snare, when, suddenly, I see a startling ray of illumination. What it portends, I am not sure. So I speak it out loud to hear, for myself, how it sounds.

"Satan's seed within man is now expressly manifested, through man, in Heaven. It bridges the previously unbridgeable gulf. What's more is the realization that Elohim, indeed like us, has a vulnerability, after all.

"It is man!

"Only Eternity will prove if it is a purposeless or purposeful weakness. It is certain though, satan, will try to use this vulnerability to trap Elohim, or us, for that matter. It is something else to consider and guard against. It seems that satan may already be probing our defenses using 'The Fatigue.'

"I am now certain that I understand the life cycle of the fatigue. Now the question is 'Is there deliverance for us all from it?' For now, I have peace in knowing that if Elohim has peace with His vulnerability then I can drink from His peace for my own. I will offer that perception to my covenant partners so they too have peace. It is enough!"

YEARS AND TEARS

"Eternity has a timeline defined by footprints of its citizens, and so does the age of man," Lairn`r says, expectantly, baiting a hook.

Although Heaven and Eternity never take a day of rest, Elohim and angels, do. Such is the rest we are taking. It is filled with refreshing indulgences in the River of Life. It is then that we are refilled with Elohim's essence, as we soak in the sound of the angels who are commissioned to worship Him.

We are sitting at a round table just on the edge of the Court of Measures. It is a large round table, formed of platinum and onyx, and serves as the harbor of choice for this taskforce of resting angels. Passing by, other angels are hustling to their appointed tasks. This respite has become possible because Earthly events have once more settled into a routine. Unexpected visitations of calamity and terminal episodes, that were so prevalent earlier on, have subsided.

Now seasons of plenty, and seasons of want, come and go following no recognizable pattern. On Earth, angels now move and minister with practiced speed and efficiency. Seasons have become years and those years accumulate into decades. Decades have now become centuries. The age of man began at Adam's creation, which was followed shortly by Eve being formed from Adam's rib. They placed the first footprints there.

"What do you mean by that?" Komodo`r asks casually, resting his square jaw on his folded hands. He hesitates to disturb the calm everyone is enjoying by beginning a long discourse about man again.

"Well, since you asked," Lairn`r continues, through a stifled grin only his closest covenant partners can see. "When you compare man's timeline with Eternity's, there are similarities and there are differences. Eternity has no beginning and has no end. Man's first footprints upon Earth are a beginning. Those mark the beginning of the timeline of the age of man. Man will now keep pace with Eternity, if the age of man does not have an end. Their sin didn't end it. The death of Abel didn't end it, because there is Seth. Cain's departure didn't end it. In fact, even though he and his kind may be reprobates, they actually expanded the time line of the age of man.

"For more than 900 Earth years now we have diligently ministered to man, while looking into mysteries surrounding man, which reveal much about Elohim, Heaven and ourselves. It was, and is, a fascinating endeavor full of unexpected twists and turns.

"For now, we sit here resting, and no matter what we are doing, man lives, works, plays, creates, suffers and grieves. Continuously, they place their footprints upon the age of man and Eternity. Nothing they do is ever beyond the life Elohim gave them. Whether we watch or not...on Earth, the heartbeat of the age of man goes on," Lairn`r says, his voice trailing off into nothing. Soon, although his voice is silent, the motion of his eyes and slight hand jesters say he is still expounding.

As we wait for Lairn`r's next philosophical treatise, we rest here, unaware that the key that opens many unrevealed mysteries is about to turn. We are soon to return to "ready" status because of satan's duplicity and, what he had claimed to be, Elohim's weakness. Of course, as you shall see, an apocalypse will forever thwart the propagation of satan's unlawful claim. His deceit, however, may continue to deny this truth.

While I silently speculate, Lairn`r's mouth twitches.

I, Yushabed, serving alongside the noted scribe Lez`n, am filling in, and adding to, the chronicle Zukher has been keeping. It is an honor to do so.

Bartke and I, Omán, reminisce about what has been our commission. We are Elohim's ministers unto Seth, the third son of Adam and Eve, the one who replaced Abel. When we were given this commission, we strengthened our resolve in the protection of Seth, because of what had befallen Abel. Cain's actions and banishment necessitated self-evaluation, which was led by Lairn`r, a covenant partner of Zukher's troupe.

After a period of reflection, Elohim explained to Heaven's citizens that the death of Abel was not a failing of angels, thus relieving the consternation suffered by Lairn`r and others. Rather, it was an event strategized by satan. His intent was to nullify Elohim's promise of a child who would redeem man.

Elohim's objectives eclipse all things. We learned Elohim intended it for good. He permitted it to happen, purposefully, even though for a short time it introduced chaotic footprints upon the age of man. In the fullness of time, those footprints were transformed into order and purpose. From the death of Abel came the righteousness of Seth.

When Abel's legacy of righteousness fell upon Seth, their third son, he proved to be more than up for the challenge. He walks in all that his father instructed him.

Lairn`r and I are enjoying working with Yushabed who has become an earnest scribe advanced from Lez'n's tutelage.

We bear witness to the seven hundred and eightieth anniversary of Seth's offering of a sacrificial lamb for his sin. He performs this ceremony just as his father, Adam, has done, since leaving the Garden. And just as Abel did, on the day he was killed by Cain, Seth's absent older brother.

At a new campsite a new growing season has started. Adam and Eve sacrifice an unblemished lamb. It is their nine hundred and twenty ninth anniversary.

Scattered around a large portion of land, east of Eden, other sons and daughters born to Adam and Eve, have spread out like seeds blown by the wind. These are souls from the womb of Eve, the mother of all living. Each soul is unique, and has a relationship with others, and with Elohim. Among those that did not move on to the land of Nod, there has been no repeat of Cain's destructive deed.

Seth, the heir to Adam's legacy, and his wife are fruitfully multiplying. Of their many progeny, Enosh is the heir to Adam's birthright. Through the passing years, Enosh and his wife have witnessed the birth of many sons and daughters, whose numbers are flourishing, as well. Kenan receives the cherished birthright that passes from Enosh. He is followed by Mahalalel then Jared, Enoch, and Methuselah. Each heir receives the family birthright passed on from the father to the firstborn son. The Earth years lived by each generation will determine the age at which a son receives the birthright's mantel.

The birthright is a result of the status of the firstborn. The mantle, however, is passed on as a result of worthiness. The actions of the heir, as witnessed by replacement of Cain by Seth, is an example of this.

Together they are the generations of Adam.

Though some of these descendants of Adam choose to live in close proximity to one another, most adopt a nomadic life style. The annual memorial celebrated by Adam and Eve is kept by some. Others, like Cain, doubt. The doubters lapse into servitude, to immorality and to debauchery, each going their own way.

Those who serve Elohim endure the curse of Adam and the blessings of Elohim. Those drifting away from Elohim to serve other sovereigns, receive the curse according to their actions. By this, we, the angels, understand the impact of Heaven's laws. The blessings and curses fall upon the individuals and families, in fair proportion. As man's numbers grow, so grows the size of the company of angels serving them in the commission of ministry. While not all of the angels serving are drawn from the troupe led by Zukher, all contributing angels are trained by that troupe. This also fulfills the purposes of Elohim, when He directed Zukher, initially, to form such a troupe.

Seth has been a faithful witness to the passage of time. Enoch, the sixth heir of the mantle from Adam, is a righteous man. He walks in all that Adam and Seth instructed him. His greatest testimony is that he walks with Elohim. Along with Adam, the man Enoch lives his days spending his time communing with, and ministering unto, Yehovah. The angels guarding him have a most pleasant commission, worshipping Elohim while Enoch sings a song of worship and praise.

"The scribes are certainly being kept busy, recording all things pertaining to man," Lairn`r observes.

We had enjoyed the time of rest proffered by Michael, but now we're in a state of readiness.

"Do you plan on reading the records, or will you be delegating that to others?" I ask, guessing at the reply.

"Well, I was able to keep up with it until the time Jared was born. Heaven now has almost eighty thousand ministering angels serving commissions upon Earth. Everything their charge says, and does, is recorded by our scribes. One or two of these scribes, per hundred serving angels, records everything done by each individual on Earth. It is overwhelmingly more than the oversight that one angel can possibly exercise. Now a scribe just hands me summaries. When something in a summary warrants my attention, I read the full record. And then I go from there," Lairn`r answers.

Soon after our season of rest, Komodo`r asks for some private time with me.

"Zukher," he begins, "I have a confession to make. It isn't something I've kept from Elohim, nothing can be. Up until now it has remained unknown to all my covenant partners."

"I understand," I say, adding, "Do you prefer to talk about this here, or is some other place preferable?"

"Let's walk a little," he says, in a matter-of-fact tone. "It is easier to think and talk, when I walk."

We walk together, silently, until we reach the Garden of Remembrance, shuffling along, nodding and waving at the angels whom we pass along the way. He decides to sit next to one of the pavilions with moon shaped, stone seats, facing away from the path.

Then he begins, "Satan accused Elohim of sin and weakness, therefore of being unworthy."

I think it unusual to base a confession upon something spoken by the avowed enemy of Elohim, but I don't interrupt. I just nod my head.

"The first time I heard him claim this was out here, in the Garden, close to that spot over there," he says, gesturing toward a different Pavilion. It is one that is surrounded by oval benches, arranged in a circle, sitting under a canopy of trees.

"It didn't seem right to me at the time, so I arranged to meet with him privately, to discuss my reservations. His persuasive tongue, even then, was difficult to resist," Komodo`r says, offering the first of several personal revelations.

"Let me mention here…all this was investigated by Elohim's inquiries following the rebellion. I realize that this you already know, because you checked my background, prior to asking me to join the troupe. There was a part of the investigation that was sealed at the time. It is that which I want to talk about. Michael has given me permission now, to disclose this," Komodo`r says, anticipating my questions.

"When we met, Lucifer, whom we now know as satan, used a series of rapid fire questions to outline what he claimed was sufficient evidence of such a weakness. I didn't understand, then, that Elohim must have permitted this encounter. At the time it was questionable, but now it seems to have been so useful, despite the source of the questions," Komodo`r continues.

"'Is it not true that Elohim shows mercy at unexpected times?' Lucifer asked me, without waiting for a reply. He continued battering me with questions, none of which he intended that I answer. 'Is it not true that He often does so, even when Michael and other counselor angels recommend a corrective action of some kind?'

"He went on, 'Is it not true that Elohim, when He does so, makes it necessary to remove various entries that the scribes have made in the records of Heaven? In fact, He directs those attending to the records to destroy all evidence of them, cutting them out of the record, leaving no trace or smudge and tossing all evidence into the Sea of Forgetfulness.' I could tell he was relishing, my undivided attention.

"He continued the questioning, picking up the pace, 'Is it not true, that because Elohim instituted the Law of Free Will, periods of chaos are introduced that can require Elohim a span of Eternity to transform?'

"Nothing was going to halt him, 'Should we not ask, therefore, if Elohim is really righteous. Why would He create a law that empowers, and justifies, someone to bring forth chaos?'

"Lucifer was ever a master of supposition. 'Why doesn't Elohim just command all creation to walk in righteousness, and make it impossible for creation not to? His unwillingness to do such things is irrational and contrary to all other laws of Heaven and the heavens above Earth.'

"Lucifer now agitated, compounded his assault. 'If Elohim is good, if Elohim is righteous, if Elohim is holy, then how is it possible for Him to permit evil, unrighteousness, or unholiness?'

"This, the last question, his closing argument, was asked while he was standing, his face pressed close to my own. He then said, 'They all, each of the three-in-one, are guilty of sinning against the laws of Heaven, by creating and permitting the Law of Freedom of Choice to exist. Elohim is keeping something hidden, by cloaking a sin in a mystery. Elohim's unrighteousness is revealed when He acts out of sentiment, instead of reason, justifying His deeds by force.'"

I recognize that Komodo'r's reiteration is straightforward and absent any angst.

"Interesting," I proffer, expecting some sort of follow-up statement. When there is none, I assume that Komodo'r is awaiting a comeback from me.

"How can I help?" I prompt.

"There's no way, really. I am just convinced you and the others need to know about that inquisition. I believe the need for your possession of that knowledge will be understood, when I ask my own series of questions."

I lean forward to close the gap between us. Without hesitation, he begins, "Satan sinned and was cast out of Heaven; man sinned and was cast out of the Garden, right?"

"Yes," I answer, already beginning to see, clearly, where he might be headed.

"Yehovah passed judgment upon satan, sentencing him to expulsion from Heaven and eradicating any future he might have. Yehovah passed judgment upon Adam and Eve, sentencing them to expulsion from the Garden and the sentence for their transgression was death. Yet man is promised a future that can include redemption, right?" Komodo'r asked.

I reply with an unsettled, "Yes."

"Is this, then, not an example of the inconsistency, or injustice, that satan was suggesting when he questioned me, before the rebellion?" Komodo'r queries me quietly, so no passersby could hear.

I am now uncomfortable with Komodo'r's assault upon my reasoning. I begin seeking a foundation upon which to build a defense.

"My understanding is that any imagined injustice is only circumstantial. Lucifer's examples were nothing more than that. I see no evidence of an injustice. Elohim's pronounced judgment upon Lucifer and his followers is just, because it righteously reflected that the measure of Elohim's wrath, within their cup of wrath, was full to overflowing. Granted every opportunity, they refused all overtures and chose to celebrate and flaunt their sin. Such a full measure demands such a sentence.

"Adam's and Eve's transgression is different. First, theirs is only a trifle compared to satan's. Satan's offense was the total overthrow of the Kingdom of Heaven. In absolute prideful conceit, Lucifer chose to attack all the good, the mercy, the sanctity and the beauty of our Heaven, and Elohim. His goal was to supplant all of that with the ugly, the merciless, the vulgar and the vile that he and his followers are. In addition, satan felt no remorse, no humility and no repentance when his violation was discovered, celebrating his licentiousness.

"Whereas Adam and Eve, instead of celebrating their sin, humbled themselves before Elohim, embraced His offer of a covering, and trusted in Elohim's mercy. They did not demand that the standing they were forced to relinquish was something to which they were entitled. On the contrary, satan did," I answer with certainty.

"Excuse me," a familiar voice. "May I join you?"

Without turning around, we recognize that Lairn`r is standing on the edge of the pathway. He looks as if he is fully prepared to move on, at the slightest hint that we prefer being alone. I look at Komodo`r whose facial expression suggests he has no problem with Lairn`r joining our discussion. Since I welcome his fair minded thinking, and know that any addition from him will surely be an asset, I motion for Lairn`r to occupy the third seat, the one next to Komodo`r.

"Elohim's actions, after the fall of man, clearly indicate the certainty that Elohim foreknew that they would fall, before they actually did," Lairn`r says, betraying that he heard some of what we were so earnestly discussing, and wants to contribute to our train of thought.

285

"His foreknowledge of the fall was evidenced in that He wrote in the heavens both a promise, and a plan, of salvation from sin. Remember, the word in the heavens was written before the fall. I wish to add that, because He foreknew man would humble himself, He waited to reveal this plan, until after they fell: After they sinned, not before. Thus, He provided a righteous way to bless them in their shameful condition, because He also foreknew they would choose to believe in the promise. Those blessings continue, not because of what they were, but because of what they will be," Lairn`r says, with his head now joining our close, and secret, setting.

At this point, he looks into the deeply concerned eyes that Komodo`r is shading under troubled lids. Lairn`r says, "Sorry. I overheard part of your discussion before interrupting you and I thought I had something to toss in. I hope you don't mind."

Lairn`r's words are a revelation and are invaluable, but he keeps staring at Komodo`r, measuring whether his uninvited input is considered presumptuous.

"I don't mind. I don't mind, at all. Really, I don't mind!" Komodo`r says with a wrinkled brow, repeating the statement, as his mind is deeply preoccupied. "As I recall, you have similar questions and concerns, too."

"Well, I did. But I don't anymore. So much has happened. As well, so much has been revealed. I now think, ah, believe, that Elohim is opening our collective understanding regarding what had appeared to be, His suspicious actions. However, with this illumination, it has become quite clear they are not suspicious," Lairn`r states.

"Let me try to explain, if I may." Neither Komodo`r nor I have anything to add, so we wait for Lairn`r to go ahead.

"Lucifer and his shadows espouse the idea that the law of Heaven, what I refer to as 'The Law,' is the principal thing, the greatest thing. They justify their rebellion upon the premise that Elohim doesn't always act in accordance with 'The Law.'

"In their perverted righteousness they claim that Elohim has an unprecedented weakness. It is Elohim's disregard for 'The Law' that precipitated their flagrant disobedience and blatant rebellion, compounded by secretive insurgence and total corruption.

"Elohim created me and conformed me to be an inquisitor. He trained me to be, and so I am, a master of 'The Law.' What I now understand, and didn't until just recently, is that holding the view that Lucifer embraces puts 'The Law' above Elohim. It makes 'The Law' sovereign and not Elohim. It makes 'The Law' the master and Adonai, the servant. It makes 'The Law' almighty and not El Shaddai. Fellow covenant partners, this should not be. It cannot be! I serve Elohim, not 'The Law.' Don't you?

"So it begs the question, is Elohim then able to judge 'The Law?' Yes of course. The creator has power to judge His creation. By what then, does He judge it? It is by the power of His endless mercy.

"Where, then, do we witness a demonstration of this power? In the Season of Trumpets! This Season comes only by Elohim's command and not by command of 'The Law.' Then and there, He exercises His power to judge all things: First those who are His and then, those who are not His.

"Those who are His, do not act in disobedience, but commit error in judgment. How is it they have power to err? They err because they are created good, but not created perfect. Only Elohim is perfect.

"Those who are not His, but were also created good, have intentionally chosen the path of disobedience. By doing so, they sinned and are not repentant. These store up unto themselves fury and rage, and a fearful expectation of judgment, which is and will be poured out from the cup of Elohim's wrath.

"Is this an arbitrary thing with Elohim, as some say? No. For those who choose to seek His mercy, receive His mercy. And all those who choose wrath, consequently receive wrath.

"From whence, then, comes this power of mercy? It comes from Elohim's favor or, as I had been thinking, *The Favor*.

"Tantzer questioned the word, quite some time ago, when he asked, 'Isn't *Favor* really *Grace*?'

"This is the *Grace*[37] that the vines sing about. The mystery of the Throne of Grace is that Elohim goes there, secretly, to judge 'The Law.' Finally...*Grace* is what the angels have been singing about, without knowing what it meant. Favor is, in fact, *Grace*. The power of mercy to judge 'The Law' comes from *Grace*. 'The Law' demands judgment. 'The Law' may judge, but it is weak, because it cannot empower those under it, to fulfill it. Free will is stronger. However, I conclude...*Grace* must be stronger than free will!

"Therefore, Elohim is just. He is the sole justifier of those upon whom He wills. He pours out mercy. Does such mercy disobey 'The Law?' No. For 'The Law' also states that the creator has power to show mercy upon whom He will.

"So what do we find then? Is there weakness in Elohim? No, for though 'The Law' is weak, through the power of *Grace*, 'The Law' is fulfilled. Therefore there is no weakness in Elohim, as Lucifer claimed."

Just as Lairn`r pauses, Gabriel swoops in and stands before us, saying, "Zukher, Michael wants to see you! Bring Tantzer and anything you both will need to descend into Sheol, immediately." Without further explanation, Gabriel lifts from the Garden, and heads toward the Citadel.

THE EULOGY

Tantzer and I stand before the Viewing Window, about to take our leave of Heaven. Our destination is Sheol. Gabriel's summons, for both Tantzer and me to appear at Michael's side, is introduced as a matter of utmost urgency and honor. As it turns out, it also is a matter of reward.

Michael has just told us that Elohim is about to summon Adam to Paradise. He will be taking his leave of Eve, Seth, and joint heirs of Elohim's salvation and he will be joining Abel, already there.

We are to lead a delegation of angels to greet him upon his arrival in Paradise.

Seth, Enosh, Kenan, Mahalalel, Jared, and Methuselah stand in the opening of Adam's tent. He had chosen a nomadic life, saying, "I want to be free to return to the Garden if *Yehovah* calls me to do so."

These heirs to the birthright, passed from Adam, are direct links to the Garden and creation. Through the years they have memorized and propagated the message of the celebrated memorial. They have also become students of the Word written in the heavens. Although others have chosen the way of Cain, these have remained faithful to all Adam has commanded them. They gather now to say their good-byes. Adam is about to take his leave of Earth. He has come to the fullness of his years.

"Eve, my wife and my helper, we have journeyed far and know much. We, here, are the only two people to have seen *Yehovah* face to face. We walked with Him, talked with Him, and ate with Him. We are also the first, and the last, to see with our eyes, the Garden," Adam says, holding her creased face in his hands.

"Thank you for sharing this life with me. It has been hard and there have been frequent tribulations, but it has been beautiful, too.

"*Yehovah* knows my heart. I love Him so and I love you so. If you handed me that fruit again, knowing what we know now, and passing through what we have been through, I would eat it from your hand, again," Adam sighs and closes his eyes. The breath of Elohim leaves his body. He is gone.

Together Dāwīd and Mehgen' lift Adam's fully conscious soul from his lifeless body. Duplicating Abel's departure, the three hover together over the family gathered in, and around, the tent.

"Well done, faithful father of all men," Dāwīd says, his face shining. He is pleased to be the first angel to visibly greet the creation, with whom he has shared a very long, one sided, companionship.

"Thank you," Mehgen' says, reaching out, taking Adam's hand. He draws Adam into his embrace, his first contact with Adam, his sole purpose for the past nine hundred and thirty years.

Adam's legs dangle in midair, lifted as he is, with his face against the angel's chest. His eyes are searching downward until he finds his target.

"Eve!" he says, reaching out his hand, trying to touch her gentleness one last time.

"You will see her again, shortly," Dāwīd says. "Then you can embrace her as often as you wish. For now you have inherited Eternity. Soon she will join you."

Adam's smile and his tears, fill his face. Gone are the pains inflicted by age. He chances a look at his hands. They aren't wrinkled like they were. He looks at his body and sees a muscular firmness. With a quizzical look, he asks, "I look younger, like I was when I was in the Garden."

"Yes," says Dāwīd. "There are many other changes to you, as well. The seed of the serpent is also gone from you. It became lifeless within your body. All the faculties, you enjoyed within the Garden, are now restored. Your oneness with Yehovah has returned. Your senses: Those loaned to the body; those residing in the soul; and those residing within your spirit, which is forever meshed with your soul; are about to reach new heights. This is what you will be like for all Eternity. Life without end. Life without separation from Yehovah. Once your redemption is complete, you will be able to explore the stars you gazed upon. You will understand things of the past, present, and many things in Eternity's future. Things we don't know about yet."

"What are you?" Adam asks, gaining confidence with each passing instant.

"I am an angel. I am a messenger from Elohim, a guardian of man, and a soldier in the army of Elohim. For now, enough questions. It is time to join Abel."

With a last look around, the angels fold back their wings. Lifting higher and higher, and then arching over into a swooping dive, they enter into the bowels of Earth.

During their descent, the scenes change, going from pale light to dark, and then dark to a black nothingness. Though the journey takes only a few seconds, for Adam it feels like hours. His refreshed vision is briefly clouded by the material of Earth's strength. He doesn't know what to expect and wonders what life, after death, will be like. Most of all, he wonders just how long 'shortly' will be, the word that this creature uses, before he sees Eve again. They were hardly ever separated. Over nine hundred and thirty years! He had occasionally wondered, if he had to do it over again, would he choose to eat the fruit Eve offered. Now he knows the answer. Though once again free from the seed of sin, and his pre-sin state restored, he knows now, like he knew the names of the animals, then. He would do it again.

It seems the velocity of their trip may be slowing, and Dāwīd turns his torso, so they are traveling feet first. Adam sees an approaching light between his legs. Bigger and bigger it grows, until the three travelers burst out into an open expanse that looks, for the most part, like parts of the Garden. The vast difference is a wall that is absent of any measure of light. It isn't his focus, but the wall insults his newly restored faculties, and he knows that that is not a place he wants to be.

The angel duet, carrying Adam gently between them, comes to rest in an open courtyard. Surrounding the brilliant opening are several hundred angels. Not wanting to insult his guardians, Adam waits patiently to be released from their arms. He knows who he wants to see first.

"Is *Yehovah* here?"

"No, I am afraid not. He is in His Kingdom of Heaven. He wants you to know He patiently waits for the time He can join you again face to face, so you can see Him as He truly is, but you will have to share His patience. First, the promised One you read about in His Word must come. One who is worthy to free those, like you, who must wait here. Until then, you can still pray to and worship the One who made your arrival here possible."

"Is anyone here I know? Is my son, Abel, here?" Adam asks.

"Here I am, Father," Adam hears his son. "Over here."

Great joy fills them both when Adam reaches out and greets his son, Abel. He has been waiting to see his father for a long time. He asked, and received permission, to help prepare a place for his father.

Adam sees an angel, larger than any in Adam's field of view. Dāwīd and Mehgen' step aside, along with the others around Adam. "Excuse me," a voice resonates.

His importance is evidenced by the hush that immediately ensues.

"Is he huge!" Adam thinks. "I would have fainted, if I had seen him first, instead of these two, my escorts."

"Adam!" a voice thunders over the heads of the homecoming crowd.

"Adam!" a second clap thunders, echoing from the walls in the distance.

"I have wanted to introduce myself to you since the day Elohim created you. I am honored to meet you."

With that pronouncement, Adam looks upon a giant of a creature, standing on a ledge. Adam falls to his knees, paying homage.

"See that you do this not," Adam is instructed. "Worship Yehovah! Not the creature, which He created," the thunder corrects.

Adam rises to his feet, a little shaken, and the creature is about to speak.

On wing, I glide down from the ledge I have been standing on, watching and waiting for a semblance of order. Adam's reaction to seeing me changes that. With unexpected emotion filling me, I extend my hand toward Adam, and introduce myself, "Adam, I am Zukher, a messenger dispatched by Yehovah. He sent me from Heaven to greet you and to tell you, 'Well done, faithful servant.'

"First, some introductions. Dāwīd and Mehgen', you already know something about. They brought you here. Let me add to that which they have already told you. What you don't know is that these two angels have been your constant companions, almost continually, since before you and Eve left the Garden."

Adam is in awe, absorbing all of this. The mention of his beloved punches Adam hard. He wishes she could be here and wonders if it is a sin to wish that.

I continue, "They were there, when you passed through the gate that, even now, is guarded by the flaming sword. They were there, when you lost your footing in the river. It was their beating wings that moved the sands of the river to give you footing to stand. It was they, who helped you reach camp and battle the serpent's advances, when Cain was born. They kept your flocks of sheep, when you went back to get Eve. Yehovah, through them, comforted you, when you found Abel's body. These many years, you have never been alone. Even when times became so difficult that it seemed impossible to continue, under Yehovah's urging, they lifted your burden and made it lighter."

Adam hears this while wrestling with his sense of reality, and humbly, says, "Thank you."

I have more to say, and more angels to introduce, but I see Adam is distracted. He is looking past my shoulder.

"I know you," Adam says. "I have seen you before," pointing at a smaller angel, behind me.

"Once you frightened me. After Eve brought me around, I thought I imagined you, but here you are. You are smaller than I remembered you to be."

From around my shoulder, Tantzer peeks out at Adam. "I am sorry, son of Elohim, father of all men. I didn't mean to, I really didn't. I was just learning and forgot to hide myself," Tantzer says, apologizing for his early mistake in judgment.

"Over there, beside Abel, Ha-brit, meaning, 'Sign of a Covenant' and Alexis, meaning 'Protector of Mankind,' they've been Abel's guardian angels. They performed the same ministry for Abel that Dāwīd and Mehgen' did for you. They were holding Abel's soul, and hovering just overhead, when you and Eve found his body.

"What about Cain?" Adam asks. "I don't see him."

"Ah, Adam. Cain, I must tell you, is in another place. He chose, exercising free will, to follow a different path from yours and Abel's. Just as Abel was the first man to take residence here in Paradise, Cain was the first man to take up residence in the abyss, a place of torment and great suffering. Although where he is, is not at a great distance, he is as distant as light is from darkness. A great chasm separates the place Cain is from where we are. He cannot come here and you cannot go there.

"For you, it is given to understand much. So understand this. You are in the heart of the Earth. It has two compartments, separated by this chasm. Where you are, it is Paradise. A Paradise, almost as wonderful as the Garden. The other place is hideous and dreadful. Cain is receiving the rewards of his choices, just as you are, the rewards of yours.

"Now we must fulfill all righteousness." I lift up to the ledge above, and pronounce, "Citizens of Heaven and Earth, hear my words. Elohim, in His eternal wisdom, has determined it is right and fitting that we rejoice in Adam's return to Paradise, from a sojourn of wandering and seasons of proving.

"Abel is a man accepted by Elohim by signs and wonders. He was delivered by the determined purpose and foreknowledge of God, struck by lawless hands, and put to death. This man, whom Elohim received into Paradise, was loosed from his body and sentence of death.

"It was needful that one should die, as a testimony, to the righteousness of faith and to the atonement in the shedding of blood. This, Abel has done, proving and preparing a way for all those who shall come after. His blood, to this day, is crying out to Elohim. It testifies to, and prophesies of, a time to come. A time when men shall enter in by a new and more perfect way. A way made possible not by the blood of a lamb, but by the blood of a promised redeemer, now spoken of by the prophetic Word written in the heavens above Earth.

"In the fullness of time, Adam comes. The first man, riding the wave of Eternity, standing in his own estate, waits for those who shall come after. The serpent has sifted and shaken you and yours, seeking to nullify the promises of Elohim. He sought to steal your inheritance. You two, and Eve, have overcome, even as Elohim.

"Here, within the foundations of Earth, amongst the mountains reaching into Eternity, rest the cornerstone winds. It is a place of custody for all men, until that promise is fulfilled.

"Let me speak to you of the patriarch, Adam. He is dead, will be buried, and his grave will lie in Earth above. His soul stands here, before us. Therefore, he, being a prophet, knows that Elohim swore unto him a covenant. Out of his and Eve's body, according to the flesh, one will be born who will rise to sit on His Throne, judging all," Zukher concludes.

The celebration continues, and Adam is shown the place Elohim and Abel have prepared for him. One by one, angels step out from the pressing crowd, to welcome Adam and greet him personally. Eternity is a long time and the sweet rejoicing lasts and lasts.

"You know, don't you, we are being watched from across the way," Tantzer whispers, privately, to me. "One creature lingered, until Adam entered his abode. It is probably Cain."

"Yes, I expect it is," I, reluctantly, answer. "The suffering there is unimaginable, layers and waves of misery, and incredible pain of the soul. The prince powers on that side are no longer constrained, once a soul reaches there. They have spent such a long span of Eternity inflicting torment upon one another. In Cain, the first soul to be imprisoned there, they find a new victim on whom to heap abuse. We are forbidden to rescue him. The assurance of the opportunity for atonement of sin, as promised by Elohim, does not apply to Cain."

A FINAL COMMENTARY

The curtain descends on this breadth of Eternity with the passing of Adam and Eve on into Paradise. Thus this chronicle must draw to a close, as well. The acts of Adam's progeny, Seth and his generation, take center stage and are now being recorded in subsequent chronicles. My troupe's pathfinder commission to man continues, and will do so, for as long as Elohim wills it.

Intending to complete the final entries, I ask Lez`n to join me in a private chamber within the Mall of Wisdom. He is a singularly well suited, trained, and vocationally qualified angel, who is a bright and witty scribe from our troupe, and the principal hand recording these works.

It is my desire to convey to all who will read these accounts, the gifting of unassuming angelic scribes, like Lez`n. Those serving in this vocation are uniquely endowed, so much so, that they are privy, not only to my thoughts, but to all thoughts of the citizens chronicled herein. His access is as a true witness, without comment or judgment, and most important, without tale bearing. Once the work is determined finished, under his eyes and mine, three knowledgeable witnesses will secure the writing by placing their handprint upon the scribe's seal.

"Lez`n, let's begin," I signal.

This, then, is Eternity's testimony. It begins at Elohim's announcement of a battle campaign, which at this closing, still marches toward Elohim's promised end. Evidence of that beginning is the Word, tossed into the heavens by Dvar HaElohim. That Word, in the form of star patterns, is filled with His promises and prophetic utterances. Our account testifies to the partial fulfillment of that Word. However, there is much that must yet come to pass.

Following the stars Elohim spoke life into the formless void, placing created man into an exquisite garden, thereby launching His campaign. Man was formed of Elohim's faith, and now lives on in hope. From the spectacle of that singular creation emerged a perpetual wind, still sweeping across Eternity.

"Lez`n, my thoughts trouble me. The mystery that man is, and what they have to do with Elohim's campaign, is just escaping us. Contemplation of this makes it difficult for me to tie up the loose ends."

In spite of this, I am ready to move forward, and close the chronicle. Just then I am beset by Tantzer whose persistent interruption isn't yielding to my eyebrow-raised "not now" look. He stands before me, his body insisting that I stop and hear what he has to say. How can I resist this tenacious partner?

"I have come straight from the Throne Room with a message on two matters of some urgency," he begins, with a knowing smile.

"Lairn`r informs me you are working on closing the chronicle. I hope you haven't sealed it yet. You should have been there."

He's got me! I smile back with patience and a modicum of indulgence. Everything that happens in the Throne Room is, in truth, important. I also know, though, that not everything that happens there must be included in the chronicle. If that were the case the chronicle would never end.

"First, a personal message from Michael. He compliments your leadership and tutelage of Gabriel. He has promoted him from novice to Captain of the host of messengers. He is now my Captain," Tantzer grins, "and Michael says it is a commission for which he was destined." With that he pauses for comment.

"I am thrilled by such a thing. His performance has been exemplary. What else do you have?" I reply, my mind already searching for a replacement messenger. The troupe can't afford a lull in our ministry.

Then…the lightning!

"I was about to leave the Throne Room. I go there as you do, just to bathe in Elohim's presence and immerse myself in the worship of the angels. Elohim was in the midst of hearing petitions. When the line diminished to a remaining few, I noticed Michael slip quietly to the end of the line. I immediately sat down to listen, and what I heard proved to be most stimulating, though one-sided. It was after this that Michael caught up to me with the message I have just delivered.

"When it was Michael's turn, he said, 'El Shaddai, hear the words of my petition. Nothing is impossible with You, and all things hidden by You are beyond finding out. You have determined, in Your wisdom, to grant great honor to those of Your servants who seek out wisdom, knowledge, and understanding. This we do, since just the effort of the activity, alone, fills us with joy and peace. Please forgive, Everlasting Father, my mentioning something that frequently intrudes upon Heaven's tranquility.'

"Whereupon Elohim smiled and nodded for Michael to proceed, and so he continued, 'The absent one has made accusation before this Throne. It is a matter of some importance to those of us who minister unto You, and for You, that this be put to rest. Through our examination, HaRuach has granted us understanding that The Law, alone, is not able to judge us. Neither is Grace, alone, able to judge us. However, Grace is able to judge The Law. Therefore, I ask, for myself and all my covenant partners, whose hands rest below Your feet, how can this be? We ask for enlightenment into the fullness of this matter.'

"El Shaddai replied, with His countenance aglow, 'Grace, indeed, judges The Law for Grace is greater than The Law, but there is one thing greater than these things. For it is Who I Am, What I Am, and Why I Am.'

"'It is a new doctrine that has always been, though until now, it has remained sealed. We have shared it with each other from Eternity past, and it will last throughout Eternity to come. And so now, since you ask, We reveal it unto all.

"'The revelation, and mystery, upon which all things rest is...*Love.*'

"Under Elohim's watchful eye, several angels rose and, quietly and respectfully, tried to exit the room. As they did this, Elohim rose to His feet. This caused them to speedily retreat to their seats. Elohim smiled, and said, 'Do not hasten to leave to search out the matter of Love. You will not find it in all the annals of Heaven. It has always been, and you are witnesses to it, but until now did not recognize it or know its name. Man's footprint upon Eternity has provided the way for all creation to know the fullness of, what has been until now, Our secret.'

"At this, everyone gave Elohim their undivided attention, and El Shaddai said, 'Though I am that I am, but have not Love, I am merely a noise in the winds of Eternity. Though I have all knowledge and understand all mysteries, and though I have all power to create and judge all things, but have not Love, I am nothing. Though I bestow all of Heaven's riches, and offer Myself as a sacrifice, but have not Love, it profits Me nothing.

"'I am merciful because Love is merciful. I am kind because Love is kind. I am humble because Love does not envy, nor does it parade about, and it is not puffed up. Love is not rude, it does not seek its own, it is not easily provoked, and it thinks no evil. Love hates iniquity because iniquity insults Love. Love rejoices in truth because truth rejoices in, and magnifies, Love. Love bears all things, believes all things, hopes all things, and endures all things. Heaven is Faith, Hope, and Love, but the greatest of these is Love. Love never fails, so I, and My kingdom, will never fail.

"'When, that which is to come, comes, and Eternity future passes in review, it will be Love that judges the law, mercy, grace and all things. By all things, I say, there is nothing that does not place its hand beneath the feet of Love.'"

After thanking Tantzer for the audacity and conviction to brave my frustration at his invasion of my deep deliberation with this knowledge, I enter it here. It is a truly fitting end to what has developed into an incontrovertibly notable endeavor. For I know that this revelation, just clarified and illuminated by El Shaddai, resolves many formerly sealed mysteries within the Hall, while openly addressing any perceived weakness or unworthiness. El Shaddai has also interpreted our 'Angel Fatigue.'

It is love.

Love will be the final judge of Elohim's deeds and Love will testify to the righteousness and holiness of Elohim.

The End

GLOSSARY OF NAMES

Names of the Sovereign

Anyone seeking a practical grasp of the names of God soon discovers a universe wherein these names reside. This book explores only the periphery of that multifaceted expanse. It does not claim, in any scholarly way, to be an exhaustive reference. For that type of study we point to several excellent works such as *Names of God* by Nathan Stone, *The Names of God* by George W. Knight, and *Praying the Names of God* by Ann Spangler.

Herein we have chosen to use certain of these names, pregnant with purpose and rich undertones. As one angel within this book says, "Our great and worthy Sovereign is too exalted to be encapsulated by a single name. Any such name that may be offered would immediately limit Him as the syllables roll off the lips of the orator."

A student of scripture knows that truth is established by examining every letter of *Holy Writ*; the order in which the letters are linked; the precise accenting of the phrases and syllables; the language in which it is written; and expertise of the hand that wrote it, while judging these by the complete *Writ*. This is particularly true when seeking understanding of the names of God.

Here we introduce just a few. Our hope is that these few might help our finite minds explore some of the infinite height, width and depth, the true magnitude of the three Ones. The names we use, listed with some of the meanings determined by experts, follows. We have also included a brief explanation, as well as, some new understanding that you will find incorporated in this book.

Elohim
The All-Powerful One, Creator

His name, Elohim, along with the names Adonai, and El Shaddai, reveals much of our creator, God. We chose to begin with this name because it is the first name in scripture and the first name God chose when He began revealing Himself unto us.

The word Elohim is the masculine plural of El (or possibly Eloah). This name, in Hebraic thinking, only occurs in Hebrew and does not occur in any other Semitic languages. The plural ending, though, does not mean "gods" when referring to the God of Israel. When used, in conjunction with the singular verb forms, adjectives, and pronouns in the scripture, it promises a unique concept. However, considering the Hashalush HaKadosh (Trinity), the form indeed allows for the plurality within the Godhead.

Each use of this name within *The Angel Chronicles* conveys all that is presently accepted when this name has been used in scripture, plus some new understanding. Our usage portrays the three Ones, acting in such unity, that witnesses to the occurrence cannot tell which of the three Ones it is.

Adonai
The Lord, Master

Adonai is also plural, like the name Elohim, identifying the Trinity. The name reveals the foundational authority of each of the three Ones and their eternal stature as the unparalleled Sovereign.

Nathan Stone in his book *Names of God* underscores Adonai conveys ownership, or mastership, of those Elohim created…the idea of a master-slave relationship.

In *The Angel Chronicles,* when a character mentions the title "Lord," we could have correctly used the name, Adonai, and combined it with the name Elohim. However, we kept it simple for the sake of readability.

When we do use the name, Adonai, it's because its use is essential to portraying the authority of God to act as He does.

El Shaddai
The All Sufficient One, The God of Mountains, God Almighty

This, the third name of God which identifies the plurality of the Godhead, denotes the mightiness of the three pre-existent Ones. We believe this compound name actually portrays the divine personification of grace. It is likely the name that Elohim chose for Himself. Other than referring to Him as Elohim, we speculate that the angels likely use this name, El Shaddai.

Abba
Father

It is the intimate name for Yehovah. Some experts suggest that it is similar to the English word Papa. The word Papa is not meant irreverently or to lessen His stature. If the practice of using "Papa" leads to a reduced reverence, it should not be used, at all.

Dvar HaElohim
The Word of God

The second person of the Trinity. In searching for what Yeshuah's name might have been before creation, we settled upon this name. Weeks later we learned that Revelation 19:13 teaches that Yeshuah is called by this name. The One that Adam and Eve refer to as *Yehovah* is referred to, by the angels, as Dvar HaElohim.

Yehovah
I AM, The one who is the Self Existent One

The first person of the Trinity. It is the formal name for Abba. There is much controversy surrounding this name which has led to much misunderstanding about Elohim. After creating all things, Elohim conveyed certain names as a means to reveal Himself. Since early in man's history it has been necessary to discipline His creation. The name Yehovah had become associated, incorrectly, with a vengeful God rather than a God inviting intimacy.

We now believe that, in scripture, both Abba and Dvar HaElohim are referred to by this name. However, we propose that when referenced as Dvar HaElohim, it occurs because He in that instance is assuming the mantle of the Father. Thus He is demonstrating the application of the scripture which states, "When you've seen the Son, you've seen the Father."

HaRuach
The Spirit

The third person of the Trinity. In reality it is the person of the Trinity with whom man interacts the most, but is least recognized as God. Man chooses to de-deify Him and therefore becomes blind to His presence. For example, what man terms "Mother Nature" is in reality "The Spirit" fulfilling His responsibilities.

An interesting side note is, this person of the Trinity is the easiest to insult. Many revivals end because the Holy Spirit is insulted or quenched.

On a very serious note, blasphemy against this person of the Trinity is unforgiveable though blasphemy against Yehovah or Dvar HaElohim can be forgiven. Yeshuah warns against this and clarifies what it is in Mark 3:22-30.

Seven Spirits of God
Seven Ministries of the Holy Spirit

The *Seven Spirits of God* mentioned in *The Angel Chronicles* is the name of a specific revelation of "The Spirit" or HaRuach. This particular revelation identifies the seven ministries HaRuach performs. Some are transparently revealed in the Hebrew Scriptures while some are mentioned outright but maybe as a different name. However, these same ministries are openly declared in what is called the New Testament. A complete study of them is impossible within these pages.

We are convinced whenever "The Spirit" is mentioned in scripture it is referring to HaRuach's seven ministries acting in concert. This is similar to the scriptural treatment of Elohim, Adonai, and El Shaddai.

Below is a list of those ministries.

Spirit of Wisdom and Revelation – Exodus 28:3, Deuteronomy 34:9, Ephesians 1:17

Spirit of Grace and Adoption – Zachariah 12:10, Hebrews 10:29, Romans 8:15

Spirit of Faith – 2 Corinthians 4:13

Spirit of Truth – Isiah 4:4, John 14:7, John 15:26, John 16:13, 1 John 14:6

Spirit of Holiness – Romans 1:4

Spirit of Life – Romans 8:2, Revelation 11:11

Spirit of Glory – 1 Peter 4:14

Names of Characters**

Name	Meaning	Vocation	Notable Comments
Abel [A'-bel]	Breath, Vapor	2nd son of Adam and Eve	First man to die; First man in Paradise
Adam [Ah'-dahm]	Man	First Man	Father of all living; Only man to walk in the Garden
Alexis [Al-lek'-sees]	Protector of Man	Sculptor	2nd Guardian of Abel
Bartke [Bart'ka]	Adventurer	Scout/Pathfinder	Stand-in Guardian of Adam; later promoted to 1st guardian of Seth
Cain [Kayn']	Possession or Possessed	Firstborn of Adam and Eve	Killed Abel, his brother; Likely killed by a descendent
Chayim [Hai'-im]	Life	Worshipper	Held a commission to worship Elohim continuously, before the Throne
Dāwīd [Dah-veed']	Beloved	Song Writer	1st Guardian of Adam
Emunah [Em'-oo-naw]	Faith	Craftsman	2nd Guardian of Eve
Eve [Eve]	Mother of All Living	Wife/Mother	First woman; First wife; First sinner; First person to know spiritual death; Only woman to see the Garden
Fernez [Fur-nez']	Longsuffering	Sculptor	Probationary Guardian of Cain
Gabriel [Gay'-bree-ul]	God is My Strength	Novice Messenger	Yes, this is the one we all know about
Gershom [Ger'-shum]	A Sojourner There	Surveyor	1st Guardian of Eve
Ha-brit [Hah'-breet]	Sign of the Covenant	Orator	1st Guardian of Abel

Holofernez [Ha-luh-fur-nez']	Love's Labor Lost	Vial Maker	1st Guardian of Cain until he reached age of accountability
Klalish [Klay'-lish]	Standard	Warrior	Guard at East Gate of Eden
Komodo`r [Kah'-ma-dor]	Commodore	Tactician	Covenant partner of Zukher
Lairn`r [Layr'-ner]	Learner	Inquisitor	Covenant partner of Zukher
Lez`n [Lez'-en]	Reader	Scribe	Principal scribe of Chronicles
Lucifer [Loos'-i-fur]	Bringing Light	Fallen Archangel	Yehovah renames him satan (Angel without a future)
Mehgen' [May-ghen']	Defender	Architect	2nd Guardian of Adam
Michael [My'-kuhl]	Who is like God	Archangel	
Omán [Oh- mahn']	Artist	Artist	Stand-in Guardian of Adam; later promoted to 2nd guardian of Seth
Phendimann [Fen'-di-men]	Full of Oneself	Physicist	This name was derived from the name of a notable physicist
Seth [Seth]	Put, Who Puts, Fixed	3rd son of Adam and Eve	Received mantle of Adam
Shtitsen [Shteet'-sen]	Support	Exhorter	Former member of Zukher's troupe, tasked to lead his own later
Sryyab`r [Sree'-yab-r]	Scribe	Scribe	Lez`n backup
satan [say'-tin]	Adversary, Beelzebub	Former Cherub	Formerly named Lucifer
Silber Lo`shen [Sil'-ber Low'-shen]	Mesmerizer	Entertainer, Orator	Demonic being encountered by Zukher in Sheol
Tantzer [Tont'-zer]	Dancer	Novice Messenger	Covenant partner of Zukher
Yushabed [Yoush'-a-bed]	Change of Mercy	Inventor	Provisional Guardian of Cain

Zukher [Zuhk'-er]	Seeker	Organizer	Leader of vanguard troupe attending man; Principal narrator of *The Angel Chronicles*.

** We selected the names of characters from several broad sources. We either took them directly from the *Pentateuch* [pen'-ta-tuuk], Yiddish names, Hebrew names, or variations or modified forms of either Hebrew names or Yiddish names, and some are simply fabricated.

For those interested in honoring a character by pronouncing the name correctly, our phonetic pronunciation is shown in [ ] brackets.

Post Script

We hope that reading *The Angel Chronicles* was an enlightening and entertaining experience.

A major element in our story is the presentation of how man was created. By that, we don't mean how God accomplished the creation, rather how He fashioned man. We hold the view that this subject is so important to us who want to be overcomers, that God sowed seeds of truth about it, in over 2000 verses of scripture.

We want to encourage serious minded ministries, and believers, to follow the example of the principled Bereans who *"received the word with all readiness of mind, and searched the scriptures daily"* to see if those things were so: Acts 17:11 KJV. We would enjoy hearing about your discoveries.

For those of you interested in learning more about that which we presented here, in imagery only, please check out our website www.windsofeternity.com.

ZUKHER'S REFERENCES

Note: All scripture references are taken from the King James Version of the Bible, unless otherwise indicated.

<u>The Prelude</u>
[1] Hebrews 13:1.

[2] See Glossary of Names – Names of Sovereign.

[3] Genesis 1:1 speaks of the "beginning." When that "beginning" was, relative to what follows in Genesis 1:2, is debated. We, the authors, are respectfully taking the view that there is an enigmatic time span that elapsed between the end of Genesis 1:1 and the start of Genesis 1:2. During that time the Earth may well have been inhabited by dinosaurs and other creatures. Some describe a selection of those creatures as "humanoid." However, there is no reliable evidence, that what is biblically defined as "man," existed on Earth before Genesis 1:2-26.

[4] When *Elohim* created all the angels, they were created as 'angels of light.' Lucifer's initial state was, therefore, as an angel of light. He was a cherub and enjoyed an exalted position among the angels, the most elevated within the ranks: Taken from Ezekiel 28:12-19. Verse 17 of this same reference, mentions he was a covering, which suggests he was once one of the two cherubs resting upon the Ark of the Covenant in Heaven.

[5] Isaiah 14:12-17 and Luke 10:18 expound, in great detail, what we refer to as 'The Rebellion,' along with the already mentioned Ezekiel 28:12-19.

<u>Noble Intromission</u>
[6] Lucifer had been granted authority only over Earth and the atmosphere above it, therefore, only the Earth was without form and void, or blemished, as mentioned. Unrevealed at this time is if man's fall blemished the entire universe, whereas satan's fall did not. Though it is not certain, several biblical references indicate this might be true. We presently hold the view that man's fall, somehow, did blemish the entire

universe, because of the implications in the references: Isaiah 34:4, Isaiah 65:17, and Revelation 6:14.

[7] In gospel accounts of one of *Yeshuah's* temptations, satan plainly says "All these things will I give thee, if you bow down and worship me." Here satan is saying he has authority over all the kingdoms of Earth and their glory. His ability to show them to *Yeshuah* supports his claim. *Yeshuah* does not rebuke satan for saying so. Therefore, we conclude that at least prior to *Yeshuah's* resurrection, satan had some level of governance upon Earth and the breadth of sky above: Matthew 4:8-10.

[8] Moses fashioned Israel's tabernacle in the wilderness after being shown Heaven's Tabernacle: Exodus 25:1-5, 7-9. Later David's son Solomon used the wilderness Tabernacle as a blueprint for the permanent Temple he built in Jerusalem. We believe that before the messiah appears, a Temple patterned after these two, will once again be built in Jerusalem.

[9] 'Seven Pillars of Wisdom' is referenced in Proverbs 8:12-14 and Proverbs 9:1. Those mentioned are Prudence, Knowledge, Fear of the Lord, Counsel, Sound Wisdom, Understanding, and Strength.

[10] 'Fall of the Seven Waters' is not mentioned specifically, anywhere, in Scripture. However, Hebrews 6:1-3 does refer to certain principals of *Yeshuah's* doctrine. The conclusion of this reference establishes that God permits only those, who are seasoned disciples of those principals, to go on to maturity. 'Fall of the Seven Waters' is an image of those principals. We believe that fully understanding them will unlock the entire Word of God and the mysteries, therein. Glen Ewing taught this concept, and the principals, extensively in *The Texas Grace Counselor.*

[11] Ezekiel 47:1-12 and Revelation 22:1-2 mention the river we refer to in this book. The Tree of Life is also mentioned: Genesis 3:23-24 and Revelation 2:7.

[12] Sin is "transgression of the law," 1 John 3:4. Therefore, when angels "transgressed" they sinned. The application of the word 'sin' is not unique to man.

The Announcement
[13] Psalms 19:1-4 tells us that the heavens are readable in every language known to man. Controversy surrounds our premise. Actually, it is plausible, and very likely, that Elohim used this means to give man the first written scriptures. By doing so, He provided fallen man the same means to faith that He gives us now. "Faith comes by hearing the Word of God," Romans 10:17, paraphrased.

Mystery - Elohim
[14] Romans 3:27 mentions "Law of Faith." All laws have statutes, provisions, and consequences. Faith and its operation in Heaven, and its operation here on Earth, are governed by this law.

[15] Sentience, as we are defining it, is the inherent ability to think, feel, perceive, and/ or experience, subjectively. It is our view that only God enjoys this capacity to its fullest extent. Angels and man experience a large measure of that. If an animal or other creature exhibits any sentience, at all, it would be the spirit part of its makeup doing so and not the entity, in and of, itself.

Let There Be
[16] See Glossary of Names – *Names of the Sovereign, the Seven Spirits of God.*

[17] Acronym for "The Joy of the Lord is my strength": Psalms 5:11

The Apokálypsis
[18] Apokálypsis means revelation, or unveiling, in a literal manner, as opposed to a spiritual one or an apparition.

[19] We hope our presentation of body, soul, and spirit was instructive. We are claiming, with the use of images, that the soul is much more than just the mental-emotional part of who we are, as some perceive. That which is our complete presence in eternity, our complete personality, complete character, and complete ego, reside only in the soul. Those of us, who are 'born again,' John 3:3, John 3:7, and 1 Peter 1:23, enjoy the benefits from the eternal union of our personal spirit with Christ's. No part of who we are, as individuals, is shared with the body or the spirit. An explanation of the 'new creation' and the 'spirit man' requires more than a brief statement, here. A complete discourse on this subject of body, soul and spirit is available on the www.windsofeternity.com web site.

Heaven on Earth
[20] This is a reference to the sun, moon, and breadth of sky. The sun is an image of *Yehovah*, the moon is an image of *Dvar HaElohim*, and the breadth of sky is an image of *HaRuach.*

The Hedge of Elohim
[21] Commonly known as 'Haley's Comet.'

[22] In Ephesians 6:12, "spiritual wickedness in high places," explains that satan, and his kind, have a limited theater of operation, and a spatial location. In Daniel 10:13, Gabriel mentions that one of satan's underlings, the "Prince of Persia," had resisted him. The reference implies that this prince exercises influence over the territory or region of Persia.

[23] Chaos, as a scientific theory, describes erratic behavior within the created universe. In the context of the Heavenly and terrestrial spheres, chaos is divided into two different categories, purposeful and purposeless, when considered from the point of view of Elohim.

[24] Commonly known as the 'North Star.'

[25] In Job 1:10, Isaiah 5.5, Ezekiel 13:5, the word "hedge" is used to illustrate God's protection of a man or a nation. The most obvious is the reference in Job.

The Season of Trumpets
[26] Should anyone not fully understand the nuances of our assertion: The intimacy we mention is that which is shared by the three holy Ones whose name is *Elohim*. See the Glossary of Names – *Names of the Sovereign*.

Elohim's Prophecy
[27] Both Ezekiel 5:5 and Ezekiel 38:12 talk about Jerusalem as the center of nations, or center (navel), of the land. We are asserting here, that at the time of Adam, there was only one continent and that the geographic center of that single continent is where, one day, the city of Jerusalem would stand.

Our premise of a single continent is not an original idea. Scientists openly talk about the possibility of this being true, two different times, in Earth's present geological history.

The Vast Unknown
[28] The song sung by Adam and Eve is a paraphrased version of Psalms 18:1, 16, 19, 32, 33 and 36.

Revelation of the Linen Kaftan
[29] Kaftan or Caftan is a coat or over-cloak with long sleeves that reaches to the ankles. It is a variant of a robe or tunic. Our source is Wikipedia.org, 2015.

The Nether Regions of Earth
[30] Tsuwr is Tyrus that is mentioned in Ezekiel 28:2 & 11. We had some fun with it and changed the name to Tsuwr (pronounced Sewer).

[31] It is clear that the text of Ezekiel 28:11-15 is speaking about Lucifer. How this works out, in relation to the chronology of creation in Genesis, remains unclear. We think our premise stands as soundly as any of others being proposed.

[32] The casting out of Lucifer is mentioned in Ezekiel 28:18, Isaiah 14:12-14, and Luke 10:18.

[33] © 'Thou Clouded Mystery' lyrics by Track Johnson copyright: 2015.

Unto Us a Child is Born
[34] The inspiring words of this song were given as a prophetic utterance, sung by Robert Ewing (son of Glen Ewing, original publisher of the periodical *The Texas Grace Counselor*), in 1969. It was during a public college student gathering in Little

Rock, Arkansas. There were many witnesses to this message. One was an author of this work.

A Blood Testimony

[35] The Hebrew version of the *Pentateuch* word "chet," is translated "sin" in English. It literally means "missing the mark." Adam and Eve's disobedience in the Garden resulted in a kernel of the sin nature being passed on to their progeny. Genesis 8:12, Psalms 51:5, and Proverbs 22:15, each confirm this contention.

An interesting side note: The kernel of satan's nature, being passed on, is through Adam and not Eve. This is because Adam knew what he was doing, while Eve was just deceived.

[36] Dead Works: A reasonable explanation of dead works is doing something independent of Elohim's working through one. Such a thing is not only frowned upon, but purchases merely unedifying results. One ministry known to us gives us a good example: "Dead works is like a man who finds the entire floor of a storehouse covered one kernel deep in grain. He picks up the grain, one kernel at a time and eats it. In the end, the energy consumed by harvesting and eating the grain, is greater than the amount of energy produced as a result of eating the grain." El Shaddai gave this excellent example to our mentor, Auseklis Zidermanis.

Years and Tears

[37] The biblical definition of grace takes many excellent forms. The favor of God, God's riches at Christ's expense, and unmerited love and favor, are but a few. You probably have a favorite. We have our own favorite, one that is much broader. It is God's goodness, in whatever form or measure it has to be, at the time it is needed.